The Three Loves OF CHARLIE DELANEY

BOOK ONE

JOEY W. KISER

iUniverse

THE THREE LOVES OF CHARLIE DELANEY
BOOK ONE

iUniverse books may be ordered through booksellers or by contacting:

iUniverse
1663 Liberty Drive
Bloomington, IN 47403
www.iuniverse.com
1-800-Authors (1-800-288-4677)

Because of the dynamic nature of the Internet, any web addresses or links contained in this book may have changed since publication and may no longer be valid. The views expressed in this work are solely those of the author and do not necessarily reflect the views of the publisher, and the publisher hereby disclaims any responsibility for them. Any people depicted in stock imagery provided by Thinkstock are models, and such images are being used for illustrative purposes only. Certain stock imagery © Thinkstock.

ISBN: 978-1-4917-8477-8 (sc)
ISBN: 978-1-4917-8475-4 (hc)
ISBN: 978-1-4917-8476-1 (e)

Library of Congress Control Number: 2015921331

Print information available on the last page.

iUniverse rev. date: 1/08/2016

CONTENTS

PREFACE

Ever since men and women have been living on this planet, they have had to struggle and cope with each other physically, mentally, and emotionally. Romance has played a large role in this long-enduring relationship between the two sexes.

Men have always turned to women for companionship—for someone to talk to, relate their problems to, share the good times with, support them in the bad times, love them, and be loved by them. But most importantly, men need women to mitigate the horrible pain of loneliness—to be their friends.

Women, on the other hand, need men for completely different reasons. These reasons range from basic needs to the very complex. Today, women aren't as dependent on men as they might have been in the past. Women have become more independent, more aggressive in the job market, and more determined to take control of their own destinies. But in this process of self-determination, women still need partners to share their achievements with and to be there when things get tough.

Women need men to satisfy their emotional needs. A woman who doesn't have someone to compliment her and tell her once in a while those special words soon will begin to feel worthless. No woman wants to feel that way. A woman needs to hear those things she would never ask to hear, because if she doesn't feel appreciated, she may become harsh, hateful, uncaring, and mean.

That is why we are always in search of romance novels—stories that let us forget about the rest of the world for a while, stories we can get caught up in, about people to whom we can relate. We want to read about characters that bring out what we want most of all and often find missing in our own lives, including love and romance.

Such a story is *The Three Loves of Charlie Delaney*. This story should help men and women understand each other better. Although the story is about fictional characters, it is based on truth, honesty, and purpose. It deals with real feelings, love, hate, good times, bad times, tragedy, and, of course, romance.

In a time in which most novels are written in such bad taste, this one may be held accountable for its respectability. I have omitted all those nasty words that most novels contain today. Most people today have the strange and perverted belief that to be a good romance novel, a book must include a lot of filthy words. I hope the reader of this book is more mature. Love and lust are not the same thing, even though they can seem the same. In today's distorted society, people have become confused with the many disillusions on the subject of love and lust.

Romance and sex are two totally different things. Romance is the enchanting, nonphysical relationship before sex takes place. It is an unselfish feeling in one's mind, heart, and soul. Romance is the general opening up of an honest conversation with a bit of incantation. The anticipation of what is about to take place makes romance an important element in the development of a relationship. Loving someone just for sheer physical pleasures without caring inner feelings is like trying to build a skyscraper without a foundation. Eventually, the main structure will collapse.

Another important element in a true loving relationship is emotion. In a relationship without emotion, something is missing. You deny yourself wondrous and magnificent feelings that make you feel warm and good, like holding a three-day-old baby close to your heart.

Most romance novels today focus on arousing sexual appetites and other physical allurements. They tell of fulfilling only the pleasurable physical aspects. Lovemaking is not what loving someone is all about. This novel is much more than that.

In our fast-paced modern society, no one wants to wait for anything. Everyone wants everything now—not next week or next month. But it takes quality time to develop a true and meaningful relationship. The small things of two people's personalities make up the nucleus of a wonderful and long-lasting relationship. Romance, that special element of enchantment, plays an important role in this development; romance ignites the mechanism that makes a person fall in love.

When a couple begins dating and jumps into bed on the first or second date, chances are the relationship will only be a temporary entertainment, not a long-lasting and meaningful relationship. In these cases, the man is using the flesh of the woman to satisfy his physical desires, and the woman is allowing the man to use her in this manner because she thinks she is being loved for what she is. In reality, she is just being used and lusted after for the man's selfish reasons. She has selfish reasons of her own. If she chooses to allow the man to do this to her, she is partially to blame when the relationship goes sour.

If a relationship is devoured by sex too early, the involved parties are to blame for not controlling their sensual lust. Just think of all the relationships that would blossom into full and meaningful unions if the man and woman involved would control their sexuality until making a true commitment, a commitment that includes God.

People think that marriage is just some words written on a piece of paper, but that is far from the truth. That's just an excuse for people not to get married. Marriage, in the true sense of the word, has nothing to do with words written on a piece of paper. A true loving and meaningful marriage is intangible. It is not something you can touch at all. A true marriage is built and developed in the heart. It is a commitment from one individual to another individual, bonded by God through his love, to create one flesh, one soul, one creation.

If people would put God's will, as opposed to their own wants, first in their marriages and try to build on His plan instead of theirs, they would come to realize that marriage is a partnership in life, a partnership that will better their lives, giving their lives more significance and meaning. They would also give and show more respect for one another. This complex world of ours is made more complex when we let our uncontrollable, lustful nature alienate God.

In this confused, self-centered, and carefree society in which we live, the average person doesn't want a long-lasting relationship with that one special person, preferring instead a temporary relationship with a lusty, sexual partner to satisfy his or her physical body. Then, after tiring of that relationship, he or she just casts that person aside like garbage. This person is uncaring, thoughtless, and selfish, an individual whose primary goal in life is to use others for sexual favors. I'm afraid our society is being consumed by lasciviousness.

If fooling around in a promiscuous manner outside of marriage was nothing more than experiencing pleasure and enjoyment, then I wouldn't be making such a ruckus. But the problem with lust is it erodes the element that makes us civilized. Once we human beings begin to give in to lust, we tend to forget what is right and wrong. The pleasure prevents us from seeing things clearly.

Promiscuous relationships eventually destroy the intelligence and moral character of the people involved. These people may even begin having affairs, tainting the sacred union of marriage. When this happens, these people begin to lie to themselves. They feel content about their sexual activity and don't think there is anything wrong with having affairs until something awful takes place or the burden of guilt or shame takes its toll. Then they come to see the false thoughts that have been planted in their minds, the false thoughts their promiscuity created.

I hope people who are having trouble with their relationships will get something positive and meaningful out of this novel. It has something for everyone. It will bring you in touch with what true love is supposed to be. It will help you realize that if two people only care about lust, they will miss out on a whole lot of life and inner peace.

The three main problems in today's marriages (and with a 50 percent divorce rate, one would wonder if there aren't more than just three) are money, sex, and lack of communication.

I will begin first with the second most common problem in marriage, the one everybody is most concerned with: sex—or, should I say, lovemaking. When two people get married, everything is wonderful for the first few months. Then the couple starts to realize that the sex that lured them into marriage is not always what they had in mind. The male partner thinks that since he is now married, he can have sex anytime he wants, as many times as he wants, and that his wife will do anything he wants. This is one of the biggest misconceptions in our culture. It just doesn't work out like that. Sometimes women are not in a romantic mood. Women do not want to feel obligated to their husbands all the time. Most men understand these feelings and do not force or intimidate their wives, but there are men who are not so understanding. A man like this makes his partner feel as though she was put on this earth just to satisfy his physical pleasures, and when she doesn't respond to his every whim, he is disrespectful and verbally abusive. That is the primary reason sex is such a problem for a lot of people. Some husbands treat their wives only as objects of lust, instead of partners in life. This attitude destroys what love their wives have for them. Luckily most individuals aren't dominating and possessive like this.

Without togetherness and mutual love and respect, a marriage isn't going to overcome the other hardships that will follow later on. When physical elements become more important than emotional ones in a marriage, then problems will arise. These petty problems may start a chain reaction of self-destructive forces that will end in divorce.

The most difficult problem to overcome after two people have made a permanent commitment is money. Young couples think they should have all the nice things that their mothers and fathers possess right now. They don't realize that their parents spent their entire lives getting where they are. Many couples go out in this sign-your-name-here world and get so far in debt that anytime one partner spends some money, it leads to a major argument. Most arguments don't stay on the main subject; they tend to branch off and create new avenues to argue. As the fighting grows more intense, personal feelings and individual characteristics get involved. The issue that brought on the argument in the first place is cast aside when feelings get hurt. This is how money issues slowly divide couples and erode their love.

The third and last main issue in marriages is lack of communication. This is the problem people have the hardest time working on. Women need to be talked to, but men have a natural instinct to keep things to themselves and not open up to their partners about problems. This annoys women. Most women have a strange and sometimes obsessive desire to help with their partners' problems. They want to be involved. If they are alienated from the problem-solving process, they may argue just to provoke responses from their spouses. It's their way of getting attention. This may lead to negative reactions from their irritated husbands.

Nagging and arguing can divide couples. When two people fail to communicate properly it could lead them to lose admiration and respect for one another. Soon the fighting devolves into stupid, completely ridiculous arguments. They start to manipulate love, respect, trust, and admiration through verbal abusiveness. The bond that God knitted commences to unravel.

These are the reasons why there are so many divorces. When the ways of the world start to attack our foundation, the American family, then the whole structure of our culture starts to crumble and break before our eyes. If people put strong family values before physical and selfish desires, then maybe our foundation will grow strong again.

Family life needs to become stronger so the children of the next generation won't grow up in one-parent homes. I hope the next generation will learn the right way to conduct themselves and not repeat the mistakes of people caught up in this material world of ours. One of the main objectives of this novel is to show that there is more to a loving relationship than jumping into bed for physical pleasures. People need to think about all the responsibilities that go along with those pleasures. This novel displays what it is to be really in love and shows all the problems love can create. Maybe people will then learn how to deal with these problems in their own lives. If men and women start to show each other respect and not let selfishness, lust, and deception control their lives, then this book will have served one of its primary purposes.

I dedicate this book to the generation that doesn't know how to develop true and meaningful relationships. I hope they will learn that it is better to wait and develop something special rather than to plunge into something that will scorch their intellects and prevent them from doing what is right. I also dedicate this book to the married couples who are struggling to keep their love alive and to the individuals who can't recognize the truth because they are caught up with the deceptions of this world. Finally, I dedicate this novel to the love-starved individuals who have been thirsting to read a true love story.

Chapter 1
AN INTRODUCTION TO CHARLIE

Charlie Delaney, born on January 7, 1961, is an only child. When Charlie is born, his father, John, is thirty-seven years old, and his mother, Sara, is twenty-five. They have only been married ten months when Charlie comes into their lives. He is the joy of their lives.

Charlie's father is a carpenter by trade; his mother is a nurse. They are neither rich nor poor. They live in a modest town house; it is nothing to brag about in size but is large enough. It is paid for before Charlie starts school.

Charlie grows up in this same house all his childhood. He goes to the same school, plays with the same neighborhood children, and keeps to himself most of the time. Although Charlie has plenty of friends, he is something of a loner. He doesn't like to get too close to any one individual. Charlie has never had a pet; his parents don't allow animals in the house.

Charlie has a distant relationship with his father. John Delaney is somewhat withdrawn and doesn't like to relate to other people. He doesn't like to communicate with Charlie or his wife, Sara, very much. The main reason John doesn't communicate well with his family is that he is always busy thinking about something, mainly his work. He is a perfectionist when it comes to his work. He is an expert carpenter and woodworker.

When he is working on a project, he doesn't like anyone asking him questions or interrupting his thoughts. He becomes agitated and sometimes angry when he has to explain something that he finds simple. His personality is one of self-determination but on a boring level. He never feels the need to explain things to anybody as long as he knows the answers himself. John just takes it for granted that everybody knows what he knows. John is the strong, silent type who doesn't think about the feelings of others when he speaks. He is quick to judge and condemn anyone who doesn't think as he does. John has a soft heart, though, when it comes to important things. He is generous to Sara and Charlie, and he has done without many times. John does a lot of charity work for his church. He gladly does any carpentry work for them when asked. He only charges the expenses for material, donating his labor as an expression of his love for the pastor and the people of the church.

Overall, John is a practical man with strong moral beliefs. He loves his wife and son very much but doesn't express his love to them very well. The only way he shows his love is with presents or money. His lack of communication about his feelings for them is his biggest shortcoming as a father and husband.

Sara, on the other hand, is quite the opposite of John. She willingly and eagerly expresses her feelings in a robust and open way. She tells people just how she feels without holding back anything. Her character is one of openness and cheerfulness but with an element of firmness. When she makes up her mind, nothing will change it, but after being married to John, she has become submissive to him to keep peace in the house. She has come to realize that John, in his stubbornness and bullheadedness, will not succumb to her pleas; therefore, she goes along with him most of the time to avoid his verbal attacks.

Since Charlie is Sara's only child, she gives him all the motherly attention he needs and then some. Her relationship with Charlie is one of warmth, love, and kindness. Their bond is so strong that she can sometimes figure out what Charlie is thinking just by the expression on his face. Charlie is truly the apple of her eye. She loves her son tremendously, and she doesn't hesitate to tell him so every chance she gets.

Sara's strong Christian beliefs prevent her from expressing hostility or anger to anyone. She yields before her anger gets too intense. John, on the other hand, expresses his fury openly when he is angered. He doesn't think about the feelings he hurts with his quick verbal strikes. His only concern is to point out his way of thinking. He is quick to judge and expresses his opinion without much thought, but most of the time John is a quiet gentleman.

Sara works at night at a local hospital. She is an LPN and works in the recovery room. She gets off work and returns home before John and Charlie wake up. She usually fixes breakfast for them before going to sleep; then John goes to work, and Charlie goes to school. This arrangement works out well for all three.

Charlie takes after his mother more than his father. He thinks before he speaks and tries not to hurt anyone's feelings. Physically, though, he looks more like his father; the resemblance of the two is uncanny.

The main trait Sara and John have in common is their mental ability to figure out anything that confronts them. They can study any problem that faces them and come to a solution without panicking or losing their composure. This strong trait has yet to surface in Charlie, but Charlie is still too young to have his character fully developed.

When Charlie is ten years old, he finds an abandoned dog wandering around in his neighborhood. He brings the dog home and shows it to his mother. Even though Charlie has taken a special liking to the dog, his mother is very strict about not having pets in the house. She tells Charlie that the dog probably has worms and that she isn't about to pay a vet bill for a dog they aren't going to keep. She suggests they call the animal shelter and have the shelter find a home for the animal.

Charlie asks what will happen to the dog if the shelter can't find a home for it. His mother's reply delivers a devastating blow to his innocent heart. She tells him in a very callous way that the dog probably will be put to sleep. When Charlie hears this, he begins to cry uncontrollably. He begs his mother not to let anybody do that to his little friend. He tells her that if she allows the shelter to take his little dog away, it will be like killing the dog herself. He says this with sincerity.

When his father comes home from work that night, Charlie pleads with him repeatedly to keep the little dog, but to no avail. His father is no more sympathetic to Charlie's love for the little dog than his mother is, so in the morning Charlie's father calls the animal shelter.

When Charlie comes home from school the next day, he finds the little dog is gone. Charlie goes through a very emotional and heartbreaking time because of his parents' actions. Although this happens when Charlie is only ten years old, the effects of this will stay with him until he is grown, causing him to becomes a quiet and somewhat-withdrawn individual. Most of the time, Charlie just stays in his room and listens to music. His other hobbies are collecting coins and baseball cards. He loves to read. History is his favorite subject in school.

One of the most difficult things for Charlie is talking to girls. Every time a pretty girl sits next to him, he gets timid and hardly says a word. One day in kindergarten, Charlie is attracted to a little girl. This little girl likes Charlie. They play together, eat lunch together, and sit together in class everyday.

Then one day toward the end of the school year, Charlie does something that puts him in the principal's office. Charlie and his little girlfriend are practicing graduation when Charlie kisses her. Suddenly, the little girl begins to cry. She runs to the teacher and tells him what Charlie did. The teacher leads Charlie by the hand to the principal's office.

After the teacher tells the principal what Charlie has done, the principal asks Charlie if it is the truth. Charlie, scared of what he has done, confesses. The principal takes a large wooden paddle from his desk. Seeing what is about to happen, Charlie starts to cry.

Before the principal gets to Charlie, another teacher brings a different student into the principal's office for disciplinary action. The principal is the only one in the entire school who can discipline the students with spanking. Teachers are not allowed to spank any child no matter how bad they behave.

Charlie listens as the teacher tells the principal that the student put his hand up a little girl's dress. It is somewhat comforting to Charlie that he isn't the only one in trouble. Misery loves company. The principal looks at the little boy and asks him if what the teacher said is the truth. The little boy denies putting his hand up the girl's dress. The teacher tells the principal he saw the boy with his own two eyes.

Seeing the paddle on the desk and afraid of a spanking, the boy keeps denying that he did the act, saying, "No! I never did it. I never put my hands up her dress. Please, you've got to believe me. I never did."

The teacher looks at the principal and says, "Sir, I saw him put his hands up her dress not only once but twice."

The boy abruptly shouts, "No! He is wrong. I didn't do it but one time."

The principal looks at the sad little boy and says, "Okay, young man, first of all, you lied to me. Second, you did put your hand up that little girl's dress. I am going to spank you twice as much as I was going to before you lied to me. After today you will learn and learn well not to lie to me. Secondly, you better not ever put your hands up another little girl's dress again. I was going to spank Charlie first, but after hearing what you have done, I'm going to let you go first."

The little boy doesn't cry one bit as the principal spanks him, lick after lick. He just pouts and holds it in. He has been to the principal several times before. So for a five-year-old boy he takes his punishment like a man, but he never seems to change his ways.

Seeing the principal swing that enormous wooden board against the boy's behind and hearing that loud popping sound each time the paddle strikes, Charlie becomes worried and terrified of his turn with the paddle. Charlie is amazed that his classmate doesn't cry at all, not even one tear.

After finishing the first spanking, the principal looks at Charlie and says, "Okay, young man, it's your turn."

Charlie gets up and goes over to where the principal is standing. The other little boy goes over and sits down in Charlie's seat.

Charlie looks up at the principal with sad, teary eyes. The principal looks down at Charlie and says, "Bend over and touch your toes."

Charlie bends over, and as soon as he gets halfway down, the principal strikes Charlie's right buttock with the large wooden board. The principal swings the paddle again and again. Finally he says, "Okay, Charlie, I guess you have had enough. I hope you have learned your lesson." Charlie, crying softly, sits down next to the other little boy. The boy gives Charlie a sad, sympathetic look.

The principal tells the two boys, "You two young men must understand why I had to paddle you. You can't go around kissing and putting your hands up little girls' dresses. Most of all, when you do something wrong, you should face up to it and not lie about it. I hope both of you have learned a good lesson from this. I hope you do not repeat the actions that landed you here ever again."

The principal tells both of them to go back to their classrooms. Charlie and his fellow classmate leave the office. Charlie, still teary eyed, returns to class and puts his head down on his desk. He doesn't want any of his classmates to see him crying. After about twenty minutes, he gets control of himself. Nobody makes fun of Charlie except the little girl.

When Charlie gets home, he doesn't tell his parents about what happened at school that day, because he knows if he does, he probably will get another spanking from them. When the school bus comes by the next day, things go on as normal. Charlie forgets all about what took place the previous day. He has learned not to be friendly to girls anymore.

This incident makes Charlie timid around girls through his adolescence. He's learned that girls can get him into trouble. He is reluctant to let that happen ever again. Charlie doesn't like anybody getting him into trouble. Maybe this is why Charlie keeps to himself so much.

When Charlie is in the second grade, he develops a crush on a pretty little girl named Ginger Edwardson. For Charlie, she is the cat's meow. She has cherry-red hair. Charlie falls in love with her at first sight. Her eyes are as blue as the sky. A strange, compelling fascination overwhelms Charlie when he is in her presence. He always tells his classmates that he doesn't like her, but he is only fooling them and himself. He wants to talk to her, but his shyness always gets in the way.

One day he is trying to get Ginger's attention by picking on her. Charlie soon learns that Ginger Edwardson does not like anyone picking on her. She quickly summons the teacher, and Charlie, for the first time, has to stand in the corner. After the teacher lets Charlie go back to his seat, some of the other kids laugh and tease him.

The next day when Charlie gets back to class, he forgets about the previous day and once again begins picking on his favorite sweetheart, Ginger. It is to no avail, however; Ginger just doesn't like any boys picking on her. Time after time, she reports Charlie to the teacher, and time after time Charlie gets into trouble.

As time goes on, Charlie begins to blame Ginger for his punishments and develops a love-hate relationship with Ginger. Sometimes he likes her immensely; but when she gets him in trouble, he dislikes her a great deal. Deep down he has a very strong liking for Ginger. I guess you would call it puppy love.

As Charlie grows up, he experiences the same things every other boy does. He is a normal, run-of-the-mill youngster. He plays baseball and football and watches cartoons on Saturday mornings. He has a mother and father who love him very much. They don't always give him everything he wants, but they show him that they love him in many other ways. His parents never drink alcohol in front of him, nor yell at him, except when it is absolutely necessary. Charlie seems to have a normal and healthy childhood.

Throughout elementary school, Charlie fears he will miss the school bus. He is terrified that one day he will not find it. In kindergarten there was only one school bus that took all the children home. Since there was only one school bus, Charlie had no problem finding it when it was time to go home. But when Charlie begins elementary school, he finds out that there are dozens of school buses in the school yard. This brings on a most difficult time for him.

He knows his bus number, but when his teacher walks the class out to the bus yard, Charlie is still afraid he won't find his bus. He is afraid he will be left at school. Even worse, he is afraid he will get on the wrong school bus and be taken to a strange neighborhood. He has a fear of being left in a strange place.

Charlie goes to the same elementary school through fourth grade. When Charlie starts fifth grade, he has to travel a long way to a different school, Ashley Elementary. Charlie finds it difficult to adapt to this new environment. A lot of his best friends also have to go to different schools and adapt. Charlie accepts the change but adapts slowly and with some difficulty to his new surroundings.

Charlie spends sixth grade at Ashley Elementary as well. He begins to overcome his fear of catching the wrong school bus. It is in his sixth school year that something important happens to Charlie. He has always liked his teachers, but in the sixth grade, Charlie takes a strange liking to a very special teacher, one whom Charlie will admire and keep in his mind all the days of his life.

On the first day of sixth grade, a chilly autumn morning, Charlie is excited and nervous. His mind is full of innocence as he arrives at school. The first thing on his mind is to find out where his class is. There are plenty of people there to help the students find their classes. When Charlie finally arrives at his class, he is delighted to find a young and attractive teacher waiting to bring the class to order. Her name is Mrs. Janice Williamson.

Her eyes show excitement when she speaks. She has a soft and pretty voice. Her hair is long, silky, and brown. She is married, is twenty-six years old, and has a fragrance of sweet-smelling flowers. She gets Charlie's complete attention when she smiles. Charlie develops a crush on her that is so strong that just the thought of her keeps him up at night. After the first few weeks of school, Charlie becomes more and more attracted to his new teacher.

Charlie, like most of his fellow classmates, is a typical rambunctious youngster. He runs around, talks abruptly, laughs loudly, and sometimes acts wild and carefree. One day, Mrs. Williamson tells the class it is time to go to the cafeteria for lunch. Charlie is still working on some of his schoolwork as the other kids form the line. By the time he puts away his schoolwork and enters the line, he is in the very back. Charlie never likes being in the back; he likes being in the front. When the class reaches the cafeteria, Charlie just runs up to the front of the line and breaks in as though there was nothing wrong with it. Some of the other kids begin an argument about what Charlie did. They call for Mrs. Williamson, who is talking to another teacher.

"Mrs. Williamson! Charlie Delaney broke in front of me, and he won't go back where he is supposed to be!"

"I will be there in a minute," Mrs. Williamson says angrily. She is upset because she has to shorten her conversation with her colleague. She looks at the children with frustration. The children are arguing about who is supposed to be at the front of the line. Four other boys have cut in line since Charlie made his daring maneuver.

Mrs. Williamson, looking sternly at Charlie, says loudly, "What do you think you are doing, Charlie? What do you think you are doing! Who gave you permission to cut in line? Look at all the chaos you have created. What do you have to say for yourself, young man?"

Charlie gives his teacher the saddest look he has ever shown in his entire life. He has never had anyone yell at him like that before. He doesn't know what to say. He just looks up at his angry teacher with a sad, pitiful look and says nothing.

His teacher looks at his tender, sad eyes and says, "Go to the end of the line right now, young man!"

Charlie, still looking at Mrs. Williamson, turns and slowly walks to the back of the line. His feelings are hurt so badly that his resulting facial expression has a most devastating effect on Mrs. Williamson's heart. She is touched greatly by his expression. She keeps looking at Charlie until all the other children have gotten their food and are sitting down to eat their noon meal.

Charlie's expression doesn't change. He still has such a sad look. Mrs. Williamson decides to go over and talk with him. She walks over and sits down beside Charlie, who is looking down at his food. She puts her hand under his chin and lifts his head until his sad, innocent eyes stare right into hers. She gazes at Charlie's face with love and compassion. Finally, she asks, "Charlie, did I hurt your feelings?"

Charlie looks at his teacher with a sad but sweet expression and says, "Yes, ma'am."

Mrs. Williamson smiles as she looks into his soft blue eyes and kindly says, "I'm sorry I yelled at you. I didn't mean to hurt your feelings."

Charlie just sits there focusing on Mrs. Williamson's tender, loving eyes.

She says softly, "I guess you're not used to having someone yell at you, are you?"

Charlie shakes his head, still showing the same hurt expression. His tender blue eyes capture Mrs. Williamson's heart.

Mrs. Williamson, still holding Charlie's head up, says tenderly, "Charlie, I just want you to know that I am real sorry for yelling at you."

Charlie breaks his sad expression and smiles lovingly at his young teacher. He says with compassion, "Yes, ma'am. I forgive you, Mrs. Williamson." He pauses for a moment and says, "I am sorry for cutting in line. Will you please forgive me too? I'll never do it again."

A tranquil look comes into her eyes. She smiles at Charlie's innocent expression and says, "I sure will, little man. You know something, Charlie? I don't think I have ever had a little boy like you."

With a tender smile Charlie says, "I don't think I have ever had such a pretty teacher as you before."

Mrs. Williamson gives Charlie a heartwarming smile. "That is the nicest compliment I have ever had. Thank you so very much for saying that. Now, I want you to eat your lunch."

Charlie grins at his teacher and says kindly, "Yes, ma'am. I will do anything you want me to."

Mrs. Williamson lets go of Charlie's chin and smiles an enchanting smile once more at her adorable student. She then gets up and walks over to where the teachers sit.

At this tender moment in Charlie's life, he feels love for the first time from another woman besides his mother. Charlie is the happiest boy in school this day. He gets to know his teacher in a whole different light. This older woman touches Charlie in a special way. After this conversation, Charlie's crush on her develops in a most powerful and unique way. This is one of the most memorable moments of his young life.

These three female crushes that Charlie experiences early in his life will play a bigger role in his future relationships. These three female personalities never leave his heart and mind.

Now that you have come to understand a little bit about Charlie, his personality, and his character, you can begin to enjoy his story. In a more understanding way, you will now walk along with Charlie as his life unfolds before your eyes. You will share his experiences. You will feel his pain. You will learn about yourself by learning more about Charlie Delaney. His story will be a lesson for all those who have felt the pain of love and who have struggled to overcome these emotional mountains. His story is a story of innocence, truth, and honor; it is a drama of falling in love, dealing with its consequences, and overcoming the adversities.

Even though this is a fictional story, it is filled with truth that we all have felt at one time or another. This is a story with excitement, intrigue, romance, humor, mystery, sadness, and a tingle of evil lurking around the corner. I hope you will continue to read the intriguing and tragic love story of *The Three Loves of Charlie Delaney*.

Chapter 2
CHARLIE'S FIRST LOVE

The year is 1975. Three years have passed. Charlie's body and spirit is changing every day. With these physical changes, a new feeling has emerged, bringing about the most wonderful sensations. Charlie has been learning more about life than what is taught in the classroom.

Charlie is about to begin ninth grade. He has to travel twenty-five miles on a one-hour bus trip to a new school, Parker High. This is his first year of high school, and he is very apprehensive about going to a different school.

At the breakfast table Charlie's parents are discussing his upcoming school year. Charlie's father, now retired at age fifty-one, and his mother, now thirty-nine, are concerned that Charlie might not like his new school.

"Do you think Charlie will enjoy his new school?" Sara continues. "He hasn't shown much enthusiasm about going."

"Oh, the boy will probably have a good time. I just wish it wasn't so far away."

"What if something comes up? You know, if something happened to Charlie and one of us needed to go pick him up, I probably couldn't even find the school." John doesn't pay much attention to Sara as he continues to read the paper.

Sara, with a worried look, says, "Well, you know how withdrawn Charlie is when he is around a bunch of new faces. I just hope he will find some good friends and some good teachers and take a liking to them."

John, turning the page of his paper, says, "Sara dear, you don't have to worry about that. I'm sure Charlie will be all right. I think after the bus comes and picks him up, I'll drive down there and find out where the school is. Then I will know, in case we have to go down there sometime."

Sara seems to be a little less worried. "I just hope Charlie enjoys going there. There have been a lot of problems in that part of town, all those winos and kids standing around looking for trouble. I bet some are selling drugs too. I just wish they had a school nearby so Charlie wouldn't have to go all the way to town."

Sara gets up and starts cooking breakfast. When she finishes and everything is on the table, she sends John to wake Charlie. Charlie resists, and his father sternly replies, "You get up now! Your mother has breakfast ready, so get up and come downstairs right now!"

As Charlie approaches the kitchen table, Sara smiles pleasantly and says, "I'm glad to see you up. I have fixed you a good breakfast. I hope you are feeling well."

"Oh, I feel okay. I just wish I didn't have to get up so early and go to a different school. When is the bus supposed to be here?"

"Around seven o'clock," Sara replies. "The bus number is one-eighty-one. There will be several buses riding by, but the one you are supposed to get on is one-eighty-one."

Charlie nods and goes on eating breakfast. He looks up at the clock and notices it is 6:10 a.m. He doesn't talk much while continuing to eat his breakfast. His mother and father continue their daily breakfast conversation.

As Charlie finishes and is leaving the kitchen, his father asks, "Charlie, what do you say I take you to school today? Just forget about riding the school bus until tomorrow."

Charlie looks at his father and abruptly says, "No! You want the other kids to think I'm a big baby that needs to have his father hold his hand on the first day of school? No thanks, Dad."

John, looking a bit annoyed, says, "I was just trying to help you get adjusted, and besides, I was thinking about going down there anyway so I will know exactly where your new school is. It has been a long time since I have been in that part of town."

Charlie looks at his father with curiosity. "You mean you don't even know where it is?"

"No, not really, but I have an idea where it is."

"Right in the middle of town, where all the colored people live. I don't think it would be a good place for you to be riding around looking, Dad. If you got lost and wanted to ask for directions, where would you stop? I'll just take my chances with the bus. I am sure the bus driver knows where the school is."

John disappointedly replies, "Whatever you think, Charlie. I just thought you might like old dad to drive you."

After breakfast, Charlie goes to his room to get dressed. He puts on his usual outfit of blue jeans, T-shirt, and tennis shoes and is ready in a matter of minutes. After combing his hair, brushing his teeth, and doing all the other normal things teenage boys do, he goes downstairs and waits by the window for the school bus.

Sara, seeing the bus first, says with excitement, "Look, Charlie, here it comes."

Charlie glances out the window and looks at the number as the large orange vehicle passes by. He says, "No, Mama, that bus is two-thirty-one. My bus number is one-eighty-one. Isn't that the number you told me earlier?"

Sara nods. The morning glistens with the dew of a simple unexpected excitement. Sara smiles briefly at her son and says, "You are right, Charlie. I believe that bus picked up the elementary-school children, the fifth and sixth graders."

Charlie looks out the window and reminisces. He thinks about where that bus is going, to his former school. He thinks of Mrs. Williamson, his sixth-grade teacher. He wonders if she is still teaching there. It has been two years and a summer since he has seen her. He remembers her well and thinks about the times he had with her in class. He thinks about her young, beautiful figure and pleasant voice and the nights he couldn't sleep because she consumed his thoughts. He remembers how he had a terrible crush on her.

His mind goes back to his last day of school; he can see her standing in front of the class. She was wearing a green dress, and her youthful smile brought a rush of happiness to everyone in the class. She said,

"Class, I just want to tell all of you how I have enjoyed being your teacher this year. I will miss all of you, and I hope you all have a happy and safe summer vacation. I will miss you all so much!" Her mouth showed a smile, but her eyes showed a tear as Charlie stared at his affectionate and devoted teacher with sadness and despair of his own.

The atmosphere was full of excitement and happiness as Mrs. Williamson got ready to make an announcement. She spotted Charlie and gave him a wink. Her smile was the most pleasant sight Charlie had ever seen. She got all the students' attention and said, "Class, I know all of you are excited about this being the last day of school, but now I want to present an award to Charlie Delaney." She went over to her desk and took out a certificate. Her eyes contained a twinkle of enthusiasm, and her voice was that of an angel.

"Charlie, would you please come to the front? There is something I want to present to you. Charlie, I want you to know it has been a pleasure being your teacher this year. You were the only student this year to have perfect attendance. I proudly present you with this little certificate stating that Charlie Delaney came to school every day this school year. Congratulations, Charlie!"

Mrs. Williamson handed Charlie the perfect-attendance certificate as his face turned red. He shyly and modestly accepted the award as the entire class applauded loudly.

Charlie looked over at his teacher with those tender, innocent blue eyes of his and said, "Mrs. Williamson, I wish I could stay in the sixth grade the rest of my life." Mrs. Williamson laughed, and her expression captured Charlie's heart.

Charlie's mother breaks his reminiscing. "Charlie, here it comes. Here comes your school bus."

Charlie looks out the window and confirms the correct number on the bright-orange school bus as it passes by the house. "So long, Ma. I'll see you when I get home," Charlie says.

Sara kisses her son on the cheek and says her good-byes as Charlie excitedly runs out the door to the bus.

As the bus turns around and comes back to pick him up, he anticipates who might be on it. The door slowly opens, and Charlie climbs up. He is amazed to see only three others on the bus. He walks to the very back and sits in the very last seat. He looks out the window and sees his parents standing outside the house waving frantically. He waves back as the school bus drives off.

He is glad to be one of the first ones to get on the bus. He feels there is nothing more horrifying for a shy fourteen-year-old than to get on a crowded bus with everyone staring at you in hopes of finding a seat, if there is one to be found. Most of the time there are plenty of seats available, but most kids try to save a seat for someone else. He knows it could have been an anxious moment if no one would let him sit down next to them.

Charlie is curious to see who else will get on the bus. While it makes its journey to its various destinations, Charlie realizes that the bus is going through the same route as last year and picking up the same old faces. The atmosphere is fresh and full of wonder, and the day is starting out just great.

All of a sudden, the bus makes an unfamiliar stop, and standing there next to the road near her driveway is a girl. The bus driver opens the door cautiously and asks, "Are you supposed to go to Parker High?" The girl doesn't utter a word. She just looks up at the driver with tender, frightened eyes and nods affirmatively. "Then you have the right bus. Please get on," the bus driver said. The attractive, slim girl steps up and gets on without saying a word. Charlie's curiosity gets the best of him, and he sits up straight and opens his eyes big and wide to get a good look at her.

The girl walks halfway back and takes a seat. Charlie gets a good look at her face and thinks, *Wow, my God, what a beautiful girl!* Charlie is dumbfounded and doesn't know what to think. She is the most beautiful girl he has ever seen. She has long blondish hair and emerald-green eyes. Her skin is a soft white with a few freckles around her nose. Her lovely face mesmerizes Charlie as if he is under a magic spell. Although she is thin, she has an alluring figure.

Charlie just can't sit there and do nothing. He gets up and casually moves to a seat across the aisle from her. When he looks over, their eyes meet for the first time, and a wonderful, magical moment happens. Cupid is near and takes aim at Charlie's heart with his arrow.

Charlie glances at her from time to time with joy and amazement glowing in his eyes. He is too shy to say anything, but when their eyes meet for the second time, she says, "Hello."

Her soft voice makes Charlie smile. "Hi," he says and puts up his hand.

That is not much for their first conversation, but the ice has been broken, and the first sparkle of a new happiness enters Charlie's heart. A robust, happy energy flows throughout his young and innocent heart. He feels the magic every time he casually looks over at her. He can't believe how pretty she is. From time to time, she glances his way and smiles at him.

The bus is soon full, and the sound of conversation fills the air. The crisp atmosphere echoes out a clatter of sound, and the noisy, crowded scene prevents Charlie from looking at his new interest. The ride takes an hour, and Charlie thinks of her every minute. He can't wait for the bus to arrive at school.

When the bus arrives, Charlie is faced with the task of finding out where he should go. This occupies his mind, and when he thinks of the new girl and looks back to see where she is, she is gone. His mind returns to classes, and he follows the other kids into school.

In his homeroom, the teacher takes roll and instructs the students about their schedules. Charlie's classes include history, chorus, shop, English, general math, and physical education. After homeroom finishes, the students make their way to their second-period classes. When Charlie finds his second-period class, the bell has already rung, and he is late. Thankfully teachers have been instructed to allow more time for students to get to their classes until everyone is familiar with their schedules. Though Charlie is not in trouble, he is stared at by the other students, which is worse than being last on the school bus. His face turns red, and he stares at the floor as he hurries to find a seat.

When he is finally able to look up, he gets a shock: sitting over at the other end of the classroom is the girl from the bus, and she is waving at him! He can't believe it. It is really her! He quickly throws up his hand and smiles. He looks for an empty seat near her, but, to his disappointment, there are none.

All through class, Charlie smiles at her. Her eyes sparkle as she smiles happily back at him, and her excited smile makes him feel pretty good. She seems to like him. Her long, straight hair; emerald-green eyes; and special happy smile totally captivate Charlie's innocent, youthful mind. He keeps watching the clock, impatient for the class to be over. He wants so much to talk with her, and the desire to know her name brings on a mysterious feeling for him, but his wish is soon to be answered.

After the history teacher jokes with the students about no homework on the first day and wishes them all a good school year, they wait for the few minutes until the bell rings. As soon as the bell rings, Charlie makes a beeline over to the girl, not wasting any time introducing himself. For a shy, somewhat-withdrawn teenager, Charlie is handling high school very well.

"Hello. My name is Charlie Delaney. Remember me? I saw you get on the bus this morning."

"Yeah, I remember you; you're the only one I know at this school."

Charlie, looking confused, says, "You mean you don't know anybody?"

"That's right. I used to live on the south side. All my friends are going to a different school this year."

Charlie says softly, "Well, I'm glad you moved here."

In response to Charlie's statement she bubbles with joy, like the bubbles of champagne being poured in a glass.

Realizing he still doesn't know her name, Charlie asks her. She replies, "Deborah, Deborah Swanson."

Charlie smiles; he finally knows her name. "Deborah, what's your next class?"

When she tells him it is chorus, Charlie is excited. "Chorus is my next class too! Isn't that great? Why don't we try and find it together?"

"Yeah, that would be great, Charlie. It's good to have somebody I know to help me find my class."

Charlie and Deborah walk off together to find their new class. On the way, he opens up to Deborah. He finds it very easy to speak with her. They both seem to like each other a great deal. As he walks alongside her in the loud and crowded hallway, he asks, "Deborah, do you mind if I call you 'Dee' for short? When I was a little boy, I used to visit my aunt, and she looked after a little girl named Deborah while the girl's mother worked. My aunt always called her 'Dee' for short."

"No, I don't mind. If that's what you want to call me, then I guess it would be all right with me."

Charlie's pet name for Deborah will soon take hold all over school. Before long everyone will be calling Deborah 'Dee.'

As the two approach chorus class, Charlie is as happy as a rat in a cheese factory. He enjoys walking with Dee. He gazes at her soft blondish hair and marvels at her innocent beauty.

When Dee and Charlie enter the classroom, Charlie finds a place where both of them can sit together. Charlie and Dee can't stop talking to one another. Even when the teacher comes in and starts class, Charlie still finds things to say to Dee.

When the class is over, Charlie and Dee have to say their good-byes. Charlie realizes that for the first time in his life he is in love. It wasn't like the puppy love he had for Mrs. Williamson or the crushes he had on other schoolgirls. It was real love, a grown-up love. Ever since he laid eyes on Dee, a strange force he has not known before has taken hold of his inner self. He welcomes this force wholeheartedly.

Charlie will soon find out that being in love is not always green pastures and rosy scenery. He will soon realize that love in the heart of a young, innocent teenager can be very harsh and sometimes bitter.

Charlie finds it difficult to make it through the rest of the day—all he can think about is Dee and what she might be doing. When he arrives in English class, he finds that this class is not going to be very enjoyable. First of all, English is a difficult subject, and Charlie doesn't enjoy it at all. With his mind cluttered up with thoughts of his new love, the class is going to be that much harder. He can't spell very well.

His English teacher is stern and demanding. She expects a lot from her class. She is ready to start the new school year off right. She passes out the English textbooks and tells her class to get familiar with the first chapter. She doesn't give any homework, but she does tell the class that she will give them a pop test at the end of tomorrow's class on what they have gone over. She tells them that it won't be a very hard test, that it is just her way of getting the class used to what she expects from them. She wants the class to learn. Charlie doesn't like this beginning at all.

He tells himself that he will just have to buckle down and work extra hard. He has to pass English.

Charlie spends the rest of the day thinking about the cute little blonde and nervously anticipating seeing her on the bus. It gives that whole day more excitement and splendor. Shortly, the first day of school will be over, and Charlie will head for the bus. As he sits in the gym in his last class of the day, he thinks, *I can't wait until I get back on the bus so I can see Dee. I can't wait.*

When the bell rings for everybody to go home, the PE instructor doesn't dismiss the class. He tells the group of boys, "No one leaves the gym until I say so, and if anyone leaves without me saying so, tomorrow everyone will run five laps around the track." The class's first impression of him is that he is in charge and that everyone better follow his instructions or the whole class will suffer! His first lesson for the first day is *I am the boss.*

Charlie waits impatiently as the PE teacher looks at him. The teacher bellows, "Hey, you."

Charlie looks around and sees that the teacher is talking to him. He says, "Are you talking to me, Coach?"

The PE instructor smiles delightfully at Charlie. "Yeah, you. You look like you're in a hurry to go somewhere."

Charlie is intimidated a little by his remark. "Yes, sir. I'm eager to find my bus so I can get a good seat. I don't want to get left here."

The PE teacher laughs loudly, and soon some of Charlie's classmates join in. Then he says, "Those buses aren't going to leave for quite a while. You won't get left."

"Coach, the bell has rung. Why don't you let us go?" Charlie says.

Seeing that Charlie is so eager to go, the PE instructor lets everyone except Charlie go.

As all the other kids leave, Charlie sits there with a confused look on his face. The PE instructor gives Charlie a smile of authority and says, "Okay, you want to know why I didn't let you go like the rest of the class?"

Charlie nods.

"I'm gonna tell you why, young man. First of all, don't ever get in such a hurry to go somewhere until I tell you so. Do you understand?"

Charlie looks up at his instructor and answers clearly, "Yes, sir."

The PE teacher walks around Charlie slowly, taking up more time and says, "Second of all, you haven't shown me why I should let you go. Why should I let you go, Charlie?"

Charlie thinks, *If I don't get out of here soon, I'll never find a seat on the bus.* He does some fast talking and says, "Coach, you said a while ago if anybody leaves before you tell them to, they have to run five laps around the track course. Right?"

The PE instructor nods. "Yes, I said that."

In a flash of an eye, Charlie jumps up bravely and yells, "Okay, put me down for five tomorrow 'cause I'm splitting this scene right now!" Charlie jolts out the door. The PE instructor tries to get him back, but Charlie is moving too fast. He is out of there before his teacher can stop him.

When Charlie arrives at the bus, he finds it nearly half-empty. He is glad he isn't faced with the awful nightmare of trying to find a seat. He spots Dee sitting near the back. He waves at her, and she waves back. Her eyes focus directly on his, and her smile melts Charlie's heart. He thinks, *She really does like me.* He's disappointed to see that someone is already sitting with her, but he finds a seat without much problem.

Charlie keeps turning around to look at her. She is talking to a bunch of boys, and Charlie realizes he is not the only one who thinks Dee is attractive. He has to wait until the bus delivers some of the kids before it thins out enough for him to go to the back. He is anxious to talk to his sweetheart, but before he does, he has to stay put for around forty minutes.

He thinks, *I hope that stupid PE teacher is happy with himself for making me late. He ruined my hopes of talking to Dee.*

The bus is full of overexcited teenagers talking about their day. The loud voices of the students fill the bus with a constant sound of exuberant laughter and loud conversation. The bus finally reaches the end of its long highway route, turns off at the exit, and begins making its stops.

As soon as Charlie sees a seat near Dee open up, he gets up quickly and takes it before anyone else can. Charlie catches Dee's eye as he says, "Hi."

She responds warmly and enthusiastically. Her expression is one of excitement and affection. "Hi, Charlie. How did your first day go?"

Charlie feels happy. "Oh, fine. Most of my classes are all right. How was your first day?"

"I'm glad the first day is over. It's difficult adjusting to a different school."

"Yeah, me too, Dee. Me too."

Dee's eyes twinkle at Charlie. "Guess what, Charlie. I am glad I have two classes with you. I don't have a single friend here besides you."

This makes Charlie feel like a million bucks. They both sit and talk about their classes and simple things. They get to know one another a little better.

When the bus arrives at Dee's house, Charlie watches as she gets up from her seat, and his eyes focus on her perfectly shaped rear. She turns around as she walks and catches Charlie staring at her. She doesn't say anything but smiles pleasantly. She waves one last time. "See you tomorrow. Save me a seat with you in the back, okay, Charlie?"

"Yes, Dee, I sure will." Charlie begins to sense an inner feeling of peace, happiness, and joy. He is as happy as he has ever been in his life. Oh, to be young, innocent, and in love for the first time! This is a very special day in Charlie's life.

As the bus approaches Charlie's house, he still has Dee on his mind. He can't seem to get her out of his thoughts. When the bus stops, Charlie happily gets off the bus. Charlie's mother isn't home but his father is. He is back in his shop working on a few projects. Since he has retired, he now spends a lot of his spare time working on things for other people. Charlie casually walks into the shop and says, "Hi, Dad, what's up?"

His father, concentrating deeply on what he is working on, doesn't speak to Charlie at first. A few moments later, his father breaks his concentration and replies, "Oh, just a few minor projects."

Charlie spends only a short time with his father before disappearing to his room. He stays in his room quite a lot. He turns on the stereo and listens to his music hour after hour. He plays it quite loudly, but his parents never complain. As he listens to his music, he forgets about everything. He is in his own little world. His thoughts are a fantasy. He is invincible while in this world of imagination.

The next day, as Charlie gets ready for school, his father once again comes to his room to wake him and make sure that he is up. Charlie soon makes his way to the breakfast table, where his mother and father are waiting.

"So how was your first day of school yesterday?" his mother asks.

Charlie shrugs his shoulders and replies, "Fine." He doesn't tell her anything about the new courtship he has embarked upon. He doesn't like talking about things with his parents, especially about things concerning girls.

Charlie's father is the typical basic-needs father. He provides the basic necessities of life but lacks the communication and understanding to be a useful father. Charlie finds it very hard to relate to either of his parents but especially his father. He gets along with them all right, but still there is something missing. Being able to talk to them openly is nearly impossible at this stage of his life.

Charlie quickly eats his breakfast and then goes back to his room to finish getting ready. He wants to make a good impression on Dee, so he puts on his best clothes. He is full of excitement as he splashes on some of his father's cologne. He gets a big surprise when the cologne burns his tender face! It takes him several minutes to get over the unpleasant surprise.

His mother sits by the window keeping an eye out for the bus, as she has always done. When Charlie's bus nears the house, she announces it with enthusiasm.

Charlie feels a great deal of excitement and happiness as the bus stops to pick him up. He goes straight to the back and sits down in the last seat. This is to become his normal place. He waits anxiously on the cold, dark school bus as it nears Dee's house. Then his nervousness gets really strong. He will be happy to see her again. He thinks, *I hope she likes me as she did yesterday. Dear God in heaven, please guide her to where I am sitting. Please let her come back here with me.*

Charlie waits impatiently as the bus finally stops at Dee's house. She is waiting outside near her garage. She gets on, and his prayers are answered. She comes all the way to the back, but instead of sitting with Charlie, she sits across the aisle from him.

"Hello, Charlie. How are you doing? Ready to start another school day?" she asks.

Charlie feels extremely happy that Dee is showing him so much attention and giving him the impression she really likes him. He smiles at her and replies, "Yes, I am really looking forward to it."

The relationship flourishes from an innocent beginning. Charlie and Dee follow this routine every morning. They sit next to each other and talk about school and other simple things.

As the weeks go by, Charlie becomes fonder of Dee, and she becomes fonder of Charlie, the more they talk to each other, the closer they become. These simple talks open up new avenues to build on and construct towers of trust upon which to lean.

Charlie soon knows Dee's entire schedule. He sometimes explores the hallways hoping to find her standing there. Charlie and Dee become the best of friends, but Charlie can't bring himself to tell her how he truly feels about her. This mistake on Charlie's part will become disastrous. As much as Charlie likes to talk to Dee, he just can't open up and ask her to be his girlfriend. His shyness will eventually allow someone else to take Dee's affections from him.

Charlie is going through a somewhat-difficult stage in his young life, a stage that is full of low self-esteem and a lot of frustration. But as long as he can be with Dee and talk with her, he is happy. The talks they have at the back of the bus are the most memorable and happiest times of Charlie's ninth-grade year.

Dee seems to like Charlie a lot and would go steady with him if he would just ask her. There is something about asking a girl to go steady that Charlie finds very difficult. He has never asked a girl before, so it is only natural for him to be apprehensive about that all-important question. As long as Dee seems interested in Charlie, that is enough for him, at least for the time being.

As time goes by, Charlie and Dee are seen everywhere together. The relationship develops into a good friendship, but Dee doesn't understand why Charlie hasn't asked her to go steady. She has gone steady with lots of guys in the past and can't understand why Charlie is taking so long to ask her. He waits for her every morning after homeroom, and then they walk to their history class together. It becomes a morning ritual. She enjoys seeing Charlie waiting for her and likes the attention he gives her, but there is something missing: that all-important question.

Dee and Charlie arrive at their history class one day to experience something long in coming, something Charlie would learn to hate—the first instance of another boy showing great interest in Dee. The jealousy begins. The teacher comes into the room and sees the class ready for their lesson. He takes the roll and tells the class to move their desks together and make six groups. Because of the assigned seating, Charlie doesn't get to be in Dee's group. He notices that one of the guys in Dee's group, Tim Simpson, is very fond of her. He is always friendly and kind to her. Charlie knows Tim all too well. Tim used to play on Charlie's Little League baseball team a few years ago.

When the bell rings, Dee has a special sparkle in her eyes. Charlie waits for Dee like always, but this time Dee leaves with Tim. Charlie, like a lost little puppy, follows behind. As Tim branches off to go to his class, he leans over and kisses Dee right on the mouth—right in front of God and everyone else who wants to see! Charlie looks on with anger and resentment, outraged at this boy's action. Charlie is hurt.

Charlie is still tagging along behind Dee at a distance. When he gets to their chorus classroom, he takes a seat next to her, saying, "Hi, Dee. How's everything going?"

"Hey, Charlie, I'm just fine." She talks to Charlie as if he is her brother.

Charlie tries to shrug off her new admirer. He manages to change the subject for a bit, but all through chorus, Dee talks about Tim. Her eyes have a special sparkle to them that Charlie ignores as much as he can. Then the bell rings. Charlie is relieved. He is getting tired of Dee going on and on about Tim.

Charlie walks with Dee until he has to branch off to his next class. Before he walks off, he gives Dee a mean look. He begins to act hostile to Dee but in a silent way. He is feeling the agony of jealousy.

After Charlie's fifth-period class, he waits for Dee. Her class is on the same floor and just a few rooms down. When she comes down the hallway, he doesn't say a word. He just gives her an angry and disappointed look.

Dee, seeing this, asks, "What's the matter, Charlie? You look like you're mad at me."

Charlie says, "Nothing, there is nothing wrong with me. What makes you think that?" Charlie is too jealous to tell her the real reason he is mad at her. He just pretends as if nothing is wrong. It is hard for Dee to understand why Charlie is acting this way. Charlie, like most young men, can't tell her that he is simply jealous.

The two head downstairs for their next class. Charlie doesn't say a word as they walk, giving her a large dose of the silent treatment. When Dee reaches her class, she turns to Charlie to say good-bye, but Charlie just looks at her coldly. He shrugs his shoulders and, without saying anything, walks away angrily.

Charlie's attitude really bothers Dee. She can't understand why Charlie doesn't speak to her. She tries to think if there is anything that she has said that might have upset him, but she can't think of anything. She is puzzled as to why Charlie's behavior had changed so dramatically. After racking her brain, she still can't figure out Charlie's sudden change. She has to find out what is the matter, but first she has to go to her sixth-period class. She feels hurt and confused all the way to her last class. She thinks of Charlie as a very close friend. Dee likes Charlie more than any other guy in school, but now she thinks Charlie doesn't like her anymore. He has had plenty of time to ask her to go steady with him but hasn't. She knows there are plenty of other guys that find her attractive, and she feels it is only natural for a girl to like other guys.

Dee worries the last few moments of her sixth period and thinks of what she wants to say to Charlie. As she sits there quietly, her green eyes get a little watery. She eagerly waits for the bell to ring so she can find Charlie and relieve her troubled mind. When the bell rings, everyone eagerly rushes to their buses.

Charlie is one of the first ones to arrive at the bus. He goes to the very back and impatiently waits for Dee. Soon Dee walks down the aisle. She has a sad look on her face, but when she sees Charlie, her sad, confused look disappears.

Charlie says to her, "I saved you a seat." He slides his legs into the aisle so she can get past him and sit next to the window. He does this so he can have Dee all to himself; this time nobody else is going to sit next to her except Charlie. Dee sits down. Soon the bus fills up, and Charlie and Dee sit together all the way home. This is the happiest time of the day for Charlie.

Dee just can't understand why Charlie was so angry before. Earlier she got the impression that he was upset with her, but now he is being friendly again. She doesn't understand why he is acting like this. She forgets what she was planning to talk to him about. She forgets the scene at school and enjoys the ride home, but she still has some doubt about him.

Three months pass. Charlie and Dee get to know each other better, and although Charlie is in love with Dee, he doesn't admit it. It is as though he is afraid to admit it even to himself. Dee begins to open up and tell Charlie all about her life. She confides in him so much that she can't wait to see him again so she can tell him her problems. He loves listening to her. Her voice is like that of an angel. Her innocent green eyes put him under a spell every time she speaks. Nothing means more to Charlie than Dee; he is always thinking of her.

Charlie has his problems too, but he locks all his problems, frustrations, and fears inside. He doesn't like to relate anything important to anyone, not even to Dee. This makes his life a little more difficult and much more complicated and prevents the communication needed to establish the special relationship he wants to have with Dee. The first three months of the ninth grade are wonderful for Charlie and Dee, but the next three months are trying for both of them. Charlie is in trouble in several of his classes, mainly English. He failed English the first quarter and is struggling this quarter. If he fails it this time, he will have to make it up in summer school. He doesn't want to do that.

Charlie gets more and more attached to Dee as time goes on. He puts other things aside, including some very important things, just to be close to her. He thinks of her morning, noon, and night, but no matter how much he cares for her or thinks about her, he still doesn't open up and tell her how he feels. This lack of communication will ultimately bring down and destroy their relationship. As long as Dee shows Charlie all her attention, he is the happiest boy at school, but Dee is growing tired of waiting.

One morning Dee, like always, gets on the bus and sits beside Charlie in the back. She looks very upset over something, so Charlie says, "Hello, Dee, why so sad?"

Dee's fawn-like eyes glance over at him. "Oh nothing, Charlie. Just me and my mom had a few words this morning."

Charlie is curious. "Would you like to tell me? I'm a good listener, you know."

"She's been on my case about my schoolwork. She keeps nagging about my grades and why I don't bring any homework home."

Charlie looks compassionately at Dee and tries to reassure her not to worry about it, telling her that parents are sometimes that way.

"Yeah, I know, but my mom is probably a little different from your folks. You see, my father and my mama broke up last summer, and it hasn't been the same since. That's the main reason we moved out here, because of their divorce."

Charlie doesn't say anything. He just listens attentively.

Dee continues, "My mama never had a chance to go to college. She wishes she had, and I guess that's why she is on me so hard. She doesn't want me to miss out on life like she did. You see, my mama got married when she was only seventeen. She had to because of me."

Charlie, with a puzzled look, asks, "How come she had to get married because of you?"

Dee looks at Charlie with a blank expression and says, "Because my father got her knocked up."

Charlie turns a deep shade of red and gives her a stupid smile.

"My father is a drunk," she says. "Last summer wasn't the first time he and my mama broke up. She has taken him back several times over the years."

"Maybe they will get back together again before too long."

Dee shakes her head. "No, this last time was the very last time. My mama made it perfectly clear to him in the divorce. If he ever comes over to the house or calls, my mama will have him thrown in jail again. When I was growing up, he was never home. He would always stay out late at night and drink with his buddies."

"Did you ever see him drunk at home?" Charlie asks.

"All the time. He would come home drunk and talk mean to me. He is a real bad father. I hate him."

Charlie sympathizes with Dee and asks, "You don't really hate him, do you?"

Dee takes a handkerchief from her purse. "Yes, Charlie, I do hate him—not for the things he has said and done to me but for what he has done to my mama. I have seen him beat her and talk ugly to her ever since I can remember."

"I know you have bitterness toward him for what he has done, but if you hate him, you will be hurting yourself even more."

Dee looks over at Charlie and tries to smile and put on a happy face before saying, "You know, Charlie, I believe you are right, but sometimes I can't help it. Hate is something that is hard to deal with. It's not something I want to think about. I just don't have much control over it. It gets in my mind and takes over my thoughts. All I can do is try to deal with it the best way I can."

Charlie reaches over and takes Dee's hand. "Well, you're going to have to deal with it while I hold your hand."

Dee smiles joyfully at Charlie and asks, "Do either of your folks ever drink in front of you?"

Charlie pauses, enjoying holding Dee's hand. "Well, my father sometimes will drink a beer in his shop, the one he works in behind our house. But my mama would never let him bring anything like that in the house. She is a hard-line Baptist woman." Dee holds Charlie's hand in a more caring manner as he continues, "My mama doesn't like alcohol at all. She has made it very clear to me and my father that no alcohol of any form will be allowed in her house." Dee listens with a smile glowing on her face. Her emerald-green eyes capture Charlie's attention, and he looks at her with love and admiration. They both sit there in a delicate, tranquil moment, simply looking at each other with tender, caring, and loving eyes.

The bus begins to get full as more and more students get on, and Charlie breaks the silence. In a gentle voice he says, "My mama's a nurse. She has told me numerous times about all the drunk drivers that have ended up in the hospital. She works in the recovery room at the hospital, and she sees firsthand all the people who get banged up after automobile crashes. So she has seen what alcohol can do."

"That's what my mother wants me to be, a nurse. She keeps telling me that college isn't going to be easy. I guess that's why she keeps nagging about my grades."

Charlie, still holding Dee's soft hand, says, "Well, I guess that's what parents are supposed to do: nag."

The school bus continues to fill, and Charlie reluctantly releases Dee's hand. They can't keep talking about this now because people are sitting close, so they instead talk about the simple things teenagers talk about until the bus reaches the school. Dee seems to be feeling better now that Charlie is there to confide in. When she gets to school, she still is filled with a little anxiety, and she tries hard to bring her grades up. She wants Charlie to ask her to be his girlfriend in the worst way, but he still doesn't.

Several weeks go by as Charlie and Dee continue to get closer and closer. She looks forward to seeing him every day. She waits and waits for Charlie to ask her to go steady, but he just can't muster up the words. Dee begins to get impatient but remains calm about the issue because she enjoys the conversations they have on the bus. These times have become their most intimate times together. Dee has come to enjoy these bus rides as much as Charlie. It is a place where they can be alone with each other for a short while without others interrupting their special talks. This has become a very carefree time for Charlie as well, a time he can find out more about her thoughts. He loves listening to her. Even though Charlie and Dee talk with each other in great detail, Charlie doesn't ever open up and tell Dee that he loves her. He can't work up the courage to tell her his true feelings. He just listens to her open up her heart.

Charlie has always been shy when it comes to talking about his true feelings. It just seems impossible for him. Being young and inexperienced, he has difficulty sharing his inner emotions. As the months continue to go by, Dee finally realizes that Charlie isn't going to ask her to go steady. She feels as if she is just wasting her time with Charlie when she could have had several other relationships by now. She is tired of waiting. A small commitment is all she wants, just to know that he feels for her the way she feels for him. A few words would establish how he feels for her, and Dee needs to hear those words. She just needs to hear Charlie's heart speak. This lack of courage will haunt Charlie Delaney all his life. He will look back years later and realize what an idiot he was then.

Dee wants a boyfriend. She has had several throughout the years; it isn't anything new for her. She just can't understand why Charlie hasn't asked her. How much he talks with her and the way he acts around her gives her the impression that he really cares for her. She just can't figure it out. She thinks, *Maybe Charlie doesn't care for me as much as I think he does. If he did, he would have asked me to go with him by now.* But shy Charlie stays the same day after day, week after week, month after month.

Around the end of the second quarter, Dee begins to realize that Charlie is never going to ask her to go steady. About that time, Tim Simpson begins to get Dee's attention again. Tim eventually asks Dee to be his girlfriend. A couple of days after second-quarter report cards are passed out, Dee quietly announces to some of her friends that she is going steady with Tim, the guy in her history class who had kissed her earlier in the year. Charlie doesn't seem to mind the news on the outside, but on the inside he hurts with a terrible left-out feeling. His heart is broken.

Soon after, Charlie becomes withdrawn and depressed. He is filled with emptiness and loneliness. He mopes around feeling sorry for himself. He tries to make Dee feel bad by pretending he is mad at her, but, in fact, he isn't mad at Dee at all. He is mad at himself for not asking her to go steady with him earlier, but he takes it out on her.

When you are young, you tend to play these immature games. Since you can't explain your true feelings, you manufacture something ridiculous that points the blame at someone else. And so Charlie pretends that Dee wronged him and acts as if he is mad. This is his way of getting back at her without feeling guilty.

Soon Dee gets tired of Charlie always giving her angry looks. She begins to ignore him, but doing this bothers her. Sometimes she goes home and cries all night, wondering what she might have said or done to Charlie. She knows that she hasn't done anything wrong, and this becomes a real problem for Dee to handle. She wants to be accepted by all her friends and classmates, but Charlie behaving so immaturely really does get her down and hurts her tremendously. She just can't figure out why he acts this way.

Dee has other problems to deal with besides Charlie—mostly problems at home. Dee's mother has been dating someone, William O'Brien, and soon this relationship becomes serious. He begins to stay over several nights a week, and then he and her mother get married, only two and a half months after they met. O'Brien wants to adopt Dee, but Dee doesn't want him to; she really doesn't like him very much. Dee's poor relationship with her new stepfather creates a very troubling time for her.

Dee's problems with her new stepfather begin to affect her schoolwork, and eventually she starts rebelling against her mother. Drugs are readily available at the high school that Dee and Charlie attend; Dee begins to hang around the wrong crowd and is slowly introduced to these substances. Charlie, on the other hand, stays clear of these people and these problems.

Neither Dee nor Charlie are making good grades by the end of the third quarter, and Dee realizes that her mother's dream of her becoming a nurse is dissolving. Charlie too realizes he has a great deal of work in front of him and is afraid that he will have to retake English in the summer. At this point, he decides to buckle down and work harder.

The stressful times continues between Charlie and Dee. Charlie keeps acting as though he is mad at Dee, but at other times he is very nice to her. She continues going steady with Tim though he really doesn't mean a great deal to her. She only goes with him because he asked her and because she really wants to have a boyfriend.

Charlie goes through periods of extreme depression. He cannot express his feelings well and begins to overeat. He feels inadequate and withdrawn from others.

One cold March morning, Dee does not get on the bus. This worries Charlie all day long. Dee has missed several days of school this year, but this time feels different.

For the next three days, Dee does not attend school. On the fourth day, Dee is standing outside ready to get on the bus and makes her short walk to the back, where Charlie is waiting for her. He is so glad to see her again.

"Hey Dee, you know we go to school around here on Mondays, Tuesdays, and Wednesdays," he says.

"Charlie, I might not be going to school around here anymore."

Charlie is horrified at her sad face and asks her what she is talking about.

"Me and my folks had a big fight the other day," she says. "My mama found something in my purse that upset her a little bit."

Of course Charlie is curious and presses her for more information.

"Charlie, if I tell you, you must promise me that you won't go around school telling everybody. Do you promise?"

Of course Charlie agrees.

"Well, my mama found a couple of joints and three little pills in my purse."

Charlie is very disappointed that Dee is using drugs.

"It's not such a big deal," she says. "A couple friends of mine gave them to me. All they do is make me feel a little bit better; that's all. Anyway, my mama and William are thinking about putting me in a different school. They think that if I go to a different school, I won't get into this stuff. Mama was also talking about putting me in some stupid drug rehabilitation center."

Dee begins to cry, and her tears affect Charlie. "Listen, Dee," he says, "if that crap is going to get you into so much trouble, why don't you stay away from it? Your mom is only looking out for what's best for you. I sure don't want you to leave me and go away." Charlie is concerned and frightened that Dee might leave the area. "You know, if you leave now and go to another school, you might have to repeat the ninth grade. I don't want to leave. If you do I'll miss you."

Dee looks happier. "You know something, Charlie? I'm glad I have a friend like you to talk with."

Charlie smiles happily at this sweet and tender girl.

"I believe when I get home, I'll tell Mama and William not to worry about me getting into trouble over this stuff anymore. I will also tell them I'll try to pull my grades up some. Maybe then they won't send me anywhere."

Charlie smiles at her again and sighs in relief. "Dee, I'm glad you're talking positively about this. I sure hope your folks don't send you away."

Charlie's influence on Dee works out. She improves her grades tremendously and does not mess with drugs anymore, at least not for the rest of the ninth grade.

Whenever Dee or Charlie have problems, they become the best of friends, but when everything is going fine and there are no problems or conflicts, they drift apart. Charlie is jealous of Dee's other male friends and begins to ignore her in the hallways once again. Sometimes he gives her mean looks or turns his head away, giving her the impression he is angry. This immature act is his way of getting more attention when he is feeling jealous, but it troubles Dee tremendously when he does this.

By the time the school year ends, Dee has gone steady with several other guys, none for very long. She wants acceptance and attention, but she has always wanted Charlie. Though he always shows her that he cares very much for her, he still doesn't ask her to go steady. The year has been a confusing one for Dee, but she has managed to bring up her grades and pass all her classes except math. She still doesn't like school, but she's managed to make the best of the year. All Dee has ever wanted is to be accepted by her fellow classmates and to be loved. Her eagerness to be accepted almost resulted in her paying a very high price when she got into the drug scene.

Charlie manages to get a C on his final in English, ending up with a D average for the year. He is just glad he didn't fail. English has been even harder for him than he thought it would be.

With the comfort of having passed all their courses, Charlie and Dee both look forward to those last few days of school. It is a time of excitement as the 1975/76 school year draws to a close. On the last day of school, the halls are filled with spontaneous and harmonious excitement. It is an innocent, joyous time. Friends say their good-byes to each other, some for the summer and some for the final time. For Charlie, it is a difficult time. He wonders how he will say good-bye to Dee. He thinks he might try to kiss her and has been thinking about it a great deal. *Will I be able to work up enough courage to do this, or will I hate myself for not trying?* he wonders.

The last hour of school finally arrives, and Charlie sits in the gym waiting for the last bell of the year to ring. He is filled with a nervous energy waiting to be released. As the boys sit and talk and wait for this bell to ring, the PE instructor walks toward them. Everyone gets silent as he gets closer.

"Okay, fellows, I want each and every one of you to have a safe and happy summer," he says. "There are a few things I would like to say to all of you before you leave for the last time." As he continues, he looks directly at Charlie. "I have picked on a few of you more so than others this year. I did this because I thought some of you needed an extra amount of discipline to overcome the problems of being a teenager. When I see someone not socializing or acting like a normal kid should act, I think that he might be going through some problems. I then pick on him a little harder so he will have me to think about rather than some girl. So if you think I have been especially hard on you, I just want you to know why. I'm not apologizing for it. I just want you to know why I did it. When you leave high school and start looking for a job, you are going to see just how rough this world really is. I just wanted to prepare you for the rough part."

The group of boys cheer and applaud, and even Charlie applauds with enthusiasm.

"So, fellas," the PE instructor says, "I am going to let you leave a little early today, so you can get to your buses and say your last good-byes. Go on; get out of here!"

Instead of tearing out like all the other guys, Charlie goes over to the PE instructor and says, "Coach, I'm glad you said all that. I needed to hear it."

"Yes, Charlie, I believe you did. One of the most important things in a teacher's life is to be sure to explain things clearly to those he or she is trying to help. If I didn't then I guess I wouldn't be doing my job properly."

"Yes, sir. I will try to remember what you just said."

The bell sounds, and the PE instructor looks at Charlie with authority and says, "Now get out of here. School is over."

Charlie walks out of the gym, turns, and waves good-bye to his PE instructor. The stocky man returns the wave.

Charlie goes to his bus, which isn't full like it usually is. He knows that the empty seats are due to the fact that some guys are driving home in cars and probably taking friends with them. Charlie's friend Larry thinks this is a great idea and can't wait until next year when they get their licenses and can drive when they want to.

Charlie is worried that he has not seen Dee yet. He wonders if she is getting a ride home from someone else. He has thought about kissing her all year long, and he knows this will be his last chance. His worrying increases until finally he sees Dee get on the bus. She walks right down the aisle to where Charlie is sitting and sits down just across from him. She is very excited that this is the last day of school; the whole bus is. There is laughter and joy all throughout the bus, and the atmosphere is alive with happy students full of positive emotions. These ninth- and tenth-grade students at Parker High are young, happy, carefree, and innocent. They are not looking toward the future but just enjoying the present.

"Hey Charlie, isn't it great? last day! I just can't believe it. It is finally here!" Dee says.

She seems happier than Charlie has ever seen her before, and this makes him happy. This fact makes a permanent impression on his young mind.

"I'm sure glad you didn't ride home with someone else today," he says. "This may be the last time we will see each other until next fall."

Dee turns her head slightly sideways and smiles sweetly at Charlie. "I am glad I didn't ride home with anyone else either. My mother wouldn't let me anyway. If I didn't get off the school bus, she would worry like the devil until I got home. Then, after I did, she'd beat me with a belt."

Charlie and Dee laugh and enjoy each other's company more and more as the bus moves up the highway.

During the year, the ride home seemed long and dreary, but today it is wonderful. No one cares how long it takes. It is the best ride ever. The ones who chose to go home by car don't know what they are missing. Everyone is happy and carefree. Since the bus is only half-full, the kids can get up and change seats whenever they want to. Everyone seems to have something to say, and this is their last opportunity to say it.

The bus gets off the exit ramp for the last time, and everyone applauds loudly, expressing a special joy. The bus then begins to unload its precious cargo, and the glorious feeling of seeing the kids depart makes the bus driver grin. Time after time, the bus stops at its appointed destinations. The bus has a happy, youthful atmosphere.

The bus reaches a part of the route where it has to go down a road and then turn back around. About three carloads of Charlie's friends are sitting out there waiting for the bus to turn around; they came here to say their last good-byes to everyone left on the bus.

Larry says, "Hey, Charlie, look. There's Wayne and Charles and David and Bobby."

Dee is waving along with the other students. The bus driver stops and lets the kids get on. They all walk around and talk to everyone who is left, amplifying the energetic atmosphere. Charlie notices the fellas kissing some of the girls good-bye, just a peck here and a peck there, nothing passionate.

As Bobby says good-bye to Dee, he hugs her and then kisses her! Charlie shakes his head in amazement. *Bobby? Dee kissed Bobby? I can't believe it! She doesn't even talk to Bobby much.* Charlie figures if she will kiss Bobby, she certainly ought to kiss him.

As the group of guys leave the bus, Charlie stays close to Dee. He remains close to her until the bus nears her house. He knows this will be his last chance. As the bus slows to a stop at her house, Charlie stands up, walks over to her, and looks at her seriously. "Good-bye, Dee."

"Bye, Charlie."

Charlie shyly says, "Let me give you a kiss."

Charlie makes his approach, and Dee responds in the same fashion. She puts her arms around his neck and shoulders as Charlie puts his arms around her waist. She turns her head slightly and presses her delicate, innocent, and tender lips against Charlie's nervous mouth. He feels the touch of a girl's soft lips pressed against his for the first time in his entire life! Charlie closes his eyes, and for one brief moment the world stops.

The kiss is over in a flash. Dee smiles at Charlie and then turns and walks off the bus. Charlie sits down and watches her walk to her house. He smiles. Something inside him erupts into a wonderful sensation throughout his soul. He has never experienced such a feeling in his entire life. He thinks about the gentle pressure of her sweet, young lips pressed against his.

Charlie cannot say another word until the bus stops at his house. He gets off slowly and departs the old orange school bus for the last time that year. He walks up the driveway to his home in a daze. He turns and watches the bus disappear from sight. He felt something today that has changed his entire life. Charlie has a special peace in his heart that he has never felt before. He feels different, but at the same time, he feels the same. This tender, youthful time in Charlie's life has brought about a change in his soul. He felt love touch his lips, then absorb into his heart, and then flood his soul.

As he enters the house, his mother is standing waiting for him. "So how did your last day of school turn out?" she asks.

He looks up at his mother with glistening eyes and says, "Oh, fine. Just fine." It was more than just fine. For today Charlie Delaney experienced his first kiss.

Chapter 3
THE LAST INNOCENT SUMMER

At nine the next morning, Charlie wakes up unusually tired, maybe because he slept too long. His father is already at work in his shop.

"Good morning, Charlie. Did you sleep well?" Sara asks as she washes dishes in the kitchen. After Charlie's sleepy response, she asks what he wants for breakfast.

"I believe I'm in the mood for a stack of pancakes and some sausage."

Charlie seems hungry, so Sara begins to fix his breakfast without delay.

After finding that Charlie's plans are merely to hang around the house and watch TV, Sara suggests, "How would you like to go swimming?"

Charlie's eyes get as big as marbles. "That would be cool! I will run and put my swimming trunks on right now!"

"You finish eating your breakfast first."

Charlie finishes eating in a hurry and quickly leaves the table to run upstairs and put on his swimming trunks.

Once he's ready, Sara drives them to Mineral Springs, one of the local swimming pools. They get out of the car and, looking through the fence, notice that the pool is very crowded.

"Just look at all the people in there," Sara says. "There are so many people in that pool you couldn't stir it with a stick. I don't know about going in there now."

Charlie is extremely disappointed. He gives his mother a depressed look and doesn't say anything. Sara sympathetically looks down at Charlie and sees his sad, innocent face.

"Charlie, I know I promised you that you could go swimming today, but there are just too many people in there."

"I understand, Mama. You're right; there are too many people in there."

Seeing Charlie's disappointment, Sara says, "I have an idea. Let's go to another pool. I don't know of any nearby, but I do know of one about forty miles from here. It is a whole lot larger than this one, a whole lot larger."

"Forty miles is a long drive from here, Mama. You don't have to drive that far just for me. I can go swimming some other time."

Sara looks at Charlie with love and admiration, "Just for saying that, I will drive one hundred forty miles to find a swimming pool for you."

Charlie hugs his mother, and they hop back in the car. Sara proudly drives forty miles to the other swimming pool.

When they arrive, Charlie is excited. "Wow! Just look at that swimming pool. It must be ten times the size of the other one!"

Sara glows at the sight of his happy expression. Sara pays only for Charlie's admission, as she has decided to sit and watch him from outside the fence. She reads and frequently looks over to see if Charlie is enjoying himself.

About noon, Sara waves to get Charlie's attention and suggests he come out for lunch. Charlie is starving and doesn't have to be told twice. Sara packed a picnic lunch of peanut-butter-and-banana sandwiches, sweet pickles, grapes, potato chips, chocolate cake, and soft drinks, which Charlie sees as a feast. She loads up plates for the both of them. Charlie gives his mother a hug and an "I love you" and digs in, as does Sara.

They sit in the cool shade and eat. As Charlie is feasting on the chocolate cake, Sara spots one of her friends walking toward them and says, "Look who's coming, Charlie. It's Cathy Lane. And it looks like she is with her daughter, Melissa."

Seeming completely unexcited, Charlie continues to devour the chocolate cake.

Cathy says, "Hello, Sara; hello, Charlie. I'm surprised to see you two all the way out here. How have you been?"

Sara smiles. "Hello, Cathy; hello, Melissa. Charlie, say hello to Melissa and Mrs. Lane."

With his mouth full of cake, Charlie just waves to both of them.

"So what brings you all the way out to this neck of the woods?" Sara asks.

"Oh, I just thought I would take Melissa swimming today. Since her last day of school was yesterday, all I have heard is 'Mama, I want to go swimming.' I thought I would do it today so I wouldn't have to hear that whining and whimpering anymore."

The two women laugh and talk for awhile. Melissa remains silent, and Charlie keeps eating cake.

Cathy complains, "Kids nag and nag about wanting you to take them somewhere, but they don't ever want to get out of bed first. We would have gotten here earlier if Melissa had gotten out of bed sooner. She thinks she can sleep all day now that she is out of school."

Sara doesn't have that problem with Charlie, so she just listens, grateful to have a son like him. She asks, "How old is Melissa now?"

Cathy replies, "Fourteen." She turns to Charlie and says, "You know, Charlie, Melissa will be going to Parker High in the fall. You two will be going to the same school."

Charlie smiles halfheartedly as he reaches for his third piece of cake.

Sara says, "They do grow up quickly, don't they?"

"They sure do. Before long Melissa will be off to college, then married. So I figure I'll do all I can for her while she is still young— even drive fifty miles to take her swimming. We tried Mineral Springs earlier, but it was so crowded."

Sara nods her agreement, commenting on how people were packed in like sardines there.

Cathy looks around to see if anyone nearby is listening and then says, "Yeah, if they wouldn't let all those Negroes in, there would be plenty of room."

Sara look at Cathy sternly. "I don't know why you would say that. Those Negroes have the same right to go there as anybody else."

Cathy gives her own stern look to Sara. "If they weren't in there, you and I wouldn't have had to drive fifty miles. That's a long way to drive just so our children can go swimming."

"But they still have the same right to be there as anybody else. And besides, I didn't drive fifty miles!"

Cathy shows a little disgust with Sara and comments that Sara is lucky that she has a son instead of a daughter. She then suggests that Melissa is not safe with all those Negro boys hanging around her while she's in a bathing suit—and not to mention where those boys' hands might be while under the water!

"Cathy, don't you think you're overreacting?"

"Overreacting! If you had a teenage daughter, you would think the same way. Melissa is fourteen now. She is developing into a very attractive girl. I don't want any of those colored boys putting their hands on my daughter."

Sara shows compassion to Cathy without necessarily agreeing with her. "I don't think any of those colored boys would touch Melissa in a swimming pool."

"Didn't you see all those little black boys running around like … like a bunch of crazy people? They don't act civilized when they're around other people. You should have seen them running around, acting wild without any control whatsoever. Melissa and I left five minutes after I paid for her to go in."

"They looked like they were only having fun to me. You're just overreacting."

"I'm not overreacting!" Cathy says loudly.

Sara's expression turns angry. "Look at you, Cathy. Your actions speak for themselves."

Cathy calms down and says in a gentler tone, "Well, just look around, Sara."

Sara looks around the picnic area and then looks down toward the swimming pool was. She notices that there aren't any black people anywhere to be seen. "So what?" she says. "What is there to look around for?"

Cathy looks proud. "You don't see any blacks here, do you? Do you know why? Because they can't afford to come here. That's why they all go to Mineral Springs, 'cause it's so cheap."

"So?"

"So that is why Mineral Springs is so crowded."

Sara doesn't reply. She just gives Cathy an annoyed look.

"Now be honest, Sara. Isn't the atmosphere here a lot better since you don't have to look at all those colored people?"

Sara is getting a little upset with Cathy. Just as she is about to say something, Cathy intervenes and says, "Don't you feel safer here knowing there are no blacks to bother you?"

"I don't know, Cathy. Maybe. I don't know."

Her face determined, Cathy says, "Well, I sure do! Just knowing I don't have to think about what they might do to me and to Melissa is worth what I paid to come here."

Melissa interrupts the conversation, whining, "Mama, I want to go swimming."

Cathy consents and says her good-byes to Sara and Charlie, who has been listening intently. She says to Charlie, "It's been good seeing you again. Since you and Melissa will be going to the same school in the fall, I hope you two will see each other and become good friends."

"Yes, ma'am. I'm sure we will. Bye, Melissa; I'll be seeing you."

Charlie, after taking the last swallow of his soda pop, casually looks over to his mother and says, "I guess I will go back to swimming now."

Sara, still watching Cathy walk away, says abruptly, "Oh no you don't, young man. You will wait at least thirty minutes before you go back in. I don't want you to get any cramps."

Charlie stares back at his mother with a bit of apprehension showing on his face. "Come on, Mama; I want to dive off the high diving board."

"Young man, you won't dive off anything until your food has time to digest, so don't keep bothering me about it, or we will just go home, you hear!"

Charlie looks so sad and hurt that Sara regrets speaking to him so harshly. She doesn't usually speak to him that way. Charlie thinks something must really be bothering her. To Sara, he looks as sad as a basset hound. His expression tears at her heart.

She tries to get him to talk, asking, "What do you think of Melissa? Do you think she is pretty?"

Charlie doesn't succumb to her questions and remains quiet. Sara continues to try to start a conversation with Charlie, but all she can get are yes-or-no answers. He doesn't say anything else; he just looks at her with those sad blue eyes. Another five minutes go by, and Sara can no longer stand the torture of seeing her son heavyhearted.

"Okay, Charlie, I give up. I can't stand to see you like this anymore. I feel so bad when you look up at me that way. Go ahead and go swimming."

Charlie's sad expression blossoms into joy. He looks at his mother with love and kindness, hugs her, and gives her a kiss. "I love you, Mama."

As Charlie runs out from the picnic area, Sara shouts, "Don't run, Charlie!"

Turning around, he sees his mother's strong, caring face and begins to walk.

Sara notices Cathy sitting alone watching Melissa play in the water. She thinks about going over and sitting with her but decides against the idea. She is still a little disturbed by what Cathy said earlier, so she opts to read her book instead.

Sara watches Charlie for a few more hours, reading a great deal of her book. After finishing a chapter, she glances at her watch. It's nearly three o'clock, so she motions to Charlie that it's time to go home. Charlie gets out of the water without having to be told twice and walks slowly to his mother.

"Did you have fun today?" she asks.

With a look of jubilation, he replies, "Yes, Mama, I sure did!"

"Good. Now let's make that long drive home."

The two head toward the car.

"You know," Charlie says, "Melissa is a pretty nice girl."

Sara smiles. "I'm glad you like her, Son. She is pretty."

"Yes, she is. We were talking about how Mineral Springs was so full today. I'm glad we came here today away from all those niggers."

Suddenly, Sara becomes extremely angry. Charlie hears a loud pop, and then his face begins to hurt. His mother just slapped him!

"Ahh, Mama, why did you do that?"

"Charlie William Delaney! Don't you ever let me hear you say that word again!"

Charlie draws back in fright. His mother's face is full of anger and fury. He says in his fear, "Melissa says that word. All the people at school say it too."

"I don't give a hoot what Melissa or anybody else says! Do you understand me, young man?"

Charlie, looking scared, says, "Yes, ma'am! I understand, Mama."

Sara's expression turns gentle—a little more kindhearted and compassionate. She says softly, "I want to tell you something, Son. That word came into being because this nation put those people into slavery. That word means a black slave. There are no more slaves in this country, so that word shouldn't be used anymore."

Charlie just stands there looking stunned, giving her his complete and undivided attention.

"That word offends people a great deal. Nobody wants to be called a word that means slave. Slavery was a bad thing this country did, Charlie. Calling them that name reminds them of slavery. That is not what good Christians should ever do. Do you understand now why I slapped you?"

Charlie nods. Then he asks, "But … but aren't Mrs. Lane and Melissa good Christians too? Mrs. Lane sings in the choir, and Melissa sings solos for the entire church."

Sara opens the car doors, and the two get in. "Charlie, just because you sing in the choir or go to church doesn't mean you are a Christian. A good Christian is someone who follows Jesus and does what he preached about. You wouldn't hear Jesus say that word, would you?"

Charlie looks at his mother and says, "I guess not."

Sara looks serenely at Charlie. "There are a whole lot of people in this world who pretend to be Christians. They pretend because it makes them feel righteous and good. The problem is that they become self-righteous and think they are better than others."

As Sara starts the car, she continues, "Son, whatever you do with your life, remember this: you are never any better than anyone else in this world. God loves everyone the same. In God's eyes, we are all the same."

"Okay, Mama, I will try to remember that."

Sara drives away from the swimming pool. After a while, Charlie looks over at her and says in a quiet tone, "Mama, I am sorry for upsetting you. Will you forgive me?"

Sara looks at his humble expression and says, "Yes, Charlie, I forgive you."

Charlie shows his love toward his mother with a single grin.

"Charlie, how would you like some ice cream?"

"Yes, ma'am! That would be great!"

Sara, hearing Charlie's enthusiasm, drives to an ice cream shop. They both go inside and have some ice cream.

When they arrive home, Charlie goes to his room and listens to his stereo while his mother prepares dinner. He thinks about what his mother told him earlier. This is a strong trait of Charlie's character, thinking about recent events and learning from them.

When dinner is ready, Charlie sits at the table with his parents. John reads the paper as he eats. Sara tries to start up a conversation, but the newspaper wins John's attention. She always gets upset with him when he reads at the table, but he doesn't seem to care.

Charlie often tries to talk to his father, but John doesn't talk much. He doesn't understand his son or what Charlie is going through. He doesn't think often about Charlie's concerns, and he is quick to judge and condemn. He thinks he knows what is right and wrong without thinking about it too long. He does not communicate as a father ought to; he speaks to Charlie not as a son but more like an object. And John doesn't have the patience to be understanding and caring.

After dinner Charlie tries to talk with his dad about Dee, whom he couldn't stop thinking about. "Dad, I am having a problem with a girl I met in school this year."

"What is it, son?"

"I like this girl a whole lot. But now that school is over, I kinda miss her. I miss seeing her."

"So?"

"I was wondering if you and I could drive over to her house and see her sometime this summer."

Charlie's father gets up from his seat. "Go ask you mother about it. If I were you, I would just occupy my mind with something else."

Charlie is distressed about his father's lack of interest. "I can't seem to think about anything else but her."

John looks as though he doesn't like talking about this subject. "Don't worry about it. You will see her when school starts next fall." Then he gets up and leaves the house, heading for his shop.

Charlie feels stupid for trying to talk to his father about his dilemma. He goes back to his room, becoming intensely depressed as he thinks about how much he wants to be with Dee. He falls asleep and has a quite unusual dream.

He sees Dee lying on a beach wearing a skimpy bathing suit. She gets up when she sees him and waves at him as he walks over to her. She wraps her arms around him and hugs him profoundly. She then kisses him. As their lips part, Charlie turns and notices something peculiar—four owls sitting together on a tree limb. They are looking into the sunrise. The second owl in the group flies over and stares at Dee, right in her face. The owl continues to do this as the others hover near her, and then they all fly away.

Then, all of a sudden, Tim Simpson steps in and bellows to Charlie, "Get away from my girlfriend, Charlie Delaney!" Tim's face is full of evil, and the pleasant dream turns into a nightmare.

Tim pushes Charlie to the ground, and Charlie fights back, saying, "You get away from my girlfriend, Tim Simpson."

Tim is holding a baseball bat and begins swinging furiously at Charlie, time after time, but each swing misses Charlie.

Behind Tim, Charlie sees his father laughing at him. "What's the matter, Charlie? Are you afraid? Ha-ha-ha."

All Charlie's friends from school are standing around and laughing too.

"Larry, Wayne, Bobby, why are you all laughing at me? Tell me! Why are you all laughing at me?"

As Dee screams for everyone to leave Charlie alone, proclaiming he is her friend, Tim picks her up and carries her away. Charlie frantically tries to get to Dee, but the crowd gets in the way.

The scene then moves on, and Tim is carrying Dee down a long dirt road. Dee is screaming for Charlie to come and get her.

Charlie cries, "Dee! Dee! I'm coming! I'm coming!"

Tears are running down her face. As Charlie follows them, Tim takes her into a little white church. The preacher at the pulpit is the principal from Charlie's school, Mr. Golding. All the pews in the entire church are full of people, all dressed in formal attire.

Charlie determinedly walks up the aisle and sees his father looking and laughing at him again. His father grabs him to prevent him from stopping the ceremony. "This is the girl I told you about," Charlie screams. "This is the girl I am in love with!"

His father convulses with laughter, as does the rest of the congregation. "You are stupid, Charlie. You don't know what love is. You are plumb stupid! You aren't going to stop anything. Now sit down beside your mother and stop making a scene."

Charlie sits down quietly with his mother. She looks at Charlie sadly and says, "Do as your father says." Charlie's father grabs his arm and pulls him in to where they are sitting.

Dee looks back at Charlie, weak-spirited and heavyhearted, and the principal progresses through the ceremony. When he reaches the part about anyone objecting, Charlie leaps out of his seat and runs down the aisle screaming, "Stop, stop! Yes, I think these two should not wed. Stop the wedding!"

Charlie's father once again steps in and drags him away as everyone in the congregation laughs again at him. The principal then pronounces Dee and Tim to be man and wife, and the wedding is complete. As Tim kisses Dee and the "Wedding March" is played, people stand and applaud.

Charlie then wakes up in a cold sweat. He jumps out of bed and takes a shower. The terrible agony of wanting to be near Dee erupts into a dark, depressive state. He submits to his sad thoughts, and the ache of loneliness and depression floods his mind and soul. He doesn't understand why the depression is so harsh and real!

From this time on, Charlie begins to spend his days at a lake near his home, never taking anyone with him. He loves fishing but doesn't ever come home with fish, because he always throws them back. It is a twenty-minute journey between the lake and his house, and he always makes sure he is home before dark so his parents will not restrict him from going back. This becomes his special place.

When Charlie is alone, he can't stop thinking about Dee. He tells himself that it was his own shyness that prevented him from being close to her. He reminisces about the school year and all those special times they had on the bus and those bad times also. He realizes that he brought on the bad times with his immature behavior.

One day at the lake, Charlie notices an elderly man fishing on the other side of the lake. Charlie is curious about the Old Man and wonders if he should go and talk to him. He decides not to. He feels a strange reluctance to meet and talk to strangers, or anyone else for that matter.

As Charlie gets ready to leave the fishing hole, he pulls up the one fish he has caught. He removes it from the string and throws it back into the water. The fish just floats to the top, dead. He wonders how it died so suddenly. It was alive only twenty minutes before. He stares at the dead fish with sadness and then looks over to where the Old Man is fishing. He can't make out the Old Man's facial features, but he does notice that the Old Man is looking directly at him, motionless.

When he gets home, his mother comes out of the house and asks in a worried tone, "Where have you been all day, young man?"

"I told you this morning I was going to the lake."

"You mean you have been there all day long? So where are all the fish you caught?"

"Oh, I only caught one, and I threw it back. It wasn't big enough to eat."

Sara is relieved she doesn't have to clean any fish. They talk about the lake and the fishing, and Sara suggests that she might join Charlie one day. He objects so quickly that Sara asks if he is up to no good, like smoking cigarettes or something.

"No, Mama, you know I don't smoke," he says. "What makes you think that?"

"Anytime you don't want me or anyone else to go somewhere you go, it makes me wonder what you're trying to hide."

"I'm not trying to hide anything from you. I just like to be alone sometimes. Don't you like to be alone sometimes and think things over?"

"Yes, there are times when I like to be by myself too. I think I know what you mean, Son."

Out in the workshop, John is refinishing a table when Charlie comes in and asks, "How is everything going?"

"I'm trying to refinish this table for Harry Hedgecock. Everything was going all right until about thirty minutes ago."

Sounding concerned, Charlie asks what went wrong.

"I was putting the final coat of stain on this table when I felt something strange in my heart."

"Are you all right? Are you feeling okay now?" Charlie asks anxiously.

John detects the fright in Charlie's speech. "Oh, it was nothing, Charlie. It was just a very strange feeling; that's all. When I felt this strange feeling, I dropped the can of stain right on the floor, and it splattered all over."

"It looks like you have cleaned it up pretty good now."

John looked disgusted, though. "That's not the worst of it. When I reached over to clean up the mess, the table slid off and hit the floor. It broke off one leg and damaged two more. I don't know what to tell Harry."

Trying to make his father feel better, Charlie says, "Oh, he will understand, Dad. It was an accident."

"You don't know Harry Hedgecock the way I do, Son. He will probably be very upset about it. You see, this table is an antique."

Charlie is concerned his father might have to pay for it and, seeing his dad's dilemma, tries to cheer him up. "Maybe it won't take too much to fix it. If you need help, I will be glad to help you with it."

John smiles. "Okay, Charlie, tomorrow me and you will try to fix it the best way we can before Harry sees it."

"We might fix it so good you won't even have to tell him about the accident."

John, looking sternly at Charlie, says, "No, Charlie, anytime you break something that doesn't belong to you, always tell the party involved what you did. If you don't, you will live with a guilty conscience the rest of your life. Always tell the truth, no matter what the costs are. Always be truthful."

"Yes, sir, I will."

John puts his arm around his son as they walk to the house for dinner. They discuss the damaged table some more during dinner. John is distressed, but Charlie reassures his father he will help him the next day. John is grateful and hopes that maybe it won't be as bad as they think.

Then John asks Charlie, "What did you do today?"

"I went fishing down at the lake again."

"You mean that lake over at Beaver Creek? You walk all the way over there to fish?"

With a casual expression, Charlie says, "Yes, Dad, I walk all the way over there nearly every day."

"How long does it take you to walk there?"

"Oh, about twenty minutes. I don't mind walking that far. I like that lake. It has a special something about it."

"So how many fish did you catch today?"

"Only one. Funny thing about that fish." Sara and John look at Charlie curiously as he continues, "When I threw it back in the water, it was dead. I can't seem to understand why. I caught him only twenty minutes earlier."

Sara says that maybe it died because of all the chemicals they dump into the lake.

"What chemicals? There are no chemicals in that lake," replies John's father.

The table falls silent as everyone thinks about how the fish could have died.

Looking perplexed, John says, "I can't understand why a fish that was caught twenty minutes before would die when it was let free."

"I don't understand it either, Dad."

"I still think it is because of chemicals," Sara adds.

Everyone sits and wonders about the fish until Charlie asks to be excused. Since he has finished his dinner, Sara excuses him, and he heads for his room.

The next morning, Charlie's father wakes him up. "Okay, Charlie, off and on. It's time to get up. We have a lot of work to do today."

Charlie wishes he could sleep longer but gets up, showers, and heads to the breakfast table anyway. Charlie and his dad go off to work in the shop after a big breakfast of scrambled eggs, bacon, and toast.

Charlie looks at the table, the broken leg, and the nasty cuts and waits for his father to show him what to do, but John doesn't direct Charlie as to what he wants. Charlie is bothered at the idea of having to read his father's mind. John is very impatient and makes it difficult for Charlie to help. Charlie feels hurt and frustrated and begins to think his name is "Stupid."

After several hours, the legs on the table are ready to be stained. Charlie looks over at his father with hurt eyes, and John looks back with disappointed eyes. Not caring about Charlie's feelings, he says, "Okay, Charlie, I believe I can finish it now."

Charlie feels relieved and replies timidly, "I guess I will go in the house now." He waits for a reply from his father but doesn't get one. His father doesn't give any thanks either.

When Charlie enters the house, Sara notices Charlie's sad expression and asks, "So how did it go? Did you two get the table fixed? Is something wrong?"

"It's Dad, Mama. Nothing I did was good enough for him. Every time I asked him a question, he would get angry. It was as if I was supposed to know everything without him telling me."

"Don't let your father's words get you down, Son. I've lived with him for a long time, and I know just what you are going through. Your father doesn't communicate very well. It is something I have come to accept from him."

"Yeah, but he didn't even say thanks. It's like he just takes me for granted. Not even one compliment for helping him!"

Sara understands what Charlie is going through. "I know, Son. He is just that way. Don't let him bother you. He will come into the house happy in a few minutes now that the table is finished."

"He isn't finished yet. He still has to put the stain on again."

Sara smiles and gives Charlie a big hug. "I'm proud of you."

Charlie smiles back, and they hug again.

John comes in for lunch, and he does seem happy, just as Sara said he would be.

"So, John, is the table fixed?" Sara asks.

"Yeah, I fixed it as good as new," John says happily.

Charlie is disturbed that his dad uses *I* instead of *we* but doesn't say anything.

"Don't you want to thank Charlie for helping you?" Sara asks.

"Oh yeah, thanks, Charlie, for helping me."

Charlie quietly replies, "You're welcome, Dad." He shakes his head at his mother, knowing his dad didn't mean it.

As the three finish their lunch, Charlie announces, "I think I will go fishing."

Sara looks over at John and says, "Why don't you drive Charlie down to the lake?"

"I can't today. I have to put another coat of stain on the table in a couple more hours."

"It won't take you long to drive Charlie down there."

"That's all right," Charlie says. "I don't mind walking. I enjoy it actually. Walking is half the fun of going."

Sara gives John a disappointed look, and John says, "The boy said he doesn't mind walking."

Sara, looking upset, says, "I guess so." Sara looks out the window at thick gray clouds. It looks as though it might rain.

Charlie hurries to his bedroom, puts on his shorts, grabs his fishing rod and tackle box, and hurries off to the lake. When he arrives at the lake, the Old Man is fishing where Charlie was the day before, so Charlie chooses another spot to fish. The Old Man gets closer to Charlie with each toss of his line, though he is still too far away Charlie to see his facial features. The Old Man watches Charlie through the day as Charlie fishes, each time throwing his catch back in the water.

It gets late, and Charlie heads home. Walking back to his house, he wonders if the Old Man owns the lake. If so, Charlie hopes the Old Man doesn't mind him fishing there.

Charlie returns home late that afternoon and finds his father in the living room. "Hey, Dad, who owns that lake over at the crossing at Beaver Creek?"

"It belongs to the power company."

"I guess it's all right for me to fish there, isn't it?"

"Yeah, I guess so."

Charlie feels more comfortable.

The next day Charlie again grabs his fishing pole and tackle box. He kisses his mother, telling her he will be home before dark. Sara gives him a bag with a couple of sandwiches and a thermos of chicken soup. She knew Charlie would be going there if he didn't have anything else planned for the day.

"I just don't see what you find so special about that lake, but go ahead, if it makes you so happy," she says.

Charlie kisses her good-bye and leaves. Sara watches him out the window, hoping it won't rain before he gets back home.

When Charlie gets to the lake he looks around for the Old Man but doesn't see him. He feels strange like someone is watching him. He fishes for about 20 minutes then hears a voice from behind him, "Charlieee ... Hello, Charlieee." Charlie is startled by the voice and turns to see the Old Man standing right behind him. He has long, curly blond hair hanging down to his shoulders and cold, beady blue eyes that glare evilly at Charlie. He is resting both his hands on a long walking cane and has a somewhat-mischievous grin on his face.

"Oh, hello there," Charlie says as the Old Man walks over to him and sits down.

"How is the fishing, Charlie?"

Charlie looks at the Old Man with great curiosity. "How do you know my name?"

The Old Man stares at Charlie as if he is looking right through him. "You are the Delaney boy, Charlie Delaney, aren't you?"

Charlie confirms this and again wonders who this man is and what his name is.

"Oh, I know you from way back. I know your father and mother too—John and Sara."

Charlie eagerly answers, "Yes, that's correct. May I ask what your name is?"

"So how is the fishing?" the Old Man interrupts.

"Oh, pretty good, I guess."

"Yes, this is a nice place for a young boy to come. I have come here for a great many years."

Charlie is intrigued by this man. "I don't see you catch too many fish. I saw you yesterday and the day before that, but I didn't see you catch any fish in that time."

The Old Man looks at Charlie with that mischievous grin.

"My dad said it was all right to fish here. He told me the power company owns the lake."

"He is right, Charlie. They do. I like to see a young lad like you fish here." His voice is peculiar, sounding like a man's and also like a woman's and also like a homosexual's in a strange eerie way. He enunciates every word clearly, making each syllable distinct. His accent has a unique tone. It sounds like it came from a faraway distant land. His voice is scary to Charlie.

The Old Man continues, "How is John doing these days?"

"He is doing fine. He and my mother are doing fine."

The Old Man smiles gladly and says, "Sara. Oh yes, I have known Sara since she was born."

Charlie says with enthusiasm, "Really! It's good to hear that. I don't like to talk to strangers, but you're no stranger, since you know my folks."

The Old Man gets up and walks over to the edge of the bank. He says, "Hey, Charlie, come here. I want to show you something." He points to a steep bank over the hill on the other side of the lake. "Do you see that bank over there?"

"Yes."

The Old Man points again. "Do you see that little platform I have put up there?"

Charlie sees a little chair on a wooden platform on the front of the bank. "Yes, sir, I see it."

"I caught a three-pound bass from up there."

Charlie excitedly responds, "Really? You caught a three-pound bass up there?"

The Old Man nods.

"It doesn't look very safe up there. If you slide down that hill, you might not be able to get out," Charlie says, sounding worried.

"Oh no, it can't be more than two or three feet deep there. You can just walk right out if you do happen to fall in. All the big fish like to hang out there because it is the shallowest part of the lake."

"Well, I will have to go up there and fish sometime."

"Why don't you go up there and fish now?" the Old Man asks. "I'm not going to fish today, so go ahead and fish there. I don't mind."

Charlie feels uneasy about the Old Man pressuring him. "Not right now. Maybe some other time, but not right now."

The Old Man senses Charlie's uneasiness and doesn't press him. "Well, anytime you want to fish at my platform, Charlie, you just go right ahead. I know you will catch a big one over there. I just know you will."

Charlie begins to feel at ease again. "Thank you. I will. By the way, you never told me your name."

The Old Man turns around and walks away, not responding to Charlie. Then he grins that same mischievous grin and says, "So long, Charrrlieee," and disappears in only a brief moment.

Charlie doesn't understand why the Old Man didn't tell him his name and decides that the Old Man is probably hard of hearing—after all, that comes with old age. But his curiosity about the platform and the fish he might catch there grows stronger and stronger.

His curiosity finally gets the better of him, and he walks over to the far side of the lake. As he walks toward the platform, he feels a raindrop. He looks up and notices the sky is getting very dark. It starts to rain, and the raindrops tell Charlie it's time for him to go home. With his fishing rod in one hand and his tackle box and thermos in the other, he begins the long walk home.

Not far from the lake, it stops raining, and the sun comes out bright and radiant. Charlie thinks about going back but decides against it. He keeps walking until he reaches his house. He walks inside and sees his mother and father sitting in the living room watching TV.

"Hey, Mama and Dad, I met an old man down at the lake today. He told me he knew both of you."

Sara and John listen to Charlie with interest.

"Yes, Charlie, what about him?" Sara asks.

"He said he has known you since you were born. Dad, he said he has known you for years."

"What is his name?" John asks.

"I don't know."

Sara asks, "Didn't you ask him his name?"

"Yes, I did, but for some reason he didn't say. I guess when you get that old, your mind doesn't work so good."

John says, "So you say he knows me?"

"Yes, he knew who I was too. He called out my name before I told him what it was. The way he talked, it sounded like he knows you really well."

John looks at Sara and asks, "Who do you think it is?"

"I don't know. I didn't think I knew anybody who lives over there."

"Charlie didn't say he lived over there, dear. He just met him there. He probably drove there."

Sara tries to think of who it might be. "It's impossible to know who he is without knowing his name or seeing what he looks like."

John says to Charlie, "I am curious to find out who he is. What do you say we both go fishing there tomorrow?"

Charlie's smiling face turns sour, and Sara picks up on this immediately. "John, I don't think Charlie wants anybody to go to his special place."

"What? What do you mean?"

"Charlie likes to go to the lake by himself, so he can think about things."

"What kind of things?"

"Don't you remember when you were his age? He just likes a place to go where nobody will interrupt his thoughts."

"I'm not going to interrupt nobody's thoughts. I just want to go fishing." Charlie remains silent, and John looks at his son. "You don't mind if I go fishing there, do you, Charlie?"

Charlie reluctantly replies, "I guess not, Dad, if you want to."

"Fine then, tomorrow me and Charlie will go fishing down at the lake near Beaver Creek."

"I tried, Charlie. Maybe you and your father will have fun," Sara says.

"I guess so, Mama. I guess so."

The next day, Charlie and his father prepare to go fishing. "Are you ready, Dad?" Charlie asks as he gets his fishing gear ready.

"I will be right with you, Son." John gets his fishing rod, and the two head off.

As Charlie starts down the driveway to walk to the lake, John asks, "Where are you going, Charlie?"

Charlie turns to his dad looking confused. "What do you mean?"

"You don't think I'm going to walk down there, do you?"

"I don't know."

"Hop in the car, Charlie. We're going to drive down there today."

They soon arrive at the lake. John parks the car not too far away, and they walk the rest of the distance to the lake. It is a beautiful day. The sun is shining, the birds are singing, and the flowers are blooming—a perfect day for fishing.

John looks around, but they are the only ones there. It's about ten thirty in the morning when they begin to fish. They talk about what a beautiful day it is. John looks for the Old Man that Charlie mentioned. "I wonder if that old man will show up today," he says.

"I don't know. I have seen him here for three days in a row."

After about an hour and a half, neither of them have had a single bite. John is getting tired and disgusted.

"Hey, Dad, you see that little platform over there on that bank? Yesterday, the Old Man told me he caught a three-pound bass from up there."

Excitedly, John says, "Well, what are we waiting for? Let's go over there. Why didn't you tell me that sooner, Charlie?"

So Charlie and his father reel their fishing lines in and walk over to the platform.

When John and Charlie get there, John looks unsurely at the steep bank and the platform. He says with a little doubt in his voice, "This doesn't look as good as I thought earlier. I wonder if it is safe to fish on that platform."

Charlie is eager to try fishing there. "The Old Man said it was plenty safe."

"What is that?" John asks, pointing to a rope with some type of noose near the bottom of the bank. "It looks like a rope of some sort." He hesitates and says, "I don't know, Charlie. If one of us slid down that bank, it might be hard to get out. The water might be deep on this side."

Charlie tells his father that it would be easy to get out because the water is only a couple of feet deep.

John says, "That's probably why the Old Man caught such a big bass there. The big ones always like to stay in the shallowest part of a lake. Let me tell you about a time when I was a boy and caught a monster of a fish. All I did was throw out my line a couple of feet from the bank. I saw this fish swim right up to me and take my bait. He was in only a couple of feet of water!"

Charlie, eager to go first, says, "Well, let me climb down there and see if I can't catch a big one."

"Let me try it first. I want to make sure it is safe for you."

Charlie reluctantly says, "Okay, Dad. But I get to fish there too."

John ruffles Charlie's hair. Then with his fishing rod in hand, he climbs down to the small platform. He throws out his line and sits down.

He turns and yells back to his son, "Hey, this is great! I believe this is going to work out just fine."

Something awful happens then. One of the legs of the platform breaks where John is sitting, and he slides down the steep bank. His foot gets caught in the noose in the rope at the bottom of the bank. As the noose pulls tight, Charlie sees that the other end of the rope is tied to a concrete block that was hidden in the red mud earlier. John plunges into the water with the block fixed tightly around his foot.

"Daddy! Daddy! Are you all right?" Charlie slides down the bank yelling at his father. He tries frantically to get him out but can't.

"Help! I can't get out! Help me! Help me!" John screams in terror.

Charlie looks down at his helpless father and cries. Charlie's face is full of panic as tears flow out of his eyes. He cries out in horror, "Daddy! Daddy! Daddy! What do you want me to do?"

John, splashing around in the cold water, says, "There is something on my foot, Charlie! It's pulling me down! It's pulling me down!"

Horrifying screams come from his father's water-soaked mouth.

Charlie screams, "Daddy! Tell me what you want me to do!. Daddy! Daddy! Please tell me to do something!"

Charlie's father screams out one more time, "Help! Help! Charlie, help me! Somebody help me!"

Charlie goes into shock. He yells back down to his father in terror, "Daddy! Daddy! Try to grab hold of the bank! Grab hold of the bank!"

The horrifying screams stop. Charlie keeps yelling down to his father with tears rushing out of his eyes, but he doesn't hear anything else down there.

He runs as fast as he can to the nearest house he can find. A woman is sitting on the porch swing reading her Bible. He runs to her screaming hysterically, "Lady, my father is in the lake! Lady! My father is drowning in the lake!" He is out of breath from running, and his voice and his horrified look scare the woman. "Please, lady, call the emergency squad! My daddy is drowning!"

The lady jumps up from her seat and runs into the house with the Bible in her hand. Charlie follows her. She picks up the phone and dials 911. She tells the dispatcher, "There is a boy here who says his father is drowning in the lake over at Beaver Creek. Please come at once!"

Charlie grabs the phone away from the lady. "Hurry! Please hurry! My daddy is in the lake drowning. Please hurry!"

The dispatcher says that there will be someone over there shortly. Charlie thanks the man and hangs the phone up. He thanks the lady for helping him. He rushes out of the house and hurries back to the lake.

When Charlie gets there, he can just barely make out his father's lifeless body—his head the only thing visible—floating underwater. Soon, Charlie hears sirens, and people come running in hopes of getting Charlie's dad out of the lake. When they spot him, one leaps in and tries to pull him from the water but cannot. They have to cut the rope around his foot. It takes them over an hour to pull his lifeless body from the lake.

Charlie is lying on the bank crying when the police arrive. They begin questioning Charlie, but he is nearly delirious, so it is difficult to talk. "My daddy and me were fishing when he slid down the hill and drowned." He breaks down again and cries uncontrollably. The police wait patiently before attempting to ask him more questions.

"I must tell my mama! I must tell her about this!" Charlie screams, leaping up from the ground. One of the officers escorts him to the squad car, where Charlie calls his mother and tells her what has happened. She rushes down to the lake right away.

With his mother holding his hand, Charlie tells the police about the Old Man who told him about fishing on the platform. Stuttering as he speaks, Charlie says, "The Old Man told me to fish up there." He points over at the steep bank where the platform is. "He told me that part of the lake was the shallowest part. He lied to me. The Old Man lied to me!" Charlie breaks down again. His tears run like a river that has been flooded. He can't talk anymore. His mother tries to comfort him, but it doesn't do much good. The paramedics rush Charlie and his mother to the hospital.

At the hospital, they give Charlie some drugs to calm him down. His mother is crying also, finally over the shock. When the police arrive at the hospital, she has a nervous breakdown. They admit her into a room next to Charlie's.

The next day, Sara and Charlie wake up at the hospital. The drugs have worn off, and the agony erupts once more. Sara, with the help of a nurse, begins to walk around her room. Soon she is ready to go home. Charlie, on the other hand, takes the tragedy the worst. The hospital brings in a psychiatrist, Dr. Paul Rose, to talk with Charlie.

Charlie is asleep when Dr. Rose first enters Charlie's room. Dr. Rose wakes Charlie up, softly saying, "Mr. Delaney. Mr. Delaney. Wake up."

Charlie looks around and sees the kind expression on the doctor's face.

"It is time to wake up."

"Could I have a glass of water?"

Dr. Rose fills up a glass from the bathroom and brings it to Charlie. "Here you go, Mr. Delaney."

"Please, call me Charlie."

"Okay, Charlie. Would you like to tell me about the bad experience you had yesterday?"

Charlie takes a drink from the glass and then pauses for a moment before saying, "I saw my daddy drown yesterday."

Dr. Rose listens as Charlie tells his story.

Back in Sara's room, sergeant Moser is there to make the report. The hospital officials won't let him talk to Charlie until Dr. Rose is finished. Sara is doing a lot better since yesterday. She is sitting in a chair next to her bed with a mournful expression on her face.

"Could you tell us about the Old Man your son spoke of yesterday?"

"Yes, sergeant. I will try." Sara tries to get a hold of herself, but she begins to cry as she remembers seeing John's lifeless body. She takes a deep breath and says, "Charlie first told us of the Old Man two days ago."

"Do you know this man's name?"

"No, sergeant, I don't know. Charlie doesn't know either. He only talked to the Old Man once."

"When was this?"

"Two days ago. Charlie asked him his name, but the Old Man wouldn't give it to him. Charlie thought he was too old to hear him. You see, my son only talked to him once."

The sergeant writes this down in his report.

"The Old Man told Charlie he knew the whole family. He called out Charlie's name when he first approached him and knew my husband's and my names. He said that he'd known me since I was born."

"Do you have any idea who he might be?"

Sara thinks and says, "None. I have racked my brain trying to think who he might be."

Sergeant Moser looks at Sara with a remorseful expression.

"You see, Mrs. Delaney, we found your husband with a rope tied around his leg. The other end of the rope was tied to a concrete block. When your husband slid down the bank, the rope was waiting to snag his foot. Whoever thought this out killed your husband. I am sorry to be the one who has to tell you this."

A tear runs down Sara's cheek. "The Old Man. The Old Man must have done it!"

"Yes, ma'am. I believe you're right. We have dispatched three squad cars to keep an eye out for that man. They will drive over to the lake at all hours of the day and night until they find him. We will do all we can to find him."

With a look of hope and inspiration, Sara says, "Thank you, sergeant. I hope you find him."

"We will do our best. Could you tell us any reason someone would want to hurt your husband or your son?"

"I can't think of one. We don't have any enemies. None, sergeant, none."

"Thank you for your time, Mrs. Delaney. I would like to ask Charlie about the incident once Dr. Rose is done. He might be able to help us locate the Old Man."

Sara nods, and the two of them wait until Dr. Rose enters the room thirty minutes later.

Dr. Rose looks at Sara with compassion and says, "Mrs. Delaney, your son will need to have intense therapy to cope with this terrible tragedy. He has taken the loss of his father very hard. It might take several months or even longer for him to get over this calamity. I have done all I can for now."

Sara sits in stunned silence for a few moments and then says in a gentle tone, "Thank you, Doctor, for your help."

"Can I talk to Mr. Delaney now, Doctor?" Sergeant Moser asks.

"Yes, but for only a few minutes, no more. And he would like to be called Charlie."

Sergeant Moser heads to Charlie's room. He finds Charlie lying on the bed staring up at the ceiling.

Sergeant Moser says softly, "Hello, Charlie. I would like to ask you a few questions, if I may."

Charlie doesn't respond. He just keeps staring at the ceiling.

The sergeant, seeing that Charlie is very disoriented by the loss of his father, waits a few moments before trying to speak to him again. "Charlie?"

Charlie looks over at the sergeant. "What?"

Sergeant Moser kneels down and softly says, "I would like to ask you a few questions."

Charlie gently replies, "What would you like to know?"

"Tell me about the Old Man."

Charlie, looking dazed and confused, replies, "He told me he caught a three-pound bass up there on that platform he built. He told me it was the shallowest part of the lake. He said I could go up there and fish anytime I wanted to."

Sergeant Moser, trying delicately to get some useful information, asks, "Do you know his name?"

Charlie speaks as though he is in a trance. "He never told me his name. I only spoke to him two days ago. I asked him his name, but he left before he told me."

"What did he look like?"

Charlie pauses for a moment and says in a soft voice, "He had long, curly blond hair. It went all the way down past his shoulders. He had blue eyes. They were very blue. It was easy to see them because they were so blue. He looked very old, maybe eighty or ninety years old. He said he knew me. He said he knew my mother and my daddy too." Charlie breaks down again and covers his head with the bedsheet as he cries.

Dr. Rose walks into the room and says, "I will give you another five minutes, Sergeant. Then I will have to ask you to leave." Dr. Rose looks at Charlie with compassion and then turns back to the sergeant. "Five minutes, sergeant." Dr. Rose leaves the room quietly.

Sergeant Moser hurries to ask Charlie a few more questions. "Is there anything else that you can tell me about this man?"

"No. I can't think of anything except …"

"What?"

"He was carrying a large walking cane, but he always held it with both hands. Please find him for me. Please find him and kill him." Charlie's face turns red with hate. "That man deceived me and my daddy to get us to fish up there."

Sergeant Moser, not knowing what to say, replies, "We will do everything we can to find him, son." Charlie returns to staring at the ceiling, and sergeant Moser looks at Charlie sadly. "We will do all we can, Charlie, to find that monster who did this to you and to your father."

Charlie turns and looks at the sergeant. He doesn't say anything, but the mournful expression on his face speaks for him. This expression is something sergeant Moser will never forget. The sergeant turns and leaves the room quietly.

A few hours pass before Charlie gets another visitor, his mother. She is accompanied by a nurse and is in a better mental state than she was earlier. Smiling, she takes Charlie's hand and gently strokes his hair. "Hello, Charlie. How are you doing?"

Charlie looks at his red-faced mother. "Mama, what are we going to do now?"

"Me and you are going to have to pull together. You will be the man of the house now. I will have to rely on you more than ever before."

Charlie looks at his mother with compassion. He's full of grief, but the presence of his mother makes him a little happier.

"When can we leave and go home?" he asks.

"We can go home anytime you want to! Would you like to go home right now?"

Charlie's face lights up. "Yes! I want to go home right now."

Sara smiles at Charlie. "I am glad to hear you say that, Charlie. The doctor wanted to move you to another place, but now I will tell him no. We are going home today. Right now."

Charlie smiles for the first time since his father's death. "I'm glad, Mama. I am glad."

Sara makes all the arrangements for them to go home. Dr. Rose disagrees with Sara about taking Charlie home so soon but doesn't protest too much. Sara signs all the papers and calls her sister-in-law, Frances, to drive them home. Before they leave the hospital, the police give Sara all the possessions John had on him at the time of his death. Soon mother and son are on their way home.

When they get home, Sara realizes that the car is still down at the lake. Frances offers to drive her down there so she can drive it back. Charlie insists on going along. Charlie thinks back to the time of his father's death. When they pull up to where the car is, Charlie has a flashback.

He jumps out of the car and starts to scream, "Where are you? Come out and show yourself! Come out, you coward!"

Sara walks over to Charlie to comfort him, and Frances follows. As the three stand there near John's car, a police car drives by. It doesn't stop, but the officer who is driving waves.

Sara says, "You see, Charlie, the police will find that man. So don't let it bother you. They will handle it for us."

Charlie hugs his mother lovingly. "Yes, Mama. I'm sorry for acting the way I did. Please forgive me."

Sara smiles down at Charlie. "There is nothing to forgive you for,

Son. I understand your anger, but we must not let it destroy us from within. Everything will be all right. Trust me, Charlie; everything will be all right."

Sara takes her son's hand as they walk over to the car. Frances walks behind them. Sara thanks Frances for driving them home and promises to call and tell her when the funeral services will be. Frances quietly gets into her car.

Lurking behind some trees, the Old Man watches the three of them leave with a frown on his face. He turns and disappears into the woods.

When Sara and Charlie arrive home, they go straight into the house. Charlie goes into the living room and turns on the TV. Sara gets on the phone to make arrangements for the funeral. Charlie begins to deal with the loss of his father.

After making all the phone calls, Sara walks into the living room and tells Charlie, "The visitation will be Sunday night. Your father will be buried Monday at the St. Andrew Cemetery. You and I need to go downtown tomorrow and buy you a suit."

Charlie doesn't say anything. He just looks at her sadly. Sara walks over and sits down beside her son. She reaches over and holds Charlie's hand. She puts her other hand under his chin and lifts his head until he is looking directly at her.

She says kindly, with a little grief on her face, "Charlie, you are going to have to be brave about this. I am going to count on you to handle yourself in a courageous manner."

Looking into his mother's eyes, Charlie says, "Yes, Mama. I will try as hard as I can. I will try, Mama."

Sara smiles at her son in a loving way. "I know you will, Son. I know you will." Sara then tells Charlie all the details of the funeral services.

The next day, Sara drives Charlie downtown and buys him a nice dark-gray three-piece suit.

While Sara and Charlie are driving home, Sara says, "I was hoping you would have liked a black suit instead. Black is traditional for funerals."

"I don't feel comfortable wearing black."

"Well, I guess the dark gray will be appropriate."

Charlie turns to his mother. "What difference does it make?"

Sara looks over at Charlie with a concerned look. "There will be a lot of people at the funeral, a lot of people your father knew all his life. It would be disrespectful to your father if you didn't look proper for his burial."

"I don't want to look disrespectful," Charlie says, staring at his mother with his tender blue eyes.

"I think that dark-gray suit will be just fine. You will look handsome in it."

Sara and Charlie journey home and prepare for the visitation the next night.

The next day, food and other gifts flood the Delaney household. The people at Charlie and Sara's church come in droves to bring things and to express their sorrow at John's passing. The pastor, Pastor Riggs, comes by and prays with Sara. Charlie doesn't want to pray with them.

After praying with Sara, Pastor Riggs says, "Charlie, we at the church express our deepest sympathy in the loss of your father. I hope you will come to church tomorrow and get involved with our youth program."

Charlie gives the pastor an angry look. He says quickly and firmly, "I am not going to church tomorrow or any other time!"

Pastor Riggs and Sara look at Charlie in surprise.

Charlie continues, "If God is so great, then why did he let my daddy drown in that lake?"

Pastor Riggs looks at Sara then back over at Charlie. He says with compassion, "Charlie, you must not blame God for what happened to your father." He gets up and walks over to sit down beside Charlie. He returns Charlie's angry stare with one of sympathy. "Charlie, I know you are confused and having a lot of misguided thoughts enter your mind now that your father has passed away. But you must understand that God is not responsible for his death. You must not be angry with God. God loves your father, he loves your mother, and he loves you too. God is love. He wouldn't have let your father die if there wasn't a good reason to back it up. Things happen every day that are just as bad as what happened to your father, but you must not blame these things on God."

Charlie listens to the pastor silently with humility showing in his eyes.

"Pastor Riggs is right," Sara says. "You must not be angry with God because of what has happened. Try to channel your hate out of your system. Hate will not benefit you. It will only make you more bitter and angry."

Charlie stands up quickly, trying to hold back the tears. He doesn't want anyone to see him cry. He turns around and says, "I am sorry, Mama. I know I shouldn't hate God for what has happened. I just can't understand why it happened." As Charlie speaks, tears creep out of his eyes. He looks over at the pastor and says, "I am sorry for speaking to you the way I did, Pastor Riggs."

"I know you will come through this tragedy, young man. Come here. I want to tell you a little story that might help you better understand this tribulation you are going through."

Charlie slowly walks back over and sits down next to Pastor Riggs.

"You see, Charlie, there are a lot of bad things going on in this world," Pastor Riggs says. "There is fighting in the Middle East, and there are civil wars all over the world. All those people fighting think that God is on their side, that they are fighting for God. I would say that ninety-nine percent of those people probably think they will get a reward from God in the hereafter because of the fighting they are doing now."

Charlie listens carefully to every word. Sara also pays close attention to the pastor.

"Charlie, I want you to know that people who kill in war will one day have to answer for their crimes against their fellow man. They will get something from God all right, but it won't be a reward. They will all have to stand before God and be judged for their actions. God will show them what the devil has deceived them into doing. You see, the devil has only one power in this world, the power to deceive mankind. A person who is deceived will not admit that he has been deceived, because he is being deceived."

Charlie scratches his head.

Pastor Riggs, with a serious look, says, "All those people fighting have been deceived to fight. As long as people are being deceived, there will always be chaos in this world."

Charlie quietly says, "I was deceived, Pastor."

"Tell me, Charlie, what you were deceived about?"

"The Old Man told me it would be all right to fish up there on that platform. So I did, or I was going to. When I told my daddy what the Old Man said about the platform being on the shallowest part of the lake, he went right ahead and sat down up there. My daddy thought it was all right to fish there because I told him it was all right. I was deceived, and then I deceived my daddy, but I didn't know I was deceiving him, because I was being deceived myself."

Pastor Riggs looks over at Sara with a very disturbed look in his eyes and then says to Charlie, "That's right; you were being deceived." He focuses an unusual stare at Charlie. "Charlie, I hope you don't blame yourself for your father's passing."

Charlie hesitates for a moment. "It is my fault. I told Daddy it would be all right for him to go up there. He would have never gone up there if I hadn't told him to."

"But you were being deceived when you told him that. You didn't know that you were telling him something wrong, so it is not your fault at all. You must believe that, Charlie."

Sara interjects, "That is right, Charlie. You must not blame yourself. You were in no way responsible for your father's death. You have to believe that."

Charlie looks at his mother with timid eyes and then looks over at the pastor. He pauses for a few moments and then turns back to his mother. "I still feel like it was my fault."

"It wasn't, though, Charlie. It wasn't your fault."

Charlie sadly looks away, still feeling responsible deep down.

Pastor Riggs says, "Charlie, would you leave me and you mother alone for a moment? I want to talk to her privately."

Charlie looks over at his mother with those sad blue eyes of his.

"It will be all right," she says. "You go take a shower. It will make you feel much better."

Charlie gets up and leaves the room, feeling very distressed. He doesn't say good-bye to the pastor.

Once Charlie is gone, Pastor Riggs says, "Mrs. Delaney, I recommend that you get Charlie some counseling to help him deal with this tragedy."

Sara's face is full of fright and anxiety. Her eyes turn red as tears trickle out of the corners. She grabs a tissue to wipe her eyes and blow her nose. "Do you really think I should take Charlie to a counselor?"

"He is blaming himself for his father's death. If he doesn't accept that he is not responsible, he might be worse off later in life. Now is the time for Charlie to see a professional, so he can understand it wasn't his fault."

Sara pauses for a moment. "The doctor at the hospital said the same thing. I just don't want Charlie to have to go to a mental hospital." Tears roll down her worried face, but soon she gets control of herself. "Well, if you and the doctor think Charlie should get some help, maybe I should look after his best interests and find someone."

"I can help you locate someone if you would like."

Sara gives him a thin smile. "Yes, I would appreciate that, Pastor. I don't know where to turn. Charlie is taking this worse than I thought he would. I am still in shock myself."

"I will see what I can do. In the meantime, try to get Charlie to come to church tomorrow."

"I will try, Pastor. He is getting old enough to make those decisions on his own now, but I will encourage him all I can."

"That is all I ask of you. We also have prayer service on Wednesday nights. Maybe he will find a pretty girl there who will help him with this tragedy. There are a lot of nice girls at the prayer service."

Sara, with a little gleam in her eyes, says, "He might like that, Pastor. I will tell him."

Pastor Riggs gets up from the couch. "I must be going now, Mrs. Delaney. I have a few more stops to make today."

"I understand. I am glad you came by, Pastor."

Pastor Riggs smiles at Sara. "I will see you Monday, then, and maybe tomorrow. Make sure you and Charlie get to the church early Monday morning for the funeral."

"I will."

"Is there anything special you want me to say at the funeral?"

Sara thinks for a moment. "Just say that John was a good husband and a good father and that we all loved him so very much."

Pastor Riggs shakes Sara's hand and says, "I will, Mrs. Delaney. I will also tell everyone at the church to pray for you and Charlie. God has a way of turning adversity into something good. So keep the faith and be strong. I hope everything will work out for you and Charlie."

"Thank you, Pastor. Thank you so very much for coming by."

Pastor Riggs turns and departs as Sara sits back down in the quiet house.

When Sunday night arrives, Charlie is nervous about going to the funeral home for the visitation. He knows there will be a lot of people staring at him. His shyness will make him feel a little uneasy, but he gets dressed and prepares to go with a positive attitude. His mother is dressed in a long black dress. Charlie doesn't talk much as they drive over to the funeral home. He tries to be strong when they get to the funeral home. He doesn't know a lot of the people that have come to pay their last respects to his father, but he puts on a sad smile for them anyway. He greets the people as best as he can. He shakes hands with strangers all night.

Finally he spots someone he knows. Charlie's heart beats faster and faster as he waits impatiently for the familiar face to get closer and closer. His wait is finally over, and Charlie gazes at the beautiful girl standing in front of him. She is wearing a dazzling yellow dress. It is so long it almost touches the floor. Her earrings reflect the light so that her face glows radiantly. Her sweet smile touches Charlie's soul.

"Hello, Dee," he says. "I am glad you came."

Dee puts on a sweet smile and says in a gentle tone, "Hello, Charlie. It's good to see you again."

Charlie smiles at her. "It sure is good to see you again too."

"My mama read about your father in the paper and showed it to me. When I read he had one son named Charlie, I knew it had to be you, so I asked Mama if she would bring me here tonight. She is standing over there." Dee points over to where her mother is standing.

Charlie, still in a trance from Dee's unexpected appearance, reaches over and holds her hand. She looks into Charlie's serene eyes. Her sad face melts away as she attempts to put on another smile. Her face blossoms like a hybrid tea rose in summer.

She says again in a soft, kind, gentle tone, "Would you like to meet my mama, Charlie?"

Charlie continues to gaze at Dee's beautiful, glowing face. "Yes, Dee. I would be honored to meet your mother."

The two walk hand in hand through the crowd of people until they come to Dee's mother, whom Charlie looks at with interest. Dee and her mother stand about the same height and look very similar. Dee's mother is wearing a dark-gray outfit. She is a beautiful woman.

"Hello, Mrs. Swanson," he says. "I am glad to meet you."

Dee's mother politely replies, "My name is now Mrs. O'Brien. I got married a while back." She smiles at Charlie. "I have heard your name all year long. I am glad I finally get to meet you."

Dee smiles as Charlie says to Mrs. O'Brien, "I am glad you brought Dee. It sure is good to see her again."

Dee's face turns a shade of magenta, as she looks at Charlie quietly with a sad, girlish embarrassment.

"I am terribly sorry about your father," Mrs. O'Brien says sadly. "This is an awful thing to happen."

Charlie puts his face down and pauses for a moment. Charlie looks back at Dee and sees a sadness he has never seen in her eyes before. A single tear runs down her ivory-white cheek as she tries to put on a smile.

"I am so very sorry about your father passing away like this. When I heard about it, I started to cry," Dee says. Another tear rushes down the other side of her face.

Mrs. O'Brien, seeing her daughter's tears, releases her own emotion in a flood of tears. She reaches over and holds Charlie's hand tenderly. "I didn't know your father, but I just want to tell you that I am sorry about the tragedy that you and your mother are going through." She kisses Charlie on his cheek. "I will leave you and Deborah alone now, so you can talk."

"Thank you, Mrs. O'Brien."

She turns and walks away, disappearing into the crowded funeral home.

Charlie looks over, dazzled at Dee's loveliness. She is simply stunning. "It sure is good to see you again," he says. "I have thought about you a whole lot since school let out. I sure have missed you."

Dee gazes at him with warm, tender eyes. "I have thought about you too, Charlie. I miss seeing you on the bus every morning."

"I don't know what I am going to do now, Dee. Every day since my father died I have been in a state of confusion. What am I going to do?"

Charlie's worried face troubles Dee. She looks at him with sympathy and compassion. "Everything will be all right, Charlie. I don't have a father either." Holding Charlie's hand, she continues, "I don't remember ever having a father—a real father, I mean. The only thing I can remember about him is that he was an alcoholic. I used to see him drink and get drunk all the time."

"It's sad that the only memories you have of your father are when he was drunk."

"Yeah, it is bad when you don't have any good memories of your father. So you see, Charlie, you do have some good memories of your father. So don't let yourself get you down too much. Everything will be all right."

As Charlie and Dee are talking, Charlie's mother calls his name and motions for him to come over to where she is talking to a strange-looking man and Pastor Riggs. Charlie takes Dee by the hand, and they slowly walk over to his mother.

"I want you to meet someone," his mother says. Then she notices Charlie holding hands with Dee and asks, "Who is your girlfriend, Charlie?"

Charlie says, "Mama, I want you to meet Dee Swanson. Dee, this is my mother."

Dee says, "Hello, Mrs. Delaney. I am glad to meet you."

"Nice to meet you too."

Sara doesn't pay much attention to Dee after their introduction. She is completely unaware that this is the girl Charlie has been in love with. She brushes Dee off unintentionally in her eagerness to introduce Charlie to the strange-looking man.

Dee looks over at Charlie with sad eyes. "Charlie, I must go now. It is good to see you again."

Charlie doesn't want Dee to leave so abruptly. He looks at her as if his heart is going to break. "Please don't leave now, Dee. I want you to stay."

Sara impatiently says, "Charlie, will you please come here? There is someone I want you to meet before he leaves."

Dee says, "Go ahead, Charlie. Your mother wants you. I must be going now."

"Will you come tomorrow for the funeral?"

"I doubt it, Charlie. You be sweet, and I will see you later."

Charlie, realizing Dee is really going to leave, says one last time, "I am glad you came by. If you can, please come to the funeral tomorrow."

Dee kisses Charlie on the cheek. Charlie just stands there in a paralyzed stupor as he watches her disappear from the crowded room. He shows no emotion on the outside, but on the inside his heart longs for her to come back. His father may not have cared much about his feelings toward Dee, but today his father brought her to him for one short, happy moment.

Sara doesn't waste any time. She takes Charlie by the hand and introduces him to the strange-looking man standing beside Pastor Riggs. "Charlie, I want you to meet Dr. Thomas Alfred Fletcher. He is a youth counselor at Richardson Hospital."

Charlie looks at the man shyly. Charlie finds the man's thick-lensed black glasses repulsive; they give him a negative feeling. He doesn't feel comfortable standing next to the man. But when the strange-looking man holds out his hand, Charlie shakes it.

"Hello, Charlie. I have heard a great deal about you," Dr. Fletcher says.

Charlie reluctantly says, "Nice to meet you," and releases Dr. Fletcher's hand. Sara, Pastor Riggs, and Dr. Fletcher talk to Charlie about certain things that have happened in his life. Charlie pretends to like Dr. Fletcher, but he feels a strange dislike and uneasiness toward him more and more as they talk. The doctor looks like Heinrich Himmler.

Soon, it is time for Charlie and his mother to leave the funeral home. Mostly everyone has left. Charlie is glad to go home and get out of his suit. His tie has been choking him all night.

As they drive home, Sara casually asks, "So tell me, Charlie, how did you like Dr. Fletcher?"

"Mama, why are you so concerned about that man?"

Sara, not hearing what she was hoping to hear, says, "I just wanted to know how you feel about him; that's all."

Charlie, a bit skeptically, says, "If you must know, I don't really care for him at all. I think he is a jerk."

Sara gets angry. "Charlie! He is a professional psychiatrist and a professor on juvenile psychology. I think he can help you with the loss of your father."

Charlie gives his mother a stunned look as he shakes his head in disbelief. "I don't need any help! Are you crazy? I'm not going to see any psychiatrist!"

"Young man, don't you talk back to me like that. I am only thinking of your well-being."

"If you are thinking of my well-being, then you can stop thinking about me going to see a shrink."

"He is not a shrink. Where did you heard such a word?"

"It doesn't matter where I heard it. I am not going to a place where crazy people are. I am not going to see that man!"

Sara sees anger in Charlie's eyes. She continues to drive. There is a long, tense silence in the car. Then she asks, "Charlie, will you go see him for my sake?"

"See him for what? I don't need any doctor helping me. What's wrong with you, Mama? Do you think I'm crazy?"

"No, I don't think you're crazy. I just thought it would be a good idea if you had some type of outlet to help you with this most difficult time we are going through. I am worried about you, Charlie."

"I don't ever want to go to someone like that. There is nothing wrong with me. Maybe you need to go see him for some help."

Sara gets very upset with this remark. She gives Charlie a mean look. "I'm not going to see him! You are the one that needs to see him, not me. I have no intention whatsoever of going and seeing a psychiatrist."

Sara is getting a little agitated with this conversation. She doesn't want to go for the same reason Charlie doesn't want to go. She says, "Okay, I won't schedule you an appointment to see him." She glances over and sees relief on Charlie's face. "I'm glad you don't think you need to go after all. I never wanted you to go anyway. The people at the hospital and Pastor Riggs are the ones who put the idea in my head in the first place. I am sorry for upsetting you about this matter."

Charlie reaches over and touches his mother's hand. "You don't have to apologize to me, Mama. I know you were only thinking of me, but I will be all right. As long as you are around me, everything will be just fine."

A tear runs down Sara's cheek. "Charlie, I am glad you are my son. I love you so much. Those people that think we have a problem are the ones with the problem."

Charlie slides over as close as he can next to his mother. "I am glad you are my mom. I love you, Mama."

Sara's teary mood turns into a happy cry. She laughs for the first time since John's death as she grips Charlie's hand. "Honey, how would you like some ice cream?"

"That would be cool!"

They get some ice cream and eat it in the car, enjoying each other's company. This time is especially precious to Sara. Soon they finish, and Sara drives them home.

Charlie, tired and worn out, goes up to his room and takes off his suit. He is relieved to finally remove his tie. He takes a shower and then goes back downstairs to see his mother before he goes to bed. He finds her in the living room reading the Bible. He quietly walks over and sits down next to her.

"I am glad we are finally home. I am bushed," he says, resting his head on his mother's shoulder as she reads.

Sara puts down the Bible and strokes Charlie's hair. "Son, I am going to have to rely on you more than ever now. It's not going to be easy for us these next few months. So I want you to try hard to help me through this difficult time."

"I will, Mama. I will."

"You are the man around the house now. I will expect you to act like a man from now on."

Charlie listens silently. Her words fill him with hope and understanding.

"I hope you accept that you are not responsible in the slightest for your father's death. I hope and pray you don't blame God for this tragedy. God is the only thing that will bring us out of this tribulation."

Charlie holds her hand and says, "Yes, Mama. I know."

"It's getting late. Tomorrow is going to be a big day. We need to be at the church by ten o'clock, so I want you ready to leave early, by nine o'clock. Tomorrow will be the last time we will see your father, so please be ready."

Charlie looks at his mother with soft, tender eyes. His voice is soft and gentle as he says, "Yes, Mama. I will be ready by nine o'clock."

Charlie and Sara kiss each other and go to bed, sleeping soundly until morning.

Charlie gets up before his mother and prepares breakfast. He scrambles the eggs, fries the bacon, and toasts the bread. He gets everything ready. Sara walks into the kitchen and smiles. This is the first time Charlie has prepared breakfast for her. She appreciates it so much she kisses him on the cheek and gives him a big hug.

After breakfast Charlie runs upstairs and puts his suit back on. The two drive first to the funeral home to see John one more time, and then they go to the church, where the funeral will soon take place.

Pastor Riggs performs a beautiful ceremony. He tells the congregation all the nice things John did in his life. He talks about how good of a husband and father he was. He asks everyone to pray for the family. He ends his service with a spiritual goal.

"I want to tell all of you who have come here today to give John Walter Delaney your last respects one last thing," he says, the congregation listening with complete and undivided attention. "Every one of us is going to leave this world someday. When that day comes, when this life is over, we will have to prepare ourselves to enter the next life, a new life that will be forever. Our maker will show us how we lived in this world. All of us will have to stand before God and give an account on how we lived our lives."

Charlie listens with great intensity to Pastor Riggs, his attention growing stronger with each passing word.

"That day will be unpleasant for some of us, for we will have to witness all our sins, every one. All those sinful things that we have never admitted before will be shown to us, so we must all be ready and prepare ourselves for this day. We will also be shown the great tribulations that we experienced while we lived on this tiny planet."

The entire church is silent and still, filled with a calm anticipation of what is to follow.

After a short pause Pastor Riggs says, "There will be people who claim to be righteous and good and even some who proclaim to be good Christians. But they will still have to stand before the great white throne and be shown how they lived their lives."

Sara's tears dry up as Pastor Riggs continues, "The only way we will join God in his paradise we call heaven is if we pour out all our sins on Jesus. We must admit our sins and ask Jesus for forgiveness. Many people will rebel against God because they can't ask Jesus for forgiveness. They will not admit their sins even after God has shown them those sins before their own eyes. It is so important that we admit our sins and ask Jesus for the forgiveness that we must have. I want all of you to know that John Delaney was a good Christian. He didn't just come to church to hear me talk, but he came to learn about Jesus. John's humbleness would not let him deny the love that Jesus showed us through his death on the cross. The suffering that our Lord endured was because of his love for us. Jesus knew that one day we would all have to stand before the great white throne and be judged for our sinful actions. He suffered terribly so we would inherit eternal life, a life after this world."

Sara reaches over and holds Charlie's hand.

"Jesus knew that some would never admit their sins because of their pride. So he took it upon himself to be the sacrificial lamb. He chose to be crucified, to suffer, to pay the price, so we all can admit our sins and be saved from eternal death. By the sacrifice that Jesus endured, we all will be saved from the shameful prison of pride we all know as hell. Because of Jesus's suffering we can go to heaven."

The congregants' emotion-filled eyes radiate beams of understanding to the pastor. With this understanding comes the triumphant glory of the realization of the true meaning of Christianity.

"If you want to know how to inherit eternal life, you must first come to Jesus and let him be your personal savior. He is the only way to have your sins rectified. John was one of those men. His life was not an easy one. Most of the fifty-two years he lived in this world were very difficult. His life was filled with adversity and hardships. Now he is with our beloved Lord for all time. He has not died; he has just left to go to another place. We must all understand that he is in a happier place. We will all miss John. His face will not be around to see, but what he has done with his life, the love he has shown, the things he has made, and the joy he has brought will never leave us. So I ask you all to pray for the family and to give God thanks for bringing John into our lives."

Tears of joy flood the congregation like a burst water pipe.

The pastor gives a prayer and then say in a soft tone, "We will all meet at the burial site now, and may Jesus come into your life and reign as Lord and Savior all the days of your life."

At the burial site Charlie searches for Dee but doesn't see her. Pastor Riggs tells Sara and Charlie and the other family members to go sit down at the chairs near John's grave.

There are a few songs, and a few more words are spoken. But soon the ceremony is over, and everyone begins to go his or her own way. Sara thanks Pastor Riggs for the nice service and for all the nice words that he spoke for John. Charlie thanks him also but still feels bad that Dee didn't show up. He needs to have her near him at this time.

After the people all leave, Sara and Charlie drive to the pastor's home for some quiet time with loved ones from the church. Several hours go by at the pastor's home.

Sara and Charlie decide to go back to the grave to see that it is filled and properly finished. They stay about thirty minutes, alone at the grave. Charlie looks down at the grave as a single tear falls from his eye.

Sara takes Charlie's hand and with a smile says, "I love you, Charlie. I love you more than anyone else in this world now. You are the only man in my life."

Charlie looks at his red-eyed mother and gently says, "I love you too, Mama. I guess this is the last time we will be next to Daddy. I hope the pastor is right about Daddy not being dead but just gone to another place."

"Yes, Charlie, the pastor is right. We will see John again one day. Everything will be all right. You must have faith that God is looking over us."

Charlie turns and looks at his father's grave one last time. Then he turns back to his mother. "Let's go home, Mama. I want to go home."

Charlie and his mother slowly walk back to the car. They leave the quiet, empty cemetery and go home to their quiet, empty house. Charlie goes into the living room and turns on the TV. He sits down on the couch and gets involved in a movie. Sara goes up to her room and undresses. She puts on a comfortable pantsuit and joins Charlie in the living room.

"Charlie? Don't you want to go upstairs and take off your suit and get into something more comfortable?"

Charlie just sits and watches the TV.

"Charlie? Are you all right?"

Charlie pauses for a moment and says, "I will take it off after the movie. I don't feel like it right now."

Sara, puzzled at his answer, says, "Whatever you want, Charlie. I just thought you might want to be more comfortable now that we are home."

"I don't want to be comfortable!"

He doesn't even take off his tie. He just quietly watches the TV. The movie takes control of his thoughts, but after it ends, he walks up to his room and removes the dark-gray suit. He puts on some blue jeans and then walks back down to the living room and gets involved in another movie.

"Dear, would you like me to cook a steak for dinner?" Charlie doesn't respond for a long time. Sara begins to worry about him. He has been doing all right when around a lot of people but has seem depressed when he isn't around people.

"No, Mama," he finally says, looking sternly toward his mother. "I don't want anything to eat. I just want to be left alone so I can watch this movie."

She says with a concerned look, "All right, dear. If you want me to cook something, I will be glad to."

"Fine. I will let you know."

Charlie lies down on the couch with a blank expression on his face. He stays glued to the TV until late in the evening. He finally heads to bed very late. He walks quietly up the steps so as not to wake his mother.

She has already gone to bed because of the late hour. As Charlie walks down the hall, he hears something coming out of his mother's room. He quietly walks over and gently opens her door. He hears his mother crying to herself. A rush of sadness floods Charlie's soul. He thinks for a moment and then decides not to intervene. He shuts the door and walks to his bedroom.

He takes off his clothes and crawls into his bed. He lies there thinking of all that has happened today. He thinks of all the things his dad did for him when he was alive. He thinks about all the good things and some of the bad things.

He remembers that his father never once said, "I love you, Son." Charlie wishes he would have said that to him at least one time. Charlie thinks, *I guess he never liked saying things like that, but I wish he had, just one time.*

Charlie also thinks about Dee. His heart begins to ache. He wishes that she would have come to be with him today. He really missed seeing her. He would have given anything if she had come. He needed to feel her presence.

Charlie is jolted by a new thought that enters his mind: *What if the Old Man tries to harm my mama? He succeeded in the death of my daddy, but what if he tries to kill Mama? I won't let that happen. No, I won't let him harm her. I will hunt him until I find him. Then I will pay him back for what he has done.* Charlie tries very hard to think about something else, so his heart won't fill up with hate.

Charlie then hears a faint sound from his mother's room. He holds his breath and can hear her crying. As her sad cries enter Charlie's still, dark room, he begins to cry as well. He lies alone in his bed and cries himself to sleep.

The night passes, and morning comes. Charlie stays in bed until late in the morning. His mother finally walks into his bedroom and tells him to get up. She is in a very cranky mood. Seeing the determined look on her face, Charlie gets up. Only a few moments go by until Charlie walks downstairs and into the kitchen. His mother has already fixed breakfast. He sits down at the kitchen table still groggy. He doesn't say much as he eats. Sara doesn't have a lot to say either. They both eat quietly. As

Sara places the dishes into the sink so she can wash them later, Charlie gets up and begins to walk back upstairs.

He stops on the stairway when his mother asks, "Charlie, what are you going to do today?"

Charlie turns to his mother and says in a casual way, "I believe I will go down to the lake today."

Sara erupts into an angry fit. "What do you mean you are going down to the lake!"

Charlie, surprised at his mother's anger, yells, "I want to find the Old Man and pay him back for what he has done!"

"Don't you raise your voice to me in this house!" his mother snaps. "Charlie Delaney, you are never to go down to that lake ever again! Do you understand me, young man?"

Charlie turns his head away for a short moment and then turns back to his mother. "I just want to find out who he is. I—"

Sara interrupts, "Charlie, I don't ever want you to go down there again. Promise me that you will never go down there. Promise me!"

Charlie, looking scared, timidly replies, "Yes, ma'am. I promise I will never go down there ever again. I promise."

Sara walks over to Charlie and wraps her arms around him in a loving hug. She says in a kinder way, "That man down there has already hurt us enough. I don't want you to get hurt by him too. That's why I don't ever want you to go anywhere near that lake. If you ever see the Old Man again, I want you to run as fast as you can away from him. Do you understand me?"

Charlie hugs his mother back and says, "Yes, ma'am. I will never go near that lake ever again."

"Promise me that if you ever see the Old Man, you will run as fast as you can away from him."

"No, Mama. A man doesn't run away from things he should deal with. The Old Man's deception caused my father to be killed. It is now my responsibility to make sure he doesn't harm you. I will not run from him if I ever see him again. I will make him run from me. Only a coward would run from his father's murderer. I will not let him make a coward out of me."

"I don't know what I would do without you, Charlie. You are everything in the world to me."

"You are everything in the world to me too. I hope nothing happens to you either, Mama."

Charlie and Sara hold each other and realize how much they love and mean to each other. Their bond is stronger than any force on earth.

As the days go on, Charlie and Sara depend on each other more and more to get through this horrible time. Charlie helps his mother with the housework and everything else he can. Sara depends on Charlie for emotional support. Just having him near her makes her feel more content with her everyday routines. Charlie is a good son to Sara. He never speaks rudely to her and always does what she wants without any back talk. They bond closer together as a result of John's tragic death.

The hot days of summer come to a close. The autumn leaves begin to turn into a wonderland of beauty, with a crisp new beginning. The new season brings a sense of change like never before. The season also brings a new school year. Before long, the school buses begin to make their usual rounds. The summer is over, and so is Charlie's innocence of being a boy. He has grown up very fast this summer. He is a little tougher and a little wiser, but he still remains Charlie Delaney.

Chapter 4
THE NEW BEGINNING

On the first day of school Charlie's mother doesn't have to come to his room and wake him up; he gets up on his own. He takes a shower and then gets dressed. He is looking forward to the school year. He can't wait to see Dee and all his other friends. He hurries downstairs to the kitchen, where his mother has prepared his favorite breakfast, hotcakes and sausages. He eagerly digs in, eating hurriedly until he is full and satisfied. His mother sits next to the window waiting to see that familiar sight, the school bus making its rounds. She tells him when the bus is coming. Charlie kisses his mother good-bye and then eagerly runs down the driveway and waits for the bus.

He gets on the mostly empty bus and walks to the very back. He sits down in the last seat. He is happy that school has started. He talks to friends as they get on. He feels good now that he has friends to be around. The dark, chilly atmosphere of the bus is full of excitement and wonder. It's a new beginning not just of the school year but also of Charlie's life. Soon, the bus stops at Dee's house. He excitedly looks out the window and sees his love for the first time since his father's funeral. He impatiently waits as she gets on and happily watches as she walks down the aisle. She doesn't stop until she gets to Charlie. She sits down right across from him.

"Hello, Charlie! How are you?"

Charlie puts on a happy smile. "Fine, Dee. Did you have a good summer?"

Dee smiles that sweet smile that Charlie has loved since he first saw her. She looks at him as if she is happy to see him. "I had a wonderful summer. I loved being away from school and all the problems it can bring, you know?"

"Yeah, I know what you mean."

He and Dee talk about everything they did over the summer as the bus slowly fills up. They continue to talk about small things until Dee brings up Charlie's father. "I am sorry about your dad, Charlie. I prayed for you about it."

"Really? You mean you actually prayed for me?"

"I sure did. It was the first time I prayed in a long time, but I did."

This makes Charlie extremely happy and gives him a boost of encouragement that Dee really does care about him.

"I had hoped you would come to the funeral and the burial."

"I'm sorry I didn't make it. My mother didn't think we knew your family well enough to come. I hope you aren't too disappointed about me not coming."

"I'm not disappointed. I'm just glad you came to the visitation and talked to me there. That made the situation a little easier for me. I thank you so much for coming."

"You're welcome, Charlie. I'm glad I came too."

The two continue to talk until the bus reaches school. The students get off the bus to go to their classes.

"I hope we have a few classes together," Charlie says.

"I hope we do too."

Dee and Charlie journey off to find their first classes and begin the new school year.

The day goes pretty smoothly for Charlie. He thinks this year will be better than last year. He is familiar with all the surroundings and finds his classes with ease. He takes to school better than he has ever before in his life. He enjoys being around all his friends again. He likes having a place to go and something to do. He is happy to be back and happy that he has two classes with Dee—chorus in second period and history in fourth period.

Before long, Charlie finishes up with his last class of the day. He leaves the class with a sense of accomplishment, having completed the first day. He thinks that he will have a good year this time. He enjoys school a tremendous amount now.

He walks to the bus in no big hurry. He gets on and finds Dee already there, sitting about halfway down the aisle. Charlie can't find a seat close enough to talk to her, so he just finds one as close as he can. He sits down and gets ready for the long journey home.

As the school bus drops off the students at their appointed destinations, Charlie gets up and finally sits down next to Dee for a few moments of simple conversation. He really likes to be around her, for she makes him feel happy and special. As the two talk about the school day, the school bus gets closer to her house. Charlie enjoys his last seconds with her. Those last few moments with Dee before she gets off are the most enjoyable for him.

The school bus finally stops at Dee's house, and she gets up from her seat, saying, "Good-bye, Charlie. I'll see you tomorrow."

"Okay, Dee, see you tomorrow."

Charlie stares at Dee's rear end as she walks away. Like a man hypnotized by a powerful force, Charlie doesn't take his eyes off her for one second. He marvels at how well she walks. Her blue jeans forge an extremely luscious and sexy view that send a mind-controlling substance through Charlie's attentive eyes. He gazes at her shapely form with complete wonder and amazement. Once she gets off the bus, Charlie rushes to the window to get one more glance at her beautiful feminine figure. She waves to Charlie one last time.

Charlie soon regains control of his mind, but the memory of her figure is branded into his mind. He has never seen a girl with such a beautiful figure. He sits patiently on the bus until he arrives at his house. He quietly gets off the bus and enters his house.

Sara is there waiting for him to see how his first day of school turned out. She is eager to see Charlie. "So how did it go today?" she asks.

"Fine. It was fine."

Sara notices that Charlie is not acting very happy and tries to cheer him up some. "How would you like a piece of chocolate cake? It's your favorite."

Charlie gives his mother a lonesome look. "No, Mama, I don't care for any right now. Maybe at dinner I will have a piece, but for now I don't want any."

"Is there anything wrong?"

Charlie gets angry at his mother. "I wish you would quit asking that same question!"

"I am just trying to help, Charlie."

"Sometimes you can help a great deal more if you would stop bothering me with 'Is there anything wrong? Is there anything wrong?' I get tired of hearing you say it over and over and over. If there is anything wrong, I will be the first to tell you so, but in the meantime, quit asking! I don't want to hear it anymore."

Sara looks hurt. She looks at Charlie sadly and then slowly walks away to her room.

Charlie doesn't feel bad for hurting his mother's feelings. He has been bothered by her constant questioning for quite some time now, and now he is beginning to express himself even at the expense of hurting her feelings. He goes up to his room to listen to his stereo. He remains there until his mother calls him for dinner around six o'clock.

As Charlie sits down at the table, he detects that his mother is still upset. He doesn't seem to care about her feelings this time. He just eats his dinner as his mother sits quietly and looks at him time to time with her hurt feelings plainly written on her face. She doesn't say much as Charlie finishes drinking his last drop of milk.

When he gets up from the table, Sara breaks her silence. "Charlie, are you still mad at me?"

Charlie looks at his mother with surprise. "No, Mama, I'm not mad at you. I haven't been mad at you. I just don't like hearing the same thing over and over and over. I just want to be left alone."

Sara looks silently at Charlie with sadness. Charlie gets up and goes to his bedroom once again. He spends most of his time there now, listening to his music, in his invincible world.

As the weeks go by, Charlie keeps to himself more and more. He and his mother grow further and further apart. When he comes home from school, he doesn't want anybody bothering him. Even when friends and relatives come over, Charlie still stays in his room like a cocoon. Sara tries not to upset Charlie, but sometimes Charlie yells at her for being overly motherly to him.

As school continues, Charlie and Dee become friendlier. They talk to each other about everything that is happening in their lives and tell each other their secrets. Dee really likes Charlie more than anyone else at school; he is that special friend she can relate things to easily.

One Saturday, Charlie gets up as he usually does. He sits down at the breakfast table. Sara is sitting down with the newspaper opened. She reads as Charlie eats his breakfast.

She asks, "How would you like to go to a yard sale today?"

Charlie's attention is aroused somewhat. "Where?"

"There are a whole bunch of them today. We could go to several if you want to."

He doesn't waste any time agreeing with her. He hurries to finish his breakfast and then gets ready to go. Sara rushes to get ready also. She is happy to see Charlie so eager to go with her. She looks in the paper for the address of the first sale on their list, and they drive away.

When they arrive, they park on the side of the road and walk up to the driveway. They begin to look over all of the stuff. Something catches Charlie's eye right away—a workout set. It is complete with barbells, dumbbells, and a weight bench. There are loads of extra weights and other things lying on the ground also. Charlie is fascinated with the set. He walks over to it quickly and looks it over more thoroughly. Meanwhile, Sara walks over to the other side of the yard sale to a table with some glassware. She looks the table over and picks up a piece of Depression glass.

As Charlie looks over the weight-lifting set, a strong, masculine voice asks, "How would you like to take home that set of weights, young man?"

Charlie turns and sees a middle-aged man standing behind him. The man is wearing blue jeans and a T-shirt. Charlie asks, "How much do you want for the entire set?"

The man smiles at Charlie and says, "I could let you have the entire set for about one hundred fifty dollars."

Charlie looks at the set and then back at the man. "All you want is one hundred fifty dollars for all of it?"

"That's all. It sure is a great buy. I have close to three hundred dollars in that set."

"Wow! I sure would like to have it, sir. Let me talk with my mama and see if she will buy it for me."

Charlie hurries over to Sara. "Mama, come over here! I want to show you something."

Sara looks at Charlie with curiosity. "What have you found?"

Charlie takes her by the hand. "Come on over here, and I will show you."

Charlie leads his mother to the weight set. The man is standing right beside it still and says to Sara, "So you must be this young lad's mother?"

"Yes," Sara says, gazing down at what Charlie has found. As she looks over the weight-lifting set, Charlie's excitement grows.

"I will let you have this set at a great deal today," the man says.

Sara looks over the weight-lifting set one more time. "First of all, what is it? And second, how much is it?"

The man looks at Sara and smiles. "This is a weight set, and I'll let you have it for only one hundred fifty dollars."

Sara looks very puzzled. She looks at Charlie, then the weight set, and then the man again. "One hundred fifty dollars for that?"

Charlie's happy moment is shattered. His facial expression turns from happy to sad in an instant. "Mama, that is a good buy on this set. He said he paid over three hundred dollars for it."

"That's right. I paid close to three hundred dollars for everything you see here."

"I don't care how much you paid for it. One hundred fifty dollars is way too much for it."

The man notices how disappointed Charlie is and says, "I'll tell you what. I will let you and you only have the entire set for only one hundred dollars. That is the lowest price I can take for it. The only reason I am doing this is because your son seems to have his heart set on it. I don't want to be the one to disappoint him."

Sara looks over at Charlie's eager face.

"Come on, Mama; buy it for me. I have been wanting a set like this one for a long time. Please buy it for me."

Sara knows he wants it a great deal just from the look of desire in his eyes. She pauses for a moment. "I am sorry, but one hundred dollars is still too much. I will give you fifty."

Charlie looks at the man with excitement waiting for his answer.

"I am sorry, lady. I can't let it go for that price. I'm sorry."

"Well, I am sorry too." Sara looks back over at Charlie. His eyes are as sad as a basset hound's. "I'm sorry, Charlie, but I can't pay that much money for something like that. Pick out something that costs five or ten dollars, and I will buy it for you. But this … what do you call it again?"

"It's a weight-lifting set," Charlie says. "A complete weight-lifting set."

"This weight-lifting set is just too much. Please don't be disappointed."

Pointing to the table of glassware, Sara says to the man, "There are a few things I want to buy over there." The two of them walk over to the glassware, leaving Charlie standing alone. Sara buys a Depression-glass butter dish, and the man puts it into a paper sack for her.

Sara asks him, "Wouldn't you take a little less for the weight set?"

The man looks at Sara with doubt in his eyes. He thinks about how much the boy clearly wants the set but says, "I'm sorry, lady. I paid close to three hundred dollars just a few months ago for that weight set. The only reason I am selling it now is because I've joined a health club. I wish I could help you, but I can't take that much of a loss."

"I understand. Charlie probably wouldn't ever use it much anyway."

The man glances over at Charlie and then looks back over at Sara, "I don't know, lady. He sure has an eagerness in his eyes."

Sara looks over at Charlie. He is looking at the weight set with a strong desire to have it.

"How would he know how to use it?" she asks.

"It comes with several workout books on what to do. They cover everything he would need to know."

"It would take everything I have to buy it, even what I paid you for this butter dish."

"Okay, lady, I'll let you have it for ninety-five bucks, but that's the lowest I'll take."

"I'm sorry; I still can't do it. Thank you so very much for the butter dish. I hope I get forty dollars' worth of use out of it."

The man thanks Sara, and she walks away.

"Come on, Charlie; let's go," she says.

As they get in the car, Sara notices Charlie is still disappointed. She looks over at him as she starts the car. "Charlie, I wanted to buy that for you, but now that your father is gone, we don't have that extra check coming in like we used to. The funeral costs alone were over three thousand dollars."

After hearing this, Charlie's attitude changes somewhat. "I didn't know that, Mama. I guess I should think more about things like that. I know one hundred dollars is a lot of money."

"Would you like to see what I bought?"

"Sure."

Sara takes the butter dish out of the paper sack.

"What is it?"

"It's a Depression-glass butter dish. It was made during the Depression, and that is why they call it Depression glass."

Charlie looks at it like any other dish. "How much did it cost?"

"Only forty dollars."

Charlie shakes his head. "Forty dollars! You mean that tiny little dish cost forty bucks?"

"Don't be so surprised, Charlie. I have seen butter dishes just like this one go for nearly a hundred dollars."

Charlie sits there stupefied at what his mother paid for the butter dish. They drive off to another yard sale. Charlie holds the dish in his hands as they drive.

He looks over at his mother. "Mama?"

"Yes, dear?"

"I'm glad you bought something you like. I know I wouldn't ever pay that much for a butter dish, but if you enjoy it, I'm glad you got it."

Sara looks over at Charlie and smiles. His face turns sour, and she knows what he must be thinking about. She drives Charlie to several other yard sales. Charlie doesn't look happy at any of them. He only looks around for a few minutes and then sadly waits close to his mother.

At the next yard sale, when Sara gets out of the car, Charlie remains inside.

"Aren't you going to get out?" she asks.

Charlie says out the window, "No, I believe I will just stay in the car this time."

Sara sees the same disappointed look on Charlie's face as when they left the first sale of the day. She turns and begins to walk around the tables of miscellaneous junk.

As Sara walks around, she notices a young boy sitting in a wheelchair. He must live there because the lady taking money from the customers keeps calling him "son." The little boy has the happiest expression on his face. Sara thinks, *How happy that boy looks. Here he is sitting in that wheelchair unable to walk, but he has a happy face.*

Sara hears the lady who is taking the money say to the boy, "David, look what I have for you." The lady pulls out a moon pie and hands it to him. "Here you go, son." As she hands it to him, his face lights up with excitement and joy.

Sara, curious, walks over to where the little boy and his mother are sitting. Sara gets their attention and asks the lady, "Is he your son?"

"Yes, ma'am, he sure is. He is my only son."

"He sure does look happy."

The woman says in a kind voice, "He sure is, because he is with his mama, ain't that right, David?"

David smiles gladly. "Uh-huh, Mama. I love my mama."

"He is the joy of my life."

"Oh, I bet he is," Sara says.

The lady looks over at her son and then back to Sara. "He is the reason I'm having this yard sale. I want to make enough money to send my precious little boy to a western camp out West."

The little boy declares, "I am going to ride the horses like the cowboys do."

Sara looks at the boy with great joy and delight. She sees in his eyes something wonderful. He may be sitting in a wheelchair, but he has something to look forward to. His tender eyes and happy expression touch Sara's heart. Sara is compelled to find something on the table and buy it. She just wants to help the little boy get to that camp and ride the horses like the cowboys do. She picks something out something cheap and pays for it.

As she walks back to the car, she thinks, *I feel so selfish. I ought to be ashamed of myself. I bought myself a stupid butter dish when I could have bought Charlie that weight set. I haven't bought Charlie anything he wanted in a long time. Seeing that happy boy in a wheelchair makes me realize how lucky I am to have a son who is healthy and strong. I should have put Charlie's wants before my own. I feel so awful for being so selfish, and all because of a stupid butter dish!*

Sara gets in the car and looks over at Charlie with a tear running down her cheek. "Charlie, I want to tell you something."

Charlie sees the tear and gets upset. "Mama! Mama, what is the matter?"

Sara reaches over and holds Charlie's hand. She calms him down by saying, "Charlie, I want to apologize to you."

Charlie shakes his head in amazement.

"I want to tell you how lucky I am to have a son like you."

"Why are you talking like this, Mama?"

"I just realize how selfish I have become. I bought that stupid butter dish instead of buying you that weight-lifting set. I feel so bad not buying it for you."

"That's all right, Mama; don't let it bother you."

Sara looks over at Charlie's unselfish and humble face. She realizes how precious Charlie is to her. "Do you think that man has sold that weight-lifting set?"

Charlie looks at his mother with surprise. "I don't know; maybe not."

"Well, there is only one way to find out. Let's drive over there and see."

Charlie's face lights up like a Christmas tree. "Oh boy! Oh boy! Well, I'm not going to talk you out of it. Let's go!"

Sara sees the joy in Charlie's eyes and is filled with joy herself. She sees the same happiness in Charlie that she saw in the eyes of the little boy in the wheelchair. Her heart fills to the brim with love and joy.

Sara starts the car, and the two drive off toward the house with the weight set. The car is full of a spontaneous excitement, Sara drives fast with a strong desire to rid herself from the selfishness that plagues her soul. The anticipation grows stronger and stronger as they get closer to their destination.

Soon the two eager individuals arrive and quickly walk up to the yard sale. The weight-lifting set is still sitting in the same place. The man is sitting at the table near the glassware.

Sara, holding the butter dish securely in her hands, says to the man, "Pardon me, sir. I am back to purchase the weight-lifting set."

The man smiles at Sara and says, "Good. I was hoping you would be back."

Charlie says, "I'm glad nobody has bought it yet."

The man looks over at Charlie and says, "Yes. I had a few people come by wanting to buy pieces of it, but I didn't want to break up the set, so they left."

"Good. We will take it," Sara says. She pauses for a moment and then asks gently, "Pardon me, but would you like to have this butter dish back?"

The man looks at Sara with a little apprehension.

"I paid you forty dollars for it, and I was wondering if you would give me a forty-dollar credit toward the weight set."

The man hesitates. He looks at Charlie and sees the eagerness in his eyes. "Well, I guess so. You look like nice people, so I guess I could do that for you."

Sara and Charlie smile joyfully. Sara lays the butter dish on the table and pulls out sixty dollars, all the money she has, and hands it to the man.

The man looks over the butter dish and then takes the money from Sara. He puts the money in the cash register and hands a five-dollar bill back to Sara.

Sara looks surprised at the change and says, "Oh no, you keep that!"

The man looks surprised now too. "I told you I would take ninety-five dollars for the set a while ago. That would leave me owing you five bucks."

"If you paid nearly three hundred dollars for that set, then I want you to have the full one hundred dollars. Go ahead and keep it. The more I pay for it, the better I will feel about it. So please, keep the five dollars. I will feel much better if you do."

"Well, thank you. I sure do appreciate it."

"I don't know how we will get it home. How much would it cost for you to deliver it to our house?"

The man pauses for a moment. "Lady, I will deliver it to your house for free. I would be glad to do it for you."

Sara has a joyful expression as she writes down the address for the man.

"How soon can you have it delivered?" she asks.

"I can deliver it just as soon as I am through with the yard sale, sometime this evening."

"That would be great!"

Charlie and Sara thank the man once more and then drive home. Before the day is out, the man brings over the weight set just as he said he would. Charlie helps the man take it up to his room. Charlie and Sara thank the man for bringing it over so soon, and the man leaves content with the good deed he has done. Charlie doesn't waste any time putting the weight set to good use. He reads over all the books and begins working out. Sara also feels content with what she has done for her son. She put herself second to him so he would have something that would make him happy.

As the weeks go by, Charlie works out everyday. He doesn't forget what his mother gave up so he could have his workout station. He begins to look lean and strong. Sara is happy to see Charlie involved with something good and beneficial.

One day, Charlie is walking down the street to a friend's house. On the way he stops and looks at a mean-looking dog chained up outside. The dog pulls and tugs on the chain, wanting to get at Charlie. Charlie quickly moves away from the dog because of its mean, violent behavior. He continues to walk until he gets to his friend's house.

Charlie visits with his friend until about suppertime. He bids farewell to his friend and begins to walk home. As he approaches the house with the mean dog, he grows cautious. He looks around before walking out in front of the house. When he looks over to where the dog was chained up earlier, he sees that the dog is gone! The collar is still on the chain, but the dog isn't there. A fright runs up his spine.

Charlie looks around frantically until he hears an awful scream. "Help! Help! Someone help me!"

Charlie turns around and sees a woman on a nearby porch. Her face is filled with horror. The dog is attacking a small girl just a few yards away from the woman. Charlie jumps at the horrible sight of the vicious dog biting the small child. He runs over and gets the dog's attention. The dog lets go of the little girl and barks loudly and ferociously. Its wicked-looking teeth get closer and closer to Charlie. Then the dog runs toward Charlie and jumps for Charlie's throat. Charlie jumps back, and the dog barely misses him.

The woman is screaming at the top of her lungs. The neighborhood begins to be aroused by her loud, shrill screeching. Charlie, meanwhile, is busy with his attacker. When the animal misses another lunge, Charlie jumps on it from behind. The dog digs its wicked teeth into Charlie's flesh. Charlie pounds on the beast with his fists. He swings hard and quick as the animal continues to snap its jaws of terror. The dog's barks and growls sound eerie and evil. Charlie strikes with all his might against the dog's eye. The dog jumps back as Charlie rushes it. Charlie gets a split second to wrap his arms around the dog's throat. He puts a choke hold on the vicious beast and holds it with all his strength. The blood rushes out of Charlie's head and arms, but he holds the choke hold as tight as he can. The animal puts up a tremendous struggle, but Charlie holds the animal firmly until it is still.

Charlie realizes after a few moments that the animal has died. Charlie picks up the lifeless corpse and throws it as far as he can. By that time, a police car drives up, and the neighborhood is full of bystanders.

The police call for an ambulance, and it soon arrives. The paramedics place the small child and Charlie in it. The small girl has been torn apart. Charlie is not too badly injured but is bleeding a lot. The mother of the child is sitting next to the little girl.

Charlie asks one of the paramedics, "Do you think she will be all right?"

The paramedic looks up at Charlie and says, "I don't know right now, young man. I just don't know. We will know more after we get her to the hospital and let a doctor look her over."

The ambulance rushes them to the hospital. The siren is loud and scary.

Sara hears the siren and walks outside. She notices all the people gathering around down the street. She runs back into the house to get a sweater and then runs down the street to the scene. She has no idea what happened. When she finds a familiar face, she walks over and asks, "Bill, what has happened?"

Bill looks at Sara with fright in his eyes. "I was hoping I wouldn't be the one to tell you, Sara."

She panics for the first time. "Tell we what? What has happened? Tell me, Bill! What has happened?"

"Charlie just saved a little girl's life. She was being attacked by that pit bull." Bill points over to the dead animal. "Charlie ran over, and I don't know how he did it, but he killed that dog."

"Where's Charlie? Where's my baby?"

A police officer overhears her and asks, "Are you, Mrs. Delaney?"

"Yes, I am Mrs. Delaney. Do you know where my son is?"

"An ambulance took him to the hospital. Would you like me to drive you there?"

"Yes, would you please do that?" Tears begin to run down Sara's face as she panics.

The tall police officer says gently, "Please come with me, Mrs. Delaney. Please don't panic. I saw your son walk to the ambulance. He is going to be all right. The little girl he saved is the one that got seriously hurt. Please come with me, and we will go to the hospital."

Sara, shaking, gets into the police car. On the way to the hospital, Sara prays hard for Charlie and the little girl. Soon they arrive at the hospital, and the police officer escorts Sara inside. She walks into Charlie's room expecting the worst, but when she gets there, the room is full of newspaper reporters. Charlie smiles at her, and she quickly walks up to the bed where he is lying.

"Hey, Mama. What took you so long?"

"Charlie Delaney! I have been worried sick ever since I heard they brought you here. I now see you aren't hurt. I ought to get a yardstick and tan your hide good."

The room erupts into relieved laughter.

One newspaper reporter says, "Mrs. Delaney, your son is a hero. He saved a little girl's life today."

The room explodes in applause as Sara hugs her son.

A doctor walks in the crowded room and announces, "The little girl will be all right now. She has had several bad bites, but she will be fine."

Everyone applauds again with triumphant excitement. Several newspaper reporters ask Charlie many questions about how he reacted when he first saw the dog attacking the little girl. Charlie tries to answer them all. Hours go by until the doctors finally run the newspaper reporters out of the room.

Before the last one leaves, he says, "Your face and name will be on the front page tomorrow morning, young man. You should be very proud of your son, Mrs. Delaney. He is a hero now!"

"Thank you so very much," Sara responds.

The last reporter leaves as the doctor walks back into the room. The doctor looks over Charlie one more time. Charlie has several bandages on his hands, arms, and shoulders.

"You are ready to go home now," he says. "If I had a son, I would want him to be just like you. You are a courageous and fearless young lad."

"Thank you, sir."

Sara, glowing with pride, says, "Thank you again, Doctor. How much do I owe you for taking care of my son?"

The doctor smiles at Sara and says, "You don't owe us anything. Those newspaper reporters paid the entire balance. Just keep him at home a few days until he feels like returning to school. He will probably be sore tomorrow, so take good care of him."

Sara looks at Charlie with pride. Then she looks back at the doctor. "Yes, sir, I will take real good care of him. You can bet on that."

A nurse comes into the room with a wheelchair. Charlie takes one look at it and says, "I ain't getting into that chair. I can walk on my own two feet."

"It's policy. We do it for insurance reasons," the doctor says.

"You do like the doctor says," Sara says. "He is only doing his job."

Charlie submits to his mother's request and gets into the wheelchair. The nurse wheels him down the hall as Sara goes to the front desk and signs all the necessary papers so Charlie can leave. When Sara turns and sees Charlie in the wheelchair, she gets a flashback to the boy in the wheelchair at the yard sale. She sheds a happy tear.

The police officer who drove Sara to the hospital is waiting at the front entrance when Charlie and Sara exit. He greets them courteously and then says, "This must be the fellow I have been hearing great things about."

"Yes. He is the hero for today," Sara says.

Charlie blushes a little as the police officer says, "My sergeant asked me to stay here so I can drive you and your son home."

"That was nice of him," Sara says.

"You mean we are going to be driven home in the police car?" Charlie asks.

"That's right, son; go ahead and hop in."

Sara and Charlie get into the squad car. As the police officer drives, he looks over at Sara, who is sitting in the front, and says, "The man who owned the pit bull is in jail."

Showing some concern, Sara asks, "What do you think will happen to him?"

"He has been charged with assault with the intent to kill. His dog attacked a very important little girl. Her father is the judge of the superior court in this district, Judge Brewer. He will make sure that man pays the price to the full extent of the law."

"Nobody should be allowed to own dogs like that one. There should be a law banning dog breeds that are a threat to the well-being of the community."

Charlie, sitting in the backseat, responds, "I agree completely! Those animals are too dangerous to be allowed near anyone."

"If you want, we can go downtown so you can fill out a judgment against that man for damages done to you."

Charlie pauses for a moment before saying, "We don't have to do that."

"I think we should," Sara says. "That man should pay for letting his dog run loose like that."

"The dog wasn't running loose; it pulled its collar off."

"I don't care if it pulled its collar off. I just know that my son got mauled by that animal. I think the owner should pay dearly for his negligence."

Charlie sits back and thinks on the subject for a few minutes. "I don't care about pressing charges for what that dog did to me, but if I could make a statement that could prevent anyone from owning dogs like that, I will do all I can to get that done."

The police officer makes a sharp turn at the light. "That is just what I wanted to hear. We are going down to the station. If you press charges against the man, we can issue a warrant for his arrest. Maybe you can help stop this tragic problem the whole country is facing with these ferocious animals."

"Didn't you say he was already in jail?" Sara asks.

"Yes, ma'am, I did, but he will soon post bail and get out. But just as soon as he gets home, we will go back to his house and put him back in jail. We must make sure the people know that this man is going to catch hell over this incident."

They get to the police station, and Charlie fills out all the necessary papers. Then the police officer drives Charlie and Sara home. They don't get home until late, and they are both very tired.

Charlie sits down at the kitchen table, and Sara asks, "Would you like me to fix you something to eat?"

"I am so hungry I could eat a horse. Fix me something good."

Sara walks over to the refrigerator and pulls out the steaks that she had planned to cook earlier. She cooks them and also fixes baked potatoes, corn on the cob, and a fresh tossed salad with Thousand Island dressing. Also on the list of goodies is Texas toast drowned in butter and, for dessert, hot apple pie with a giant scoop of vanilla ice cream on top. Yum-yum!

Charlie digs in. As they eat their feast, Sara looks over at Charlie and sees how much he is enjoying his meal. She is content having a son that is so happy. She loves him so much. She eats her dinner and enjoys it greatly because she has Charlie there to share the moment. Sara is really proud of Charlie.

When the two happy souls are finished, they go to the living room to watch the eleven o'clock news. As they watch the news, Sara says to Charlie in a very soft voice, "Charlie, did you know that it was three months ago today that John died?"

Charlie pauses for a moment. "Yes, Mama, I know."

"I think we have overcome that tragedy pretty well, don't you?"

"Yes, I think we have done pretty well, Mama. I just wish Daddy were here now to enjoy what I did today."

Sara shows Charlie a look of love. "Me too, Charlie, me too." Sara gets up and moves to sit down beside Charlie on the couch. She cuddles him with a loving hug. "Your father would be proud of you today,

Charlie. I am so proud of you." Sara's eyes gleam as she speaks these words, and Charlie turns red. He just sits there in a quiet, tranquil mood until the TV shows a picture of him on the screen. Sara jumps up and turns the volume up as they both listen with excitement.

"This just in, a few hours ago a young man named Charlie Delaney saved a little girl from a vicious pit bull attack. This is our state's thirtieth dog attack this year, which is the most cases of any state in the country. The little girl's father, Judge John H. Brewer, said today that he has had it with people owning animals that are dangerous to the community. He said that when small children are being mauled and killed in large numbers in our state, then it's time to do something about it. He is planning a visit to the governor tomorrow to try to get a law passed that would make it illegal to own pit bulls and other dangerous breeds."

Sara claps her hands in applause.

"For his negligence in allowing his dog to run loose in the neighborhood, the owner of the animal, Paul Martin, has been charged with assault with the intent to kill. He was placed under arrest with bond set at three thousand dollars. As soon as Martin posted bail, police officers went back and arrested him again on secondary charges from the young man that saved the little girl, Charlie Delaney."

The newscast then shows a picture of Martin, with a big smile on his face, being released from the police station. He is slender and of average height with a long, bushy black beard and black hair that hangs down to his shoulders. He is wearing cut-up blue jeans and a black leather jacket with "Harley Davidson riders are the only ones fit to live" on the back.

The TV broadcast cuts to a police officer and a reporter. The reporter asks, "What do you think will be done about all this?"

The police officer says, "I hope tomorrow the governor will sit down with Judge Brewer and try to get a law passed so this kind of thing will never happen again."

"What about the man who is responsible for the mauling? Will he have to serve any time?"

With an expression of doubt, the police officer says, "I don't think he will serve much time, but you can bet your last dollar that we at the police department will do everything possible to make sure that this irresponsible individual gets punished to the full extent of the law. I hate to see little children torn up by these vicious animals. I hope something will be done to stop this."

The TV broadcast goes to another story, and Sara and Charlie sit back with a robust energy of excitement.

The next day, Sara keeps Charlie out of school. Charlie still gets up early anyway. He watches the school bus go by with a sad but also somewhat-glad feeling. He is happy he won't have to deal with all that schoolwork, but he would like to see his friends.

As Sara fixes breakfast, the phone begins to ring. People from all over call Charlie to congratulate him for his deed yesterday. Just as soon as Charlie puts down the phone, it rings again. This happens all day long. Sara doesn't know what to think about all the phone calls. She and Charlie have to take turns answering the phone so the other can rest.

About three o'clock in the afternoon, Sara answers the phone yet again. As soon as the caller introduces himself, she calls, "Charlie! Charlie! Come here right now!"

Charlie runs into the living room. "What is it, Mama?"

"The governor is on the phone. Come here and talk to him!"

Charlie takes the phone. "Hello, this is Charlie Delaney speaking."

The man on the other end replies, "Hello, Charlie. This is your governor speaking. How are you making out today?"

"Oh, I am all right. How are you doing?"

"I am doing just fine. I heard of your bravery yesterday, and I just wanted to call you up to tell you how proud I am of you and to see if you would like to come to the state capitol sometime this week. We could talk about how we could stop animals like the one you fought yesterday from ever hurting anyone in our state again."

"Sure, that would be great! You really want me to come to the state capitol and talk to you?"

"That's right, young man. I want you, me, and a few others to sit down and have ourselves a nice long talk about the subject."

"That would be great! Can I bring my mama along too?"

Someone laughs in the background, and then the governor says, "Yes, Charlie, you can bring your mother too. I would really like to meet her."

"Oh boy!"

"They tell me you killed that pit bull with your bare hands. Is that true?"

Charlie replies with an excited expression on his face, "Yes, sir! I put a choke hold on that dog like the wrestlers on TV do. I applied all the strength I had until the dog finally stopped moving. After I knew it was dead, I picked it up and threw it as far as I could. That dog won't be hurting any more little girls; I guarantee you that, sir."

The governor laughs with pride. "Well, Charlie, I want to thank you one more time for acting the way you did. You are a fine, upstanding citizen. I bet your father is proud of you."

"Governor, my father died three months ago yesterday."

There is a long pause on the other end of the phone line. "I am sorry to hear that, Charlie; I really am. I will be sending someone to your house tomorrow to see when you can come up here and see me."

"I'm looking forward to that. I will wait to hear from you tomorrow."

"You have a good day, Charlie. I will be seeing you soon, and thank you once again for your brave act."

"Good-bye, Governor. It sure has been a pleasure talking to you." Charlie hangs up.

Tomorrow comes quickly, and Charlie prepares for the visitor from the governor's office. People from all over come by to see Charlie. The mayor even comes by and visits with him. Sara can't comprehend all the attention he is getting, but she manages well. There hasn't been this many people over since Charlie's father passed away. Pastor Riggs also comes by and wishes Charlie well, along with several others from the church.

As the people come and go, Sara tries to fix sandwiches for everyone. There is laughter and joy at the Delaney residence. As Charlie entertains some guests, a limousine pulls up outside the house. Sara goes outside to greet the new visitor.

A man gets out of the limousine and slowly walks up to Sara. He asks, "Is this where Charlie Delaney lives?"

Sara smiles gracefully at the man. "Yes, it is. I am Charlie's mother. To whom am I speaking?"

"My name is John H. Brewer, Judge John H. Brewer. I would like to see the young man who saved my little girl's life."

With great pride and delight, Sara takes the man's hand and walks him into the house and up to Charlie. "Charlie, this is Judge John H. Brewer. This is the man whose daughter you saved."

Charlie gets up and greets the man. As the man grips Charlie's hand in a firm handshake, Charlie sees a twinkle in his eyes.

"I am honored to meet you, young man," Judge Brewer says. "I owe you the world for saving my little daughter's life yesterday. I just wanted to come by and thank you in person."

Charlie blushes a little. "Well, you are quite welcome. I'm just glad your daughter didn't get more hurt than she did. I'm glad I was there to stop that dog from killing her."

"I have been talking to the governor about getting a law passed to make it illegal for anyone to own such dog breeds. He has sent me down here to see if you could journey with me back to the state capitol for a conference with him on Saturday."

"I would be honored to go with you, sir."

The judge smiles gladly at Charlie. "I was hoping you would say that. I don't know how to thank you for what you have done. I owe you a great deal for your courageous act."

"If you could help me get a law passed so no one can own a dog like the one I killed the other day, then that's all I would ever ask of you."

Judge Brewer turns to Sara. "You have the finest son in the whole world, Mrs. Delaney."

Sara's face is full of pride for Charlie. A tear runs down her face. "I believe you are right, Judge. I do have the finest son in the whole world."

The judge gives Charlie a warm, caring hug as if Charlie were his own son. He visits for a little while longer. He tells Charlie and Sara to be ready Saturday morning for the big trip to see the governor and then leaves.

The house is still full of people when he leaves. The people cheer Charlie and praise him. This is the most Charlie has been praised for something in his life. When it starts to get dark, the people leave. Soon the house is once again quiet and still.

Charlie gets up the next day, Friday, as he usually does. He watches the school bus stop and then leave without him once again. Charlie is feeling very sore now. His stiffness concerns Sara, and she wonders if he will be able to go to the state capitol Saturday. She walks into the bathroom and takes down the prescription the doctor gave her at the hospital. She reads the label carefully once more and then takes out two of the tablets. She walks back into the living room, where she finds Charlie looking out the window.

"Here you go, young man." She gives Charlie the medicine and then gets him a glass of water from the kitchen. "I hope that makes you feel better."

"Me too, Mama," he says and takes the medicine. "I sure feel rough this morning. I am as sore as I have ever been in my life."

Sara shows her motherly concern once more before she walks back into the kitchen to fix breakfast. She prepares Charlie's favorite meal again, hotcakes and sausages drowning in maple syrup. As he finishes drinking his third glass of milk, he retires into the living room and starts to watch a little TV.

At school that day, Dee hears for the first time about Charlie's heroic feat. She wondered yesterday why Charlie wasn't at school, and now she knows why. She overhears some of her classmates talking about Charlie in her chorus class.

Tom asks, "Did you hear about Charlie?"

Sue, Ron, and Lucy look at Tom with intense interest.

Sue asks, "What happened?"

Tom replies, "I heard he saved some little girl's life the other day."

"How did he do that?" Ron asks.

"A pit bull attacked the little girl," Tom says, "and, believe it or not, Charlie strangled the dog with his bare hands. Can you believe that!"

Ron says with disbelief, "Come on, Tom! You don't expect us to believe that, do you?"

Tom replies, "It's the truth! I swear! It's all over school. Charlie killed a pit bull with his own two hands."

Lucy says, "That's right! I heard Charlie's name on the news last night. He did save a little girl's life."

Dee doesn't like Sue, Ron, Lucy, or Tom, because of the way they talk about people. She keeps to herself but continues to listen to the conversation from her seat.

Sue says, "It's hard to believe someone like Charlie Delaney could save anybody's life. You know?"

All four laugh a ridiculing laugh.

Ron says, "I didn't think Charlie would have the courage to battle with such a dog. Just wait and see: they will probably say the dog was really a toy poodle with a bad haircut."

All four of them burst out laughing again. Dee looks at the four with anger and hate but manages to control herself and not say anything.

The teacher walks into the room then and takes roll. He says a few words to the class and then sits down at the piano and begins to play. He sings a few songs and jokes around with the few students who stand near him. He plays a little longer and then gets up and leaves the classroom. As soon as he leaves, the students walk around and assemble into little groups of gossipers.

Dee gathers with the group of people she likes to be around. She tries to ignore the group of snobs that she doesn't like very much, but as much as she tries to ignore them, she still manages to overhear their conversation.

Ron asks, "How long do you think Charlie will be out of school?"

Tom replies, "I don't know. His ordeal with that toy poodle probably will keep him out for the rest of the year."

The entire class begins to laugh loudly, except for Dee. As the different groups converse, Charlie's name keeps coming up in all of them. Soon he becomes the main subject of conversation. Most of the students talk admiringly about what Charlie did, but the group of snobs touches a sensitive nerve with Dee. They ridicule Charlie more and more.

Sue says, "I think Charlie is a little strange. He acts so weird sometimes."

Tom laughs as he replies, "Yeah, I know what you mean."

Sue continues, "Ever since he saw his old man drown, he has been a little crazy." Sue takes her right index finger and makes a circle around the right side of her head.

Dee jumps up in a rage of fury and bellows, "You all shut up!" She points her finger at Sue. "You shut up!"

The whole class stops talking and looks at Dee in complete awe and silence.

"Don't let me hear any of you snobs say anything bad about Charlie Delaney again!" Dee's anger explodes with a vengeance.

Sue turns a bright shade of red, as do the others in her group.

Dee gets up in their faces and shouts, "Why don't you all just shut up! There is nothing wrong with Charlie. He lost his father in a tragic accident, but there is nothing wrong with him. There is something definitely wrong with all of you, though." She takes a breath and stares at Sue. "If I ever hear any of you snobs say anything about Charlie again, I will personally slap you!"

Sue doesn't speak back; she just gets up and, with tears in her eyes, runs out of the classroom. The other students cheer Dee.

The teacher soon comes back into the classroom. He detects something is wrong by the students' expressions. He looks around and notices that Sue Parker isn't there anymore. He looks with curiosity at his class. The class is silent as he asks, "What's going on in here?" The class remains silent. "I said, what is going on in here?"

Lucy goes over to the teacher and speaks quietly to him. She points over at Dee as she explains what just happened. The teacher looks over at Dee and motions for her to come up to the front. Dee gets up and sits down next to the piano. She tells her side of the story. Most of the students in the class stick up for Dee. They all tell the teacher what they witnessed right up to the end of class.

When the bell rings, everyone gets up and goes to his or her next class. The teacher tells Dee to stay, though. He frowns at her and says, "Deborah, I am going to have to take you to the principal."

Dee is worried, and her eyes begin to tear. She looks at the teacher with sad eyes and asks, "Why? I haven't done anything wrong. Why should I have to go to see the principal?"

The teacher sees how upset Dee is. He sternly looks at her, deep in thought. "I can't let you go around school threatening other students because of something they said that you didn't like."

Dee becomes scared and sad. Tears run down her cheeks more freely. She looks back up at the teacher. "I promise I won't threaten anybody anymore. Please, Mr. Jones, don't take me to see the principal, please."

As the next class begins to arrive, Mr. Jones gets up with a determined look. He says quickly and callously, "Come with me, young lady!"

Dee walks with Mr. Jones to the principal's office. She sits and waits outside while Mr. Jones talks with the principal alone. After five minutes pass by, the door opens, and the two authority figures walk out of the room and stare at Dee with scrutiny.

With a stern look, the principal says, "Young lady, will you please come into my office?"

Dee, looking scared and frightened, walks into his office and sits down. The principal sits down at his desk, and Mr. Jones stays standing near the door.

The principal looks over at Mr. Jones and says, "That will be all. You can go back to your class. I believe I can handle this situation now."

Mr. Jones looks over at Dee, glances over at the principal, and then leaves the room without uttering a sound.

The principal pauses for a moment as he stares at Dee with his same stern look. "Young lady, I have been told you threatened to use violence on another student a while ago. Do you want to tell me about it?"

Dee's eyes begin to tear. She holds her composure as she says, "I didn't like what she was saying about one of my friends. She had no right to say the things she said."

The principal looks curiously at Dee. "You mean if someone says something you don't like, you think you have the right to threaten them with violence?"

Dee looks at him and then looks away. She pauses for a moment. "Well, I don't know …"

"I don't care what she said," the principal says. "What she said isn't the problem. The problem is you not being able to control your emotions. Just because you don't like what someone says doesn't give you the right to threaten that person."

Dee draws up and becomes silent. She looks like a frightened fawn in the woods looking for her mother. Her tender eyes turn anxious.

"Young lady, I don't have a lot of time to talk to you about this matter. I am going to call your mother and talk to her instead. Parents have a way of disciplining their children a lot better than people like me."

Dee just looks at the rough-looking man and begins to cry.

"When I talk to your mother, I am going to tell her that you threatened a student today and that this attitude will not be tolerated in this school. Then I am going to tell her to keep you home for three school days. You need to be kept away, for the safety of the other students."

Dee looks at him in shock. She can't believe what is happening! Her melancholy voice and face of anguish would make an angel cry. "Please don't call my mama and talk to her. I promise I won't threaten anyone else. I promise."

The principal looks at Dee with remorseless eyes. "I am sorry, young lady. I can't do that. You need to be taught a little lesson about making threats to other students."

Dee cries even harder.

"After you come back next Thursday, you and the girl you threatened will sit down with me for a nice little talk. I will expect you to apologize to this girl for your unruly and uncontrollable behavior."

Dee tears stop like a valve being turned off. She looks at the principal with a stern look of her own. "Oh, no, I'm not! I don't care if you don't ever let me come back to school. I will not apologize to that snob!"

The principal gets very angry. "You listen to me, young lady. You will apologize to that girl, or you won't be allowed to come back to this school, ever!"

Dee says boldly, "Forget it!"

The principal jumps up and leaves his office in a rush. Dee sits there smiling, as she feels proud of herself. She thinks about what Charlie might be doing right now. After ten minutes, a woman walks into the room and asks Dee to come with her. Dee gets up and follows the woman to another room. The woman tells Dee to stay there until her mother arrives.

Dee smiles and says, "Fine. I will stay right here until my mama gets here."

The woman frowns at Dee and then leaves.

Dee waits impatiently for her mother to come pick her up. When

Mrs. O'Brien finally gets there over an hour later, she and the principal have a long talk alone. He tells her about all the things Dee said and did. He also tells her to keep her at home until next Thursday. He doesn't let Dee speak on her own behalf. He doesn't even see Dee again. He just shows Mrs. O'Brien where Dee is waiting after they have finished talking. He tells Mrs. O'Brien to take her daughter home and have a long talk with her.

Mrs. O'Brien is very upset with Dee. They walk out to the car with distraught faces. They remain quiet until they start to drive off. About a mile up the road, Mrs. O'Brien looks over angrily at Dee. There is a tense feeling in the air as she asks, "What exactly is your problem, young lady?"

Dee pauses for a long time. "I don't know."

"What do you mean, you don't know?"

Dee realizes her mother is on the principal's side and that nothing she says will help. She just remains silent as her mother chews her out. Once they get home, Dee tries to explain her side of the story, but her mother is too upset to keep an open mind. They argue and argue about Dee being suspended from school for three days.

As the fight grows worse, Dee yells at her mother, "I don't care if you believe me or not! I don't love you anymore!"

Mrs. O'Brien looks at her daughter with tremendous anger. She slaps Dee hard across her crying face. The blow brings the room to a sudden quiet. Dee collapses on the couch and hides her face with her hands. She cries helplessly as her mother stands over her with tears of her own. Dee quickly jumps up and runs to her bedroom and slams the door shut. Mrs. O'Brien falls on the couch and begins to cry. Her tears pour out until she has no more to shed.

As Mrs. O'Brien lies on the couch, she looks up to the ceiling and prays, "Dear God in heaven, please help me! Please Lord, help me!" She looks down and quietly says to herself, "Oh, I wish I had you here, Tom, to help me with Deborah. I need someone to help me with her. I can't handle this by myself. William can't help. I need you, Tom." Mrs. O'Brien looks back up to the ceiling and prays once more, "Dear God in heaven, help me with Deborah. Please help me with her." Mrs. O'Brien gets up from the couch and retires to her room for the evening.

The next day is Saturday. As Dee and her mother try to mend their wounds, Charlie is getting ready to go to the state capitol for his meeting with the governor. Judge John H. Brewer arrives at the Delaney household to drive them. Sara greets him at the door.

"Hello Mrs. Delaney. How are you doing this nice Saturday morning?"

"I am doing just fine. I hope you are doing fine also. Come on in. Charlie should be ready soon."

The judge walks inside, and Sara asks, "Would you like a cup of coffee?"

"That would be nice."

The Judge sits down and has a cup of coffee as they wait for Charlie to come down, which he soon does. He is eager to get started on the long drive to the capitol. He is very nervous now. Charlie, Sara, and Judge Brewer all pile into the judge's automobile.

As the judge drives, he advises Charlie on what to expect from the governor and describes the format of the meeting. He explains to Charlie that the governor has a busy schedule and that the meeting must be done in a way that everything will be covered in a quick time frame. The judge explains everything to Charlie so that Charlie will be ready and willing to accomplish the task he has set for himself.

When they arrive, they are greeted by the governor himself. He has news media there as he welcomes them to the state capitol. They waste no time starting their meeting. The governor has prepared a conference room for their talk.

As the meeting begins, the governor and his associates listen with intense concentration as the judge stands and says, "I want to thank you all for letting me partake in this endeavor. I hope that our talk today will lay the foundation of a new understanding about the problem of vicious animals being unleashed on society. I hope this will be the beginning of the end for the ownership of these animals. This problem needs to be dealt with seriously. The lives of innocent people are in our hands. This is not just about what happened to my daughter; it's about all people. This problem should be given great importance because innocent individuals—the elderly; young children; women; and plain, ordinary people—are being victimized by these savage creatures. These vicious dogs must be banned once and for all!"

The judge's opening statement is met with great applause and jubilation. Even the governor applauds loudly. As the meeting continues, the governor doesn't do much of the talking. He just points to an individual and asks him or her to speak. He listens to everyone's concerns. The governor finally asks Charlie to speak on the topic.

Charlie stands up and shyly looks at the crowded room of distinguished individuals. He says, "I know everyone here is greatly concerned with the problem of vicious animals harming innocent people, but whatever we think isn't what is important."

The room becomes extremely quiet. The people look with curiosity at Charlie.

"We are only a small group of people. If anything good is going to come out of this meeting, we must put the ones who will benefit from this meeting first—the people of North Carolina. They are the ones who must decide what type of law should be passed on this issue. They are the ones who matter the most. What we decide isn't going to matter one way or the other. If anything is going to develop out of this meeting, we need to convince the people of the state of North Carolina that there needs to be a law banning the ownership of these animals. We should not let this meeting become just another good intention that doesn't go anywhere. We must make sure that we accomplish something out of this so the people of North Carolina will be protected!"

The room erupts in applause. The applause grows louder, and the people in the room begin to stand. Soon, everyone in the room is standing and applauding, even the governor.

As the applause dies down and the people take their seats, the governor looks over at Charlie and smiles, exceptionally proud. "Charlie, how would you like to speak to the state legislature, right now?"

The people focus their eyes on Charlie in complete silence. Charlie looks at the governor with reluctance. He then sees his mother looking at him with pride and admiration. The judge is staring at him with great admiration too. The judge nods toward Charlie with a smile of acceptance.

Charlie turns back to the governor and, with a face of excitement, says, "Yes, I would like to do that, Governor. I will speak to the people who are in charge of making laws."

The room erupts into a triumphant jubilation of applause. All stand and applaud Charlie and his determined beliefs in democracy. The governor gets on the phone and makes a few calls. The conference room becomes busy as everyone gets ready for Charlie's address to the state legislature. Sara and Judge Brewer sit on opposite sides of Charlie. They give him moral support as they all wait for the governor to set the stage for Charlie's speech. The governor has someone help Charlie write down what he wants to say. Charlie puts the notes in his shirt pocket, and the governor nods at Charlie, giving Charlie some added assurance about his decision.

It takes about an hour for the governor to get everything ready. It is highly unusual for the governor to interrupt the legislature when it is in session, but when the state representatives hear what the topic will be and who will be talking to them, they eagerly welcome the interruption.

The news media walk along with the governor, Charlie, and the rest of the group, asking questions on top of questions to give adequate coverage on what is about to take place. Everything is set when the group enters the building. The entire audience of the legislature gives the governor and Charlie an exhilarating welcome.

The governor walks up to the podium, and Charlie follows right behind. "Good evening to you all," the governor says. "I know this is quite unusual and very unexpected, but there is a lad here that wants to tell you all something. It is something very important. It is something I support with all my heart. Having heard what this lad has done makes me feel proud that I chose to serve as governor of the state of North Carolina."

The entire assembly listens with complete and undivided attention. A strong sense of excitement builds as the governor continues, "This week this lad fought off a vicious pit bull and saved a little girl's life in doing so. He is bright and very intelligent. He, not I, wanted to come here and talk to you all about passing a bill. Well, I think I will let him tell you what he came here for." The governor looks over at Charlie and smiles gladly at him. "So without further interruptions, I want to introduce Charlie Delaney!"

The entire assembly stands and applauds as Charlie walks up to the podium. He pulls out his speech and waits for all the representatives to stop applauding. As they sit down, Charlie still waits. The audience watches and wonders impatiently as Charlie waits even longer. He looks out to his audience and waits until the atmosphere is at a fever pitch.

He then slowly begins his speech. He mumbles a few words that no one can understand. Then he glances out into the auditorium and, with a gleam in his eye, says, "I came here today to talk to the governor, to see if there is any way a law can be passed that will prevent anyone from owning animals like pit bulls that have violent natures. As I talked with the governor today, I felt that no matter what we agreed on, it wouldn't make any difference in the world unless the people of North Carolina are involved in this decision. The people of North Carolina must be protected from any type of vicious creature that will attack anyone at anytime without warning."

Charlie raises his hands and points to the sky as he continues, "This must stop! This must be stopped! This will be stopped!"

The audience erupts with applause on a grand scale. Charlie looks out into his audience with a strong, determined gaze. "When I walked into the auditorium today, I heard you all talking about some matter on the budget." Charlie leaves the podium and begins to walk around. He takes the microphone with him as he stares deep into his audience. He waits until he has everyone's attention. There is complete silence before Charlie continues, "As you all debate on whether or not you should spend X amount of dollars on some state project, there is another violent animal out there ready to pounce on another little girl."

Charlie points out at the state representatives and asks, "What are you going to do about that?" The auditorium is filled with a deafening silence as Charlie again pauses. Charlie doesn't let the silence interfere with his eye contact with his audience. He looks at the attentive representatives until the atmosphere is where he wants it to be. The audience eagerly waits for Charlie to continue. He waits and waits until finally he says in a bold, strong voice, "What are you going to do about that?" Everyone listens in complete silence.

Charlie's voice gets softer, and his tone becomes gentle and mild, but he still looks at his audience with a powerful stern expression. "I was walking down the street I live on this week when I saw a vicious pit bull. It began to snap at me like it wanted to eat me for dinner. It snarled and growled at me wickedly. I looked at the four-legged monster and quickly moved down the street."

Charlie walks back to the podium. "As I was walking back home from a friend's house that evening, I noticed that the vicious dog wasn't at its doghouse anymore. Its collar was there. Its chain was there. But it wasn't there! My heart began to beat fast. Sweat ran down my face, and a horrible fear ran up my spine. I knew the dog was loose somewhere."

Charlie pauses again as his audience becomes completely controlled by his words and mesmerized by his facial expressions. "Then I heard a awful cry—'Help! Help! Someone help me! My daughter is being attacked by a dog! Please someone help me!' I looked and saw a vicious animal biting and chewing up an innocent little girl. I didn't have time to think. I jumped over the fence and got the animal's attention. It let go of the little girl and came after me. The dog jumped at my throat, but I dodged just in time. Then me and the dog had a knock-down, drag-out fight. It bit me several times while I tried to get my composure."

Everyone in the auditorium stares at Charlie with intrigue as he continues, "I started to pound on its head with all my might, its teeth digging into my flesh like a knife cutting bread. I punched it in the eye. I finally got my arm around its throat and with all my strength strangled it until it was dead!"

His audience applauds with a robust excitement.

"After I knew it was dead, I picked the dead beast up and threw it as far as I could."

More applause roars from the auditorium. Charlie puts up his hands to stop the roaring jubilation. He waits for the entire auditorium to become quiet and calm. He takes his time before he speaks again, waiting until the mood is once again at a fever pitch.

"Now! How many other little children will be exposed to such a tragic event?" Charlie pauses again and then bellows, "How many other little children will be killed because of such animals as this one? As long as they are allowed to roam free or to be near innocent people of North Carolina, there will be more vicious attacks. How many more people will have a confrontation with these vicious dogs? How many little children will die or be maimed because of the negligence of these dog owners?" There is another long pause. The entire auditorium is completely silent as Charlie says in a very soft tone, "Tell me, how many will die because of the negligence of you people?" Charlie points at his audience. The entire auditorium is filled with a deafening quiet. The legislators look around at each other.

Charlie, looking sternly at his audience, says, "Tell me, gentlemen, how many little children and how many others will die because there isn't a law to protect them? Tell me, gentlemen, how many?" The auditorium remains quiet as Charlie begins to walk around the stage. Charlie points out toward his audience again and cries out with a loud, blistering voice, "What are you people going to do about this problem?" There's anger in his face as he asks, "What are you people doing here?" Charlie waits a few moments and says, "What is your main purpose here?" He again pauses as he feels out his audience. When everything is quiet and still, he asks, "Are you here to serve the people of North Carolina or just to live the million-dollar lifestyle that they provide for you? Are you here just to feel important as a big-time state representative? There should have been a law against owning vicious creatures like the one I fought this week a long time ago."

The representatives look great concerned. Charlie pauses again before saying, "I mean, you can't own a lion or a tiger or a bear, can you? Of course not! Then why can someone own a pit bull or some other similar animal? Do you think that these pit bulls are not as dangerous as those other animals?"

Charlie walks around the stage as he looks some of the representatives in the eye. After a long pause, he points his finger at them and with a burst of emotion says, "I want to tell you all something: those pit bulls are more dangerous because they are not taken seriously. If people see a lion in the neighborhood, they will run for their lives. But if they see a pit bull, they will not be alarmed, because people take it for granted that pit bulls are just domestic pets. Then these dogs can attack and chew people up because people don't suspect what these animals can do. Take it from me: by the bandages I have on me, I know what these animals can do. Did you hear me? People think that these animals are just another domestic pet! Huh!" Charlie points his finger at the audience and says boldly, "That type of deceptive attitude is going to stop!"

The auditorium erupts into a loud, delirious round of applause.

"Now, what are you going to do about this problem? Are you all going to go back and talk about some silly budget proposal now?" Charlie pauses, and the room begins to show activity. People begin to get up and walk around and talk to each other as quietly as possible. Charlie points his finger at one of the legislators and says, "Hey you! I hope you aren't talking about that budget matter!" The entire auditorium erupts with laughter as Charlie walks back to the podium.

Sara's eyes are full of pride, wonder, and amazement. She looks over at the judge with a surprised look on her face and asks, "Is that my son?"

"I don't know, Mrs. Delaney. It looks like Charlie, but after hearing him talk so robustly, I just don't know! How old did you say he is?"

"I believe he is fifteen years old. At least that was what he was on his last birthday, but after hearing him talk today, I think he is more like thirty-five."

Sara and the judge gaze back to the podium to hear Charlie continue with his address to the state legislature.

"I hope I have got to each and every one of you today. I don't know what you all must do before a law is passed to stop these vicious animals from attacking innocent people, but I hope and pray that you all will do something about this problem. I hope you do something about this problem fast. The longer you wait, the bigger the chance someone will be hurt by these unsuspected monsters. Life is too short; there is no time to wait. It is time to act! Try to see it my way. Do I have to keep saying it until I can't go on? There must be a ban on ownership of pit bulls and any other animal that is a threat to the well-being of society."

The legislators' eyes and faces radiate a gleam of understanding toward Charlie as he pauses. He continues, "I've always thought it is a crime to turn away from something I think I can change. If I had turned away from that dog and run away when I saw it chewing on that little girl, it would have felt like breaking the law. It would have been a crime to leave that little girl while she was being attacked. She would have died if I hadn't acted when I had."

Charlie's face turns a light shade of red as he says in a gentler tone,

"I am not up here to brag about what I have done. I am up here so the next little girl will not be subjected to such an awful ordeal. There is still a chance of accomplishing that if we all join together and bring a law into being. I hope that law will be passed so the people of our great state will be protected. I thank you all for your time. I hope you all have a nice rest of the day, and may God richly bless each and every one of you all. Thank you."

The entire assembly stands and applauds Charlie for ten minutes complete.

Sara, Judge Brewer, the governor, and several others come by and shake Charlie's hand before he leaves the auditorium. Everyone congratulates Charlie for his outstanding speech. Later on in the day, Charlie, Sara, and Judge Brewer wish the governor and his aides a final good-bye. They all pile into the judge's automobile and make the long drive home.

When the judge pulls into Charlie's driveway, the news media hounds are there, waiting for a story. News reporters with microphones are all over, asking everyone on the street questions. Judge Brewer handles the ordeal, and Charlie and Sara walk into the house as quickly as possible. They don't let anyone in the house because of all the chaos going on outside. Charlie and Sara look outside and wonder at all the attention they are getting until people start to stare back at them. Sara then pulls the curtains closed so the onlookers outside won't be encouraged.

Soon it gets dark, and all the news media leave the scene. Judge Brewer and his wife come over after things settle down somewhat. The two thankful individuals knock on the door, hoping to thank Charlie together for the first time. Sara looks out the window and gladly hurries to open the door.

"Well, come on in!" Sara says, staring at Mrs. Brewer with excitement. "It is so good to see you, Mrs. Brewer; please come in. Charlie has been eager to meet you."

"Thank you so very much, Mrs. Delaney."

"Please call me Sara."

"Okay, Sara. I am so glad to meet you. I am very eager to meet

Charlie. I'm sorry for not coming sooner, but I have been at the hospital with my little girl."

Sara leads the Brewers into the living room, where they both sit on the couch.

"Charlie!" Sara calls upstairs. "There are some people here that want to see you."

Charlie comes down the stairs and sees the Brewers' happy faces looking back at him.

Mrs. Brewer gets up and rushes over to Charlie and hugs him gratefully. "Hello there, young man! It is so good to meet you! I didn't get a chance to thank you in the ambulance early this week, so I thought I would do that right now. Thank you so much for fighting off the dog that attacked my little girl."

Charlie embraces Mrs. Brewer and politely says, "It was my pleasure, Mrs. Brewer."

Tears run down Mrs. Brewer's face as she continues to hold Charlie in a loving hug. Then she takes Charlie by the hand and walks him over to the couch. They sit down, and Mrs. Brewer holds his hand as she says, "Charlie, you don't know how happy I was to see you fend off that mean dog. When I saw it chewing on my little daughter, I just didn't know what to do! When you jumped over that fence and fought that dog, I knew, then and there, that God in heaven was watching over my precious little girl. I just don't know how to ever repay you for your bravery."

Charlie smiles at Mrs. Brewer with an humble expression. "You don't have to repay me for a thing. I'm just glad I was there when I was."

Mrs. Brewer picks up her purse and pulls out some money. "Here you go, young man. I would feel better if you would accept this as a token of my appreciation."

Charlie looks at the money in surprise. "Oh no, Mrs. Brewer! I can't take that money! I would feel awfully bad if I did. Please don't give me any money for fighting off that dog."

Mrs. Brewer insists, "I will not take no for an answer. I want you to have it, so please take it."

Mrs. Brewer places the money into Charlie's hand, and he looks at her with sadness in his eyes. Charlie looks over at his mother and then at the judge. The look on his face is not a happy one. He looks back over at Mrs. Brewer and says, "If you make me take this money, I will feel offended. If you like me, try to understand that your good intentions are going to make me feel very bad. I ask you to please put aside your good intentions this time and take back this money. Sometimes, we think we are doing good based on our intentions, but if you make me take this money, I will feel very hurt. You don't want to make me feel hurt, do you?"

Mrs. Brewer pauses for a moment and says kindly, "No, Charlie, I don't want to make you feel hurt. I sometimes get blinded by my intentions and think I am doing good when I'm not. I will just accept your decision and not press you anymore, for I see in your eyes a look of sadness brought on by my intentions of goodwill. Since you won't take this money, would it be all right if I donated one hundred dollars in your name to your favorite charity?"

Charlie looks over at Mrs. Brewer with a humble smile. "I guess so, Mrs. Brewer, except one thing."

"Oh, what is that, Charlie?"

"I don't have a favorite charity."

The whole room erupts into laughter. Everyone marvels at Charlie's humility.

Judge Brewer, looking over at Charlie with admiration, says, "Charlie, you just don't know how much of an impression you left on the whole country today. The *CBS Evening News* even had a story on you today."

"Really? I was on the *CBS Evening News*?"

"You sure were! The whole country is waiting impatiently on the results on what our legislators will come up with about the ban on pit bulls. Just think, Charlie: you might be a national hero before next week is out."

Mrs. Brewer says, "What do you mean he 'might' be a national hero? As far as I am concerned, he already is a hero! He saved my little girl's life, and after today, Charlie might be the one responsible for saving the lives of other little girls just like mine."

The room of admirers erupts into spontaneous applause for Charlie.

"Gosh!" Sara says. "The *CBS Evening News* really showed my son's face on TV?"

Mrs. Brewer says, "Yes, they sure did! I saw it with my own two eyes."

Judge Brewer says, "They are even calling the bill the Charlie Delaney Bill."

"Well, isn't that something? My son a national hero. I just can't get over that."

As Charlie, Sara, and Mr. and Mrs. Brewer sit and talk, Sara keeps having to get up and answer the phone calls coming in congratulating Charlie. She just can't stand hearing that phone ring and interrupt the visit with the Brewers anymore, so she takes it off the hook. When it gets late, the Brewers bid their farewells to Sara and Charlie. Mrs. Brewer hugs Charlie one last time before she leaves. Judge Brewer shakes Charlie's hand with a firm, proud handshake. They both wish Charlie well as they leave to go home. When Sara walks them to the door, she thanks them for coming by and wishes them well. They leave with smiles on their faces.

Soon after the Brewers leave, it is time for Charlie and Sara to go to bed. As Sara wishes Charlie good night, she thanks him one last time for being such a good son and tells him how proud she is of him. Charlie kisses his mother good night, and the two happy individuals go to their rooms and go peacefully to sleep.

The next morning, Sara fixes Charlie his favorite breakfast, hotcakes and sausages with pure maple syrup. Charlie wolfs down a tall stack of the fluffy light cakes and devours a plate of sausage. He washes it all down with several glasses of ice-cold milk.

Charlie and Sara get ready for church. It has been several Sundays since Charlie has been to church. He puts on his best suit and tie. Sara wears the prettiest dress she has. They both look like something out of a society magazine as they walk into the little white church for morning worship services. They are greeted warmly by everyone they come into contact with. Charlie has become a celebrity. He enjoys the special attention greatly but not nearly as much as Sara does. They find a seat up in the balcony as the morning worship services begin.

The choir sings a song of joy and inspiration. Then the choir director makes a few announcements pertaining to upcoming church activities. He then asks the congregation to stand for a hymn. They all stand and sing with a sensation of joy and faith. After the congregation finishes with the hymn, the choir director motions for everyone to sit down.

The church becomes silent as Pastor Riggs walks up to the podium for his sermon. He shuffles a few papers around, taking his time getting ready. When he gets everything the way he wants, he says, "I want to thank you all for coming today. I hope my message today will be a blessing for you all. Before I begin my sermon today, I just want to know if anybody saw the *CBS Evening News* last night."

There's a gentle noise as people focus on Charlie up in the balcony.

"I hope everyone saw it," Pastor Riggs says, looking up into the balcony where Charlie is sitting. "There is the young man, up there." He points, and some more people turn and look at Charlie up in the balcony. "He is the one who saved a little girl's life this week, Charlie Delaney."

The congregation applauds Charlie, and he turns red.

Pastor Riggs continues, "He fought off a vicious animal at the risk of his own life. He slew the beast with his own two hands. On the *CBS Evening News* last night, they said that our hero went to the state capitol to talk with our state legislators to see if a law could be passed so animals like the one he fought off will not hurt any other children. I hope and pray, and I hope everyone else prays as well, that there will be such a law passed so that these vicious animals won't harm anyone else."

The congregation applauds the pastor.

"When I was looking over my sermons this morning, I wanted to find one that is somewhat related to what happened this week. I found one that fits into this subject just fine. It is about something everyone on this planet goes through at least once in his or her life." The pastor pauses for a moment as he begins to walk around. "Everyone in the world has a purpose that God has laid out for him or her. The problem is that most people don't follow that path to find out what their purpose in life is. They decide to push God aside and live their lives the way they want to, not the way God wants them to. They end up destroying their purpose and replace it with a selfish existence, a selfish existence that will make them feel miserable and unhappy."

The congregation listens quietly with intense concentration as Pastor Riggs continues, "When I chose to become a preacher, I had to push aside my own wants and desires. I had to put God first in my life; everything else had to come second. If I had lived my life the way I wanted to, I would never had finished at seminary. I would have failed God, and I would have failed myself. You see, if you don't fulfill the purpose that God has laid out for you, then you will bear a heavy burden of guilt. That brings me to the story of Jonah.

"You see, Jonah had a purpose laid out for him too. God told Jonah to go to the city of Nineveh. God knew the people's souls there were in jeopardy, and he needed Jonah to go there and preach to them so they wouldn't perish forever. It was a dangerous purpose God had for Jonah, for the evil ones in Nineveh, the ones who didn't want God's work to be done there, could have killed Jonah. Jonah, because of his selfishness and fear, disobeyed God. He wanted to live his own life and not fulfill the life God set aside for him.

"I guess you all know what happened to Jonah." The pastor pauses as the congregation gets settled. "It wasn't long until this giant whale decided to make a meal of Jonah." The congregation laughs a little.

Pastor Riggs continues, "You see, God has ways of showing us our misconceptions. God knew it would be better for Jonah to be swallowed up by a whale than for the people of Nineveh to lose their souls. Jonah had to be taught a lesson. God didn't make Jonah preach to the people of Nineveh; he just gave Jonah a little encouragement." The congregation enjoys another laugh as Pastor Riggs walks around the podium.

"How many people here are like Jonah?" Pastor Riggs pauses for a moment until the church is quiet once again. "Tell me, how many of you sitting out there today know that God has given you a purpose in your life? And how many of you are afraid to fulfill that purpose? How many of you are living your lives for yourselves? How many of you will never complete that main purpose God has laid out for you?" Pastor Riggs pauses for a long time as the people of the church start to look down.

He raises his voice and says in a loud and powerful way, "The only person you are hurting when you disobey God are yourselves! He is looking out for your best interests all the time. He wants you to be successful in every part of your life. He wants you to be content with yourself, but He also wants you to do things for others. God knows He can use us to perform great things if we will only let Him, just like our hero of the week, Charlie Delaney."

Pastor Riggs points up to the balcony and says, "Charlie, would you please stand up for a moment? I want everybody to see what a man who has done what God wanted him to do looks like."

Charlie, with a red face, nervously stands up for all to see.

"Okay, Charlie, you can sit down now."

Charlie smiles somewhat and then sits down.

"You see that young man everyone? That young man's father died about three months ago. He died, but Charlie lived. You see, God had a purpose for Charlie Delaney. When that pit bull was attacking that small child, Charlie could have been like Jonah. He could have walked away, decided not to do what needed to be done. But Charlie didn't live his life just for Charlie. No, he began to live his life for that little girl. Sure, there was fear in Charlie's heart when that animal was growling and showing its fierce teeth. Charlie knew that he may have to sacrifice his own life just to save that little girl. He chose to live out one of the purposes God had for him. He chose to defend that little girl even at the risk of his own life. He obeyed God, and for that, a little girl is alive today. We should all try to be like Charlie Delaney. We should try to obey God and live out the purpose he has laid out for us."

Charlie's face turns a darker shade of red, but he doesn't mind. As the pastor keeps on preaching, Sara reaches over and holds her son's hand. She whispers, "I am so proud of you, Charlie. I can't tell you how much I love you for being my son." Charlie smiles at his mother, and she kisses him on the cheek.

The pastor continues with his sermon. "Think of how Jesus must have felt when he knew he was going to be crucified. He knew what his purpose in life was. He knew it wasn't going to be easy to hang on that cross and be sacrificed for the sins of the world, but he made that decision to be the sacrificial lamb. Don't let me give you the impression that the purpose God has laid out for you is going to be easy, because it isn't! No, it isn't going to be easy at all. You must willingly accept the responsibilities of that purpose and achieve it without turning away because of fear or selfishness. You must be ready to take up your own cross and willingly bear any suffering required. You will one day receive the glory that is yours if you obey and follow God's glorious purpose for your own existence.

"The message I want you to receive today is to follow your conscience. Find out what God wants you to do with your life, and persevere through the suffering until you have finally accomplished that purpose. It might be something you have to study for a long time, or it might be something like Charlie Delaney experienced, a sudden task that needs to be dealt with immediately without much thought. You, and you only, will be the one who decides what that purpose is. One day we will be shown how we lived our lives. Everything we have ever said and done will be shown to us on a grand scale. We will get a detailed explanation of what God wanted us to do, and if we didn't accomplish it, we will be the ones to feel the agony of shame for not fulfilling his purpose for us. So I ask you all to start thinking of what grand purpose you contain in yourself. I hope none of you end up in the belly of a whale."

The entire congregation erupts into laughter, and the pastor waits for them to settle down before he continues, "I know not many of you will end up in the belly of a whale, but some of you out there need to be swallowed up by something so you will see the light and act before it is too late. I want to end my sermon a little differently today than I usually do. After church ends today, don't leave in a mad dash; instead look around and get to know the people around you. Pick out someone you don't know, introduce yourself to him or her, and get to know that person. Invite that person over to your house sometime so you will know them even better."

The people of the church smile at the pastor as he asks if there is anyone who wants to accept Jesus as his or her personal savior. Several people come forward, mostly young people. The choir sings "Just As I Am" several times before the pastor holds up his hands for them to stop. "I hope you all got something out of the sermon today. I sure did. I hope you all have a pleasant week." The pastor ends the service with a prayer, and then the choir sings quietly as he walks down the aisle to end the services.

Everyone does what the pastor told them to. They walk around and speak to each other in a pleasant Christian way. Charlie and Sara don't have to walk far, as people they don't know walk up and introduce themselves. Charlie and Sara shake their hands in kindness and love. All the congregants show the true meaning of Christianity with the tranquil expressions on their faces. Charlie and Sara are the last ones to leave the little white church. When they finally get outside, they shake hands with the pastor and then happily drive home with a joyous and content peace of mind. When they arrive home, they are welcomed by more friends and neighbors who want to congratulate Charlie. Sara and Charlie entertain guests all afternoon. Charlie takes in all the attention very well. He manages to shake all the hands with his natural humility.

That evening, after all the guests have left, Sara and Charlie sit back in the living room, tired from entertaining. Sara looks over at Charlie with her legs stretched out on the couch. She has a happy smile on her face as she says, "Charlie, I don't know how long I can keep up this pace."

Charlie smiles back and says, "Me either, Mama. I never knew that this many people lived on this street. I hope I can remember all their names tomorrow."

Sara, still smiling that happy, content smile, says, "I don't know about you, Charlie, but I am going upstairs, taking a long bath, and then going straight to bed. I am tired!"

"I am right behind you. I think I will just go to bed now. Tomorrow is going to be here soon, and I want to be ready for school. I am going to school tomorrow?"

Sara looks over at Charlie with a grin. "I guess I will let you go to school tomorrow. Do you think you are ready?"

"Sure, Mama. My soreness is almost gone. I feel fine."

"I'm not talking about your injuries, Charlie."

Charlie pauses for a moment. "You're not? Then what are you talking about?"

"I was referring to whether you're ready to fight off all those girls tomorrow."

Charlie, shaking his head, replies, "Oh, Mama, cut it out. I won't have to fight off any girls."

"Oh, yes you will. You will have to beat them off with a stick." Sara laughs. Charlie gets up from the couch and, without saying anything else, goes to his room while his mother continues to laugh.

Tomorrow arrives, and Charlie is eager to get on the school bus and see all his friends again. He especially can't wait to see Dee. He thinks about her the moment he wakes up. He is full of excitement and anticipation as he thinks about what he is going to say when he sees her happy, smiling face on the bus.

Sara prepares Charlie's breakfast. He gobbles it down quickly and then sits near the window, eagerly waiting for the bus to come. Before long, his wait is over. When he sees the orange school bus approaching his house, he anxiously hurries down the driveway and waits for it. He leaps on the first step and makes the easy climb upward.

The bus driver is smiling from ear to ear, looking at Charlie with wonder and amazement. "Well, hello, Charlie! It is good to see you back on the bus."

"Thank you. It is good to be back."

"You sure have made a name for yourself. Everybody I talk to has heard of your heroic feat! Good to have you on my bus."

"Thanks."

Charlie walks down the aisle to the very back and sits down in his usual place. He waits impatiently for Dee's arrival. As the other students get on the bus, they all wave at Charlie. Most of the students walk back to Charlie and congratulate him personally. Everyone is excited when they see him. He is the main topic of conversation on the bus. Charlie gets very excited when the bus gets closer to Dee's house. He can't wait to see her again.

The bus stops at Dee's house. Charlie looks out the window with great anticipation as the bus waits for Dee to get on. Then the driver closes the door and begins to drive off. Charlie jumps up and runs to the front and says, "Hey! What's the deal? Why didn't you wait longer for Dee to get on?"

The driver looks over his shoulder. "I waited long enough for her. I can't wait all day for one student."

With surprise on his face Charlie hurries back to the back of the bus. He watches with intense sadness as Dee's house slowly disappears from sight. A strange depression sets in for Charlie as the bus continues its rounds. This bad feeling numbs the pleasure of praise from his fellow students. Even with all the recognition his fellow classmates show him, he still feels alone. Without Dee there to share his triumphant accomplishment, his victory is hollow and without much joy. The bus ride to the school is the longest one he has ever had in his life. He gets off the bus sad and depressed despite all the attention he is getting. Charlie doesn't understand why, of all times, Dee had to be absent from school today. He is angry at her for not being there to share his coming back to school. Even with his anger, he misses her an awful lot. He tries to put on a smile and get to class, but his heart has been scarred by her absence. He really needs her today.

As Charlie goes through the daily grind of being a student, he finally hears about why Dee isn't in school in chorus class. The chorus teacher takes roll and then leaves the room like he usually does.

One of Charlie's good friends, Wayne Scott, walks over to where Charlie is sitting and says, "Hey, buddy! How's everything going?"

Charlie tries to put on a smile. "Oh, I guess everything is okay."

"Then why do you look so sad, man? You should be the happiest guy in the world right now."

"I would be if Dee Swanson had come to school today."

Wayne pauses for a moment. "You kinda like her, don't you, man?"

"Yeah, man, I sure do. Don't go and tell the whole world though, all right?"

"Sure, man, whatever you say."

There is a long pause before Wayne says, "I guess you haven't heard why she isn't here today?"

Charlie's sad expression disappears and is replaced with a look of curiosity. "No, I haven't. What's going on?"

"I hate to be the one to tell you about Dee, but … you see, she got suspended from school for three days last week."

Charlie's eyes get big as marbles. "What?"

"Yeah, man, Dee and Sue Parker almost got into this knock-out, drag-out fight over you in class on Friday. Mr. Jones sent her up to the principal's office, and the principal threw her out for three days."

"You mean it happened in here?"

"Yeah, I saw the whole thing go down. Dee was hot! I have never seen a girl get so mad in all my life."

"Tell me everything about that fight, man. You mean Dee was fighting over me?"

"Yeah, man, it was about you all right. Sue Parker made this remark about you and your father—you know, about you witnessing him drown in that lake."

Anger flares up in Charlie.

Wayne says, "I don't know exactly what she said, but it was something about how you were a little, you know, kinda crazy about witnessing the thing."

"Oh, I see. She said I was crazy," snarled Charlie.

"Something like that. Hey man, I don't think that. I like you, man. Everyone was on Sue's case after that went down. We all told Mr. Jones that Sue started it, but Dee got sent up anyway. After Dee told Sue off, Sue ran out of the classroom. I guess that is why Dee went to the principal's office. I hate that it happened, man, and I hate I am the one who had to tell you."

"Hey man, I'm glad you did."

"No hard feelings?"

"Hard feelings toward you? Huh? Nah, I'm glad you had the guts to tell me about it."

"Cool, man, cool."

Sue and her bunch are sitting right across from Charlie. Charlie gets up and walks over to Sue. The whole class stops talking.

"Hey you!" Charlie says, pointing his finger at Sue. The whole class stares with excitement and anticipation.

Sue timidly asks, "What do you want?"

Charlie's anger shows in his eyes and becomes noticeable to all in the classroom. He says in a loud tone, "So you think I'm crazy?"

Sue looks at Charlie like a scared rabbit. "No, Charlie, I don't think you're crazy. What makes you say that?"

"You thought I was crazy last week. Have you changed your mind?"

"I don't know what happened last week. We were just talking, and your name came up. Someone said something about you and your father, and things got out of control."

"You bet things got out of control! Dee Swanson got suspended because of you!"

Sue looks at Charlie nonchalantly. "So what?"

"What do you mean, so what?" Charlie's anger intensifies. "If you got something you want to say about me or my father, you come say it to me. Don't you go around saying things behind my back, girl!"

Sue doesn't know what to say. She just sits there with a dumb look on her face.

"Because of you, Dee got suspended from school. I don't like that! I don't like that at all!"

Charlie points his finger in her face right as the teacher walks in. Sue jumps up and runs to the water fountain on the other side of the room.

Mr. Jones looks around and asks, "What is going on?"

The class gets silent as Charlie looks at Mr. Jones with anger and indignation and asks, "Why did you get Dee suspended?"

"Hey, Charlie, I didn't get anyone suspended. I only took her to the principal's office because she threatened Sue Parker. That's all I did. If you have a complaint about Dee's suspension, you need to talk with the principal."

Giving Sue a mean look, Charlie walks over to his seat and sits down.

Mr. Jones looks at Sue, who is still standing near the water fountain, and says, "Young lady, I want you to come here, right now!" Mr. Jones stares at Sue with anger in his eyes as she timidly walks over. "You have caused a ruckus around here!"

Sue looks at Mr. Jones with surprise. Mr. Jones continues, "This all started with you talking about Charlie and his father. A girl was suspended from school because of your callous and thoughtless remarks. I think first of all you owe Charlie an apology for your unsympathetic remarks!"

Sue looks at Mr. Jones with apprehension and then looks toward Charlie as the class gives her a mean look. "Charlie, I am sorry about the remarks I made about you and your father. I didn't mean any harm, and I just want you to know that I am sorry."

Charlie pauses for a moment and says, "Well, since you have apologized, I guess I can forget about it."

Mr. Jones smiles and says, "Good! I am glad we have buried the hatchet on this matter for good. I hope in the future, Sue, you will be a little kinder when you talk about people. Now let's put all this behind us and get back to learning how to sing."

Mr. Jones and the class get back to their usual routine.

The day goes by slowly for Charlie. Everyone in the halls congratulates him on his brave act, but he feels, deep in his heart, a missing piece. He gets on the bus still feeling an emptiness in his soul that wants to be filled. All the commotion about his heroic deed only exacerbates the pain.

Charlie gets off the bus and walks up to his house in misery. Sara opens the front door as Charlie reaches the top step. She notices Charlie's sad expression and asks, "What's the matter, dear? Are you all right?"

Charlie tries to put on a smile but doesn't do it very well. He shrugs his tired shoulders. "I am all right, Mama. I'm just tired."

Sara looks on in silence as Charlie walks up the stairs to his room. She doesn't go up and talk with him but is concerned about his behavior. Charlie retreats once again into his shell. Sara knows Charlie doesn't like her asking too many questions. He yells back at her when she does, so she controls her motherly ways once again. She doesn't want to anger her lonesome son.

On Tuesday, Charlie's loneliness reaches a climax. His only enjoyment is his weight lifting. As soon as he gets home from school, he rushes up to his room. Like a drug addict looking for a fix, he works out with all his might. The mental anguish of wanting something he can't have makes him feel so inadequate. All he wants is to be with Dee, to hear her voice. Wanting something so badly and not getting it causes him an agony that hampers his emotions and his intellect. Although he is denied Dee's love, his character is strengthened and raised higher than the clouds in the sky.

On Wednesday, Charlie puts in another lonely day of school. As he rides the bus home, he thinks about what Dee might be doing. The special attention that Charlie has gotten used to is wearing off somewhat. These last three days of school have been the longest days of his life. The only person Charlie wants to praise him for his brave deed is unable to be there.

As the school bus makes that long drive home, Charlie gets an idea. He thinks, *I'll find Dee's phone number in the telephone book! I will call her up and talk to her at home. I don't know why I didn't think of that sooner. Yes, that's exactly what I will do!* Soon the bus stops at Charlie's house. He gets off in a flash and quickly runs into the house. He grabs the phone book and heads for his room. He finds her last name with her address and writes down the number. He begins to dial, but before he dials the last number, he puts the phone down. He is nervous about hearing Dee's voice, so he just sits back on his bed and thinks about what he is going to say to her. He thinks about the call for ten minutes and then dials the number once again. He is filled with stress and anxiety. When he hears the phone ringing, his lack of courage gets the best of him, and he puts the phone down once again.

He makes himself dial the number again after another ten minutes, telling himself, "I will not put the phone down. I will not yield to my own weak self. I will not hang up."

Someone pick up and says, "Hello."

Charlie gets very nervous at hearing the strange voice. "Hello. Is Dee—I mean, is Deborah—there?"

"Yes. Who may I say is calling?"

"This is Charlie Delaney."

There's a long pause. "Oh, so you are the fellow who has caused all the trouble?"

Charlie doesn't know how to respond. "Excuse me?"

"This is Deborah's mother. Do you know that because of you me and my daughter aren't speaking to each other?"

"Would you mind explaining to me what you are talking about?"

"She got suspended from school for three days because of you!"

"Please! You have it wrong, Mrs. Swanson. I like Dee. She is one of the best friends I have."

Deborah's mom says loudly, "Her name isn't Dee! Her name is Deborah. Do you understand, young man? Her name is Deborah! And my name isn't Mrs. Swanson anymore; it's Mrs. O'Brien!"

"Yes, ma'am. That's what I meant to say," Charlie nervously replies.

"Huh! With friends like you, Deborah doesn't need any enemies."

"Please, Mrs. O'Brien, let me try to explain the situation to you."

"Don't you try to explain anything to me! I don't want to hear it. I don't want you to ever call this number again. Do you understand me?"

Charlie waits for a moment and then says gently, "Yes, ma'am, I understand you completely."

"Fine! And another thing, I want you to stay away from my daughter. She doesn't need to hang around people like you."

Charlie, not knowing what she meant, says, "Mrs. O'Brien, haven't you heard that I saved a little girl's life last week? I have been to the state capitol to talk with the governor."

"I don't care if you have saved a dozen little girls' lives. You have torn me and my daughter apart. You aren't anything special to me, young man. Some hero you are. Is that what you think you are, a hero?"

Charlie pauses in humiliated silence. "Mrs. O'Brien, I feel real bad about Dee getting suspended."

"I told you, her name is Deborah!"

Charlie's face turns as red as a stop sign. "Yes, ma'am. I am sorry again. Please don't be upset with me. I am only trying..."

"Sorry? You can say that again. Listen, I am only going to say this one more time. I want you to stay away from my daughter. I have instructed Deborah to stay away from you. I don't want her to be suspended from school any more because of a crazy nut like you!"

Charlie gets very angry. He says loudly and boldly, "Hey! You listen here. I am not a crazy nut! I see why you're having a problem with Deborah. You won't listen to anything anybody's got to say. You think you know everything that is going on, but you don't! You need to start listening to your daughter, and maybe then the deception in your head will be corrected. Then you might not be so indignant."

"Don't you tell me how to raise my daughter! I am raising her the best way I know how, and that way is just fine. I don't want to hear you on this phone line ever again. If I do, I will have the police come to your house and have you arrested, Mr. Hero."

"Do what?"

"You heard me, young man. I have nothing else to say to you. Good-bye!"

Mrs. O'Brien slams the phone down, and Charlie is left with nothing but his hurt feelings.

Charlie tries not to show that anything is wrong around his mother. He eats his supper as he usually does so she won't suspect anything different. He goes to bed early with a strong pain of depression on his weary, scarred soul.

Charlie sleeps restlessly and wakes up the next day tired and weak. It is all he can do to take his clothes off and get into the shower. After he gets out of the shower, he feels somewhat better but still feels tired. He goes downstairs to the kitchen, where his mother has breakfast ready. He eats only half of his breakfast and then waits impatiently for the school bus. Soon the bus arrives. He kisses his mother good-bye and eagerly runs and gets on. He walks all the way to the very back like usual and sits down in the very last seat. He eagerly waits as the bus makes its rounds. It finally stops at Dee's house. He sees her standing and waiting outside. She gets on and looks at Charlie sitting in the back. She sits down up front in the third row. Charlie slumps in his seat, sad and unhappy. As the bus makes the long, slow drive to school, Charlie sits quietly and thinks about Dee.

The bus finally reaches its destination, and all the kids begin to get off. Charlie tries to catch up with Dee, but when he finally gets off, Dee is nowhere to be found. Charlie goes to his first class with a frown on his face. As the class goes on, he can't wait to see Dee in chorus class. He thinks he may finally get to talk to her there. Soon the bell rings. As he walks quickly to chorus class, he begins to get a bad feeling about it.

By the time the second bell rings, Dee still hasn't walked into the classroom. Mr. Jones and Sue Parker also are not there. Charlie and the rest of the class wait. Finally the door opens, and Dee, Mr. Jones, and Sue enter the classroom.

Sue sits down with her friends, and Dee sits down next to Charlie. With a happy face Charlie says, "Hello, stranger, long time, no see."

"Hello, Charlie. How have you been?"

Charlie reaches over and holds Dee's hand. "I have been doing all right, I guess. How have you been?"

"Not so good, Charlie, not so good. My mother told me you called last night. She kinda blames you for me being suspended."

"Yeah, I know. I tried to explain to her, but she didn't seem to want to listen to me. I feel awful about what you had to go through because of me." Charlie looks at Dee with sympathy as Mr. Jones takes roll.

Dee says softly, "My mama made me promise that I wouldn't sit near you on the bus. That is why I sat up front this morning."

Her tender eyes touch Charlie's heart, and he says, "I thought so. I understand, Dee—I mean, Deborah. Your mother made it clear to me that your name is Deborah."

Dee laughs. "You don't have to call me Deborah. I like Dee much better, but if you ever talk to my mother, make sure you call me Deborah."

"I understand."

Dee and Charlie laugh as Mr. Jones sits at the piano and plays and sings for the class. When the class is over, Charlie and Dee talk only a little, as they both have to go to their next class. Charlie waves bye and watches her disappear down the crowded hallway. He is mesmerized by the way she walks. He next sees her in history class, but he doesn't get a chance to speak to her there. Then, after class, she is gone before Charlie can speak to her. He doesn't see her again until he gets on the school bus.

As Charlie gets on the bus, he spots her sitting next to a couple of her girlfriends. The atmosphere is filled with the commotion of eager students talking about all the things teenagers talk about. Charlie and Dee get involved in conversations with others that are around them. He doesn't get to talk to her until the crowd on the bus thins out a bit.

Finally, Charlie gets up and walks over to where Dee is sitting. "Hello, Dee. What's up."

"Hey, Charlie. I was hoping you would come over and talk to me. My mama didn't make you mad, did she?"

"No, not too much. Are you going to listen to her and stay away from me?"

"Well, no, I'm not. I'll talk to whoever I want to, but ..."

"But what?"

"But I believe I will start sitting up in the front of the bus in the mornings."

Charlie is disappointed and asks with a sad expression, "How come,

Dee? I like to see you in the mornings. It is about the only time I get to talk to you."

"Well, my mother told me not to sit with you on the bus, and this way, if she happens to ask about it, I won't have to lie to her. You know what I mean, Charlie?"

Charlie, looking disappointed, replies, "Well, I don't want you to lie to your mother. I sure will miss talking to you, though. Maybe after a week or two you might change your mind?"

"We'll see. I kinda like sitting up front, but maybe later I might come back to the back. I don't know. But for right now, I'll just sit up front."

Charlie stares deeply into Dee's eyes. "By the way, where did you and Mr. Jones and Sue Parker go this morning? I saw you all walk in together in chorus."

"Oh, that. I had to go up to the principal's office this morning and apologize to Sue for, you know, what happened last week."

"I want to thank you for taking up for me. I guess you are the best friend I have."

"Well, thank you. I guess you are still my best friend too." Dee pauses for a moment and then says in a delicate way, "Is that all I am, Charlie, just a friend?"

"Well, I don't … well, I guess so. What do you mean?"

Dee gets a little angry. "What do I mean? Aren't I more than just a friend? I just got suspended from school for three days because of how I feel for you. Is that all you have to say?"

"Well, I guess you are more than just a friend."

"You guess! Well! Why don't you tell me when you know!" Dee gets up and sits down a few seats back.

Charlie just sits there and scratches his head. He thinks over what Dee said but doesn't speak to her again until she gets ready to get off at her house. Charlie turns back and watches her walk up the aisle.

He says in a gentle voice, "Bye, Dee. I will see you tomorrow."

Dee looks angrily at Charlie but doesn't say anything. She storms off the bus. Charlie looks out the window and watches her go straight into her house. He keeps his eyes focused on her house until it disappears from sight. Charlie, with his feelings hurt, sits alone and thinks about

Dee. He realizes why Dee is angry at him. His shyness has again defeated his chances of happiness. He sinks into a depressed state. When the bus arrives at his house, he gets off slowly and walks sadly up the driveway.

The next day comes before Charlie is ready. He doesn't feel much like going to school. Most of the attention he has been getting is dying down, and he is going through a withdrawal period. He does manage to get his clothes on and make his way to the breakfast table. His mother has his breakfast ready on the table when he gets there. She is reading the morning newspaper as Charlie sits down at the table.

"Good morning," she says. "Did you sleep well?"

Charlie mumbles at first and then says, "Oh, I guess so. Not really. Oh, I guess I did."

Sara shakes her head a little. "Well, can't you make up your mind?"

"I don't know. I guess I slept all right."

Sara notices that Charlie is not in one of his better moods. She keeps reading the newspaper while Charlie begins to eat his breakfast. Something in the paper catches her eye, and she says, "Hey, Charlie! Look here in the paper!"

Charlie looks up at his mother as she shows him an article. "So? What about it?"

"What about it? I can see you're not too happy this morning," Sara says. "It says that the state legislature is going to vote on a bill today to ban the ownership of pit bulls. It also says that the bill will put some restrictions on other vicious animals if it passes. Listen to this, Mr. Grumpy: they are calling the bill the Charlie Delaney Bill! Isn't that great? They are naming it after you."

Charlie stops eating his breakfast. He takes the newspaper from his mother and reads the entire article for himself. After he reads it, he gently puts the paper down and nonchalantly begins to eat his breakfast again without saying another word.

Sara looks at him with enthusiasm. "So? What do you think about that, Charlie?"

Charlie keeps eating his breakfast like a cow chewing its cud. "Oh boy. Could you pass me the salt?"

Sara shakes her head. "Charlie! How can you just sit there with no emotions in the world about this?"

Charlie swallows his food and then drinks half of his glass of milk. He looks over at his mother and quietly says, "It only said they are going to vote on the bill. It didn't say it was passed. There is no reason to get all excited about something that hasn't even come to pass yet." Charlie chugs the rest of his milk without coming up for air.

Sara just looks at Charlie dumbfounded.

"Is there any more milk?" he asks.

Sara shakes her head. "You have already turned into a man, Charlie. You act just like your father used to. When something of great importance happened, he would just sit there like the price of coffee in China had just risen three cents a pound."

"What does the price of coffee in China have to do with having another glass of milk?"

Sara shakes her head in bewilderment as she gets up and gets Charlie another glass of milk.

Soon the bus arrives, and Charlie sluggishly walks toward the door. Sara hands him his lunch and leans over for him to kiss her good-bye. Charlie says, "Mama, don't you think I am getting a little too old to be kissing you good-bye every morning?"

"No, I don't, young man. Even your father kissed me good-bye when he left to go to work."

Charlie looks at her and, without saying a word, tells her that she isn't going to get a kiss.

"If you don't want to kiss me good-bye anymore," Sara says, "then you don't have to."

"Whatever you say."

"Whatever I say? You make it sound like it's my idea. Maybe you are too old to kiss me good-bye, but I'm not too old to kiss you good-bye." Sara lays a big kiss right on Charlie's lips.

"Ugh! You're not supposed to kiss me there! Ugh!" Charlie wipes away his mother's kiss.

"Don't you wipe my love off your face. Now I'm going to have to kiss you again."

"No, Mama. I'll just kiss you instead." As Charlie kisses his mother on the cheek, the school bus blows its horn. "Gotta go, Mama!"

"Have a good day."

Charlie runs out to the school bus and jumps on. The bus drives off to pick up the other students and soon arrives at Dee's house. She gets on and again sits down in the front. She does wave at Charlie, though. Charlie sits back in a silent state of mind. He doesn't talk much to the others who sit next to him. His loneliness increases as the bus fills up. The more people around him, the more left out he feels. All the chatter of voices makes Charlie feel worse. He is glad when the bus finally arrive at school. He gets off and proceeds to his first class. He doesn't even look around for Dee this time.

As the day goes on, Charlie feels a little bit better. Most of his classes occupy his mind enough that he doesn't have to think of Dee and the emptiness in his heart. Charlie doesn't exactly care much for chorus. He only registered for it because Dee did. Mr. Jones usually doesn't teach. He just sits at the piano and sings to the class. He tries to get the students to sing along so they will cooperate when the class has to prepare for a concert.

Today happens to be the day that they start preparations for their next concert. There is so much going on that Charlie and Dee don't have much time to talk with one another. Dee does manage to smile at Charlie with that sweet, innocent, tender smile of hers. It is just enough to let Charlie know that she is not angry at him. He returns the smile and waves happily to his pretty young love. She waves back as Mr. Jones tells the class what he expects of them for the upcoming concert, which is scheduled for sometime next month. The class ends after a long, intense session of singing. When the bell does ring, everyone is caught by surprise. They all stop what they are doing and rush off to their next classes.

Charlie catches up with Dee. "Hey, Dee. Are you still mad at me?"

Dee's emerald-green eyes twinkle. "No, I'm not mad at you."

"Well, I am glad to hear that. I like you a whole lot and ..."

"And what?"

"Well, I like you a whole lot, you know."

Dee, waiting to hear something else, says, "Yes, I know. I like you a whole lot too."

"You do? I'm glad to hear you say that."

"Is there something else you want to say to me, Charlie?"

"Well … kinda."

"Well, what is it?"

"Well, I just want you to know that I like you more than any other girl."

Dee waits in silence for Charlie to continue.

"I just want you to know that I think about you all the time," he says.

Dee continues to stand and stare at Charlie in total silence.

"I will have to talk to you later, Dee. I have got to go all the way up to the forth floor to my English class."

Dee, disappointed at not hearing what she wants to hear, simply says, "Okay, I will see you later."

"Okay, Dee, so long."

Charlie and Dee go their separate ways.

In English class, Charlie tries hard to do what the teacher expects from him. It is Charlie's hardest class and the most important. He knows he has to pass English or go to summer school. His grade is a high D as of now.

As the teacher is talking to the class, the principal comes over the loudspeaker. "Attention! Attention! I have an important message to bring to all of you students."

All the students put down their pencils and listen to the principal's message.

"The governor of North Carolina has just informed me that our legislature has passed a law preventing the ownership of pit bulls for any reason."

Charlie's classmates stare directly at him, and then they begin to applaud loudly. He can hear students from other classrooms doing the same thing.

The principal waits until he hears the applause die down a little before he continues, "The governor also told me that any type of animal that is a danger to the well-being of the community will also be prohibited. Any person who thinks his or her community is at threat from any such animal is asked to bring it to the attention of the local authorities as soon as possible."

The classroom erupts into another applauding frenzy, and students look at Charlie with excitement. The teacher tries to calm them down as the principal continues, "This law was passed unanimously and will take effect by the first of next month. I am happy to announce to all of you that this law has been named the Charlie Delaney Law. I just want to thank Charlie Delaney for his brave act in saving a little girl's life and for his sheer determination in creating a law that will protect thousands and thousands of lives. I feel proud to be the principal of this school and to have such an honored and courageous student like Charlie Delaney. Thank you!"

After the principal finishes his message, the kids in Charlie's class stand and applaud with great excitement and jubilation. Charlie can hear other classrooms applauding as well. Charlie turns as red as a stop sign but manages to keep his composure. After five minutes of applauding, other teachers rush into the English class to congratulate Charlie personally.

After Charlie spends a few moments shaking hands, the principal comes over the loudspeaker once again. "Mr. Bishop, would you send Charlie Delaney to my office?"

The class claps once more as Charlie rises from his seat and walks to the door.

Right before Charlie leaves the classroom, Mr. Bishop says, "Charlie, I just want you to know that I am so proud of you. If I had a son, I would want him to be just like you. You are someone special."

Charlie smiles at his English teacher with a red face. "Whenever you record my grade this quarter, you can reward me then."

The whole class bursts out with laughter as Charlie leaves to go see the principal.

When Charlie arrives at the principal's office, the whole room is filled with happy faces and excited individuals eager to meet the lucky guy. Charlie shakes hands with teachers and other staff of Parker High School. The principal keeps Charlie there for a while. They all shake their heads in amazement at how Charlie has become such a well-liked celebrity.

The whole school is talking about Charlie. He has made a tremendous impression on everyone. Every girl in school will be after him now. No one can get over how a student from their school has made such a distinguished name for himself.

Charlie enjoys the special attention. He is as happy as he has ever been in his life, but with all the special attention, Charlie still feels a void in his life. There is something missing in Charlie's heart. He hasn't seen the joy and jubilation in Dee's eyes yet. He thinks about how wonderful it will be to see Dee's reaction.

Dee, on the other hand, is not as happy as one might think. She is sitting in her English class hearing all the wonderful things about Charlie. The more she hears, the lonelier she becomes. Her jealousy grows. She feels left out because she isn't going steady with him. She feels as if she is being cheated out of something. Her mind begins to deceive her. Wild and crazy thoughts, including visions of abandonment and rejection, start to fill her head. She pictures Charlie kissing other girls. The deception in her mind is of her own doing, but she can't seem to stop thinking about those ridiculously false thoughts.

One of Dee's friends, Betty Moore, says, "Hey, Dee. Isn't it great about Charlie?"

Dee tries to put on a happy face but doesn't do a very good job. "Yeah, I'm happy for him."

Betty detects a little bit of apprehension in Dee's voice and expression. "What's the matter? Is there something wrong?"

Dee looks at her friend like a fawn in the woods. She says quietly, "Yeah, there is. I like Charlie so much I am beginning to feel bad. He gives me the impression that he really likes me, but he hasn't asked me to go steady with him. I don't know why he won't just come out and ask me. Why are guys like that?"

"Guys are a little strange when they have to ask a girl something like that. They are a little strange anyway. Don't worry about it, though. He might come around and ask you sometime."

"I sure hope so. I have turned down three fellows who have asked me to go steady so far this year. Every one I said no to hasn't spoken to me since."

"Who has asked you, if you don't mind me asking?"

"Well, there was James Sapp, Jeff Hoots, and then Steve Gregory."

"Do what? You mean you turned down Steve Gregory to be your boyfriend? Are you crazy? He is the best-looking guy in the entire school. I can't believe you did that!"

Dee blushes a little. "Well, it's the truth. He hasn't liked me ever since I told him no."

"But why on God's green earth did you say no to him?"

"I don't really know him that well. He asked me to go with him the day after we met. I am not going with any guy that asks me the day after I meet him."

Betty shakes her head in disbelief.

"I'm just not that type of girl, Betty. I know he is good looking, but I don't know him well enough. Now that he is mad at me for telling him no, I couldn't care less about him."

Betty shakes her head again. "It's your life, Dee. I sure wish he would ask me to go with him. I wouldn't hesitate. I would accept so quickly it would make his head spin."

They both laugh and talk some more. Despite what Dee said, the real reason she doesn't go with Steve Gregory or anybody else is because she is waiting for Charlie to come around and ask her to be his sweetheart.

"I hope Charlie comes around and asks you," Betty says. "I really do. Your competition will increase now. Every girl in the school will be after him now for sure. But if he really likes you the way you say, you might be the lucky girl."

Dee smiles. "I hope so, Betty; I sure do hope so."

"When will you see him next?"

"Charlie's in my next class, history."

"With all the excitement going on he might not make it to history class. It looks like Charlie is making history himself."

The girls laugh a little and continue to talk.

Betty ends up being right, and Charlie doesn't make it to history class. After history class, Dee, disappointed at not seeing Charlie, walks to his locker in hopes of congratulating him. Once again Dee is disappointed. She finds Charlie surrounded by girls. They are all over him like black on molasses. Dee can't even get his attention. They are hugging him, and some are even kissing him, on the cheek of course.

Dee stands by and watches until she can't take it anymore. She turns around and, with tears in her eyes, walks to her next class with a wounded heart. She is extremely upset at all the attention Charlie is getting. Her mind begins to deceive her again. She feels resentment and outrage. She blames Charlie for not showing her the affections she most desperately needs. Her jealousy grows at a horrendous rate. She realizes for the first time that she is definitely in love with Charlie. She doesn't know how to tell him her feelings. Her mind twists the situation around until she puts herself in a depressive state. She knows that Charlie's sudden rush of fame will make all the other girls like him even more. She burns on the inside like a forest fire in a whirlwind. She eagerly waits to see him again, but the seed of resentment has been planted in her mind and is germinating.

As Dee sits down in her last class, she is still upset at what she has experienced. She tries to get control of herself as she hears the bell to start class ring. She remains completely mesmerized by the thought of all those pretty girls kissing on Charlie. The hour seems to take forever, but finally the last bell of the day is sounded. Everyone rushes to their buses to go home.

Before Charlie goes to the bus, he finds Dee standing next to her locker. As he approaches her, some other girls close in on him. They all act so prissy and silly and ask those silly things girls like to ask. Charlie finds it difficult to answer their silly questions but manages to find the words so as not to offend any of them.

Dee, seeing Charlie, listens in. She gets his attention and walks up to him. "Well, Charlie, I guess you won't have much time for me now that you have all these other girls after you."

"Oh, cut it out, Dee. They are just excited for now. Tomorrow they will forget all about me."

One of the girls says, "Oh no we won't, Charlie. We won't forget about you."

Several other girls chime in as well.

"I won't forget about you either, Charlie."

"Me either, Charlie."

"Me either."

Charlie is flooded once again with silly questions. He manages to answer some of them as Dee impatiently looks on. Charlie sees a sad, disheartened look in Dee's tender eyes.

Charlie says nicely and politely to the girls, "I am going to have to leave to go to my bus now. I will see you all tomorrow, but for now I must run."

Charlie hurries along to his bus. Some of the girls follow him a little way and then break off in other directions to get to their buses. Dee, on the other hand, follows right behind him. Charlie, noticing this, waits up for Dee, and the two walk together to the bus.

Charlie looks at Dee with a sweet smile. "I am so glad to finally get to talk to you, Dee. It has been a madhouse since the principal made his announcement."

Dee, speaking in a soft, delicate voice, says, "You don't look like it's bothering you very much. Now that all these other girls are paying you so much attention, I'm surprised you will have any time for me."

"Oh, cut it out, Dee. I will always have time for you."

"Is that so, Charlie? Isn't there something that you want to ask me?"

"Well, I don't know. What do you want me to say?"

Dee gets furious. "Charlie Delaney, I just don't understand you at all! I just can't understand why you haven't—"

Dee is interrupted by another one of Charlie's admirers. Charlie recognizes the girl as Melissa Lane, the daughter of his mother's friend that he met at the pool. Melissa pulls Charlie by the arm and says to Dee, "Would you please excuse me one moment? There is something important I must ask Charlie in private."

Dee gives Melissa a mad look and says, "Yes, I do mind! I am talking to Charlie right now, sweetheart, so get lost!"

Charlie, with a surprised look on his face, says, "Dee, you shouldn't talk to people like that. She is a real nice girl. Please don't be angry. She probably just wants to congratulate me. I will see you on the bus."

Dee gives Charlie a mean look. "If that is what you want, fine! I know when I'm not wanted!"

Charlie grabs her arm as she tries to flee. "Hey, come on, Dee," Charlie whispers in her ear. "Please don't be mad at me. You know you are my favorite girl. I like you better than anyone else. I will see you on the bus. There is something I want to ask you, but I can't ask you if you are going to be mad at me."

Dee's angry look turns into a joyful smile. Her emerald-green eyes turn radiant as she gazes into Charlie's eyes with a lure of love and a sparkle of a tender sweetness. "All right, Charlie. I will save you a seat on the bus, okay?"

Charlie's face blossoms into a happy smile. "Oh boy, I can't wait!"

Dee sticks her tongue out at Melissa and then walks off.

"What is her problem?" Melissa asks.

"What do you mean?"

"Oh nothing, it's not important. She isn't what I wanted to talk to you about anyway."

"What did you want to talk about, Melissa?"

Melissa grins a devious, seductive grin at Charlie, her mind scheming how to trap him for her own. "I just want to congratulate you on your success in the mission God has planned out for you. I think you have been chosen to do God's work in a great way."

Charlie shakes his head in amazement.

"My mother told me this morning that the legislature was going to vote on your bill today. My mother thinks you are a great blessing to the white people of this country," Melissa says, making Charlie start to blush.

"I know all the girls have been hanging around you in droves, so I wanted to talk to you before any of them dig their selfish claws into you," she says. Charlie listens in silence as Melissa continues, "I think you are one of the nicest guys I have ever met. When I saw you at the swimming pool, I thought, *I sure would like to marry a man like that one day.*"

"Well, I don't know what to say," Charlie stammers.

Melissa gives him a girlish grin. "I know you don't understand why I am so attracted to you, but ever since we met at the swimming pool, I have thought of you as someone special."

Charlie sees a sweet, innocent smile portrayed on her youthful face. "Well, thank you, Melissa. I think you are a nice girl too."

Before Charlie has a chance to say anything else, Melissa throws her arms around his neck and gives him a powerful hug. She kisses him with intensity and then says with an excited expression, "Oh, I was hoping you would like me as much as I like you, Charlie. You could ask me to go steady with you right now, and I would accept."

Charlie pauses with a scared look. "Well, I-I mean I don't really know you well enough right now."

"I understand. You want to get to know me and my mother a little bit more. I understand that. I just didn't want some floozy to come by and take advantage of you just because you are famous now." Charlie blushes as Melissa continues, "I know you could have any girl in school right now, so would you just promise me that you won't give in to any of them until we have time to get to know one another better?"

With a scared, confused look on his face, Charlie says, "Huh? What do you want me to do again?"

Melissa laughs at seeing Charlie so disarranged. "Just promise me that you won't ask anyone to go steady until you talk to me first."

Charlie, being put on the spot, reluctantly answers, "Well, okay."

Melissa wraps her arms around Charlie's neck again and gives him a kiss on his cheek. "Oh boy! You have made my day, Charlie. I can't wait to go home and tell Mama all about our little talk. I would like to stand here and talk to you some more, but I have to get on my bus now. I will see you tomorrow."

"Yeah, right."

Melissa turns and walks away, leaving Charlie dazed and confused. As Charlie walks away he realizes what a terrible mistake he has just made. He shakes his head in disgust. As he walks out the door of the school, he thinks, *Why did I promise Melissa that? Why did I make her such a promise! I could kick myself. I finally get my courage up to ask Dee to go steady with me, and I go and screw up the whole day.*

Charlie looks up to the sky and says, "Dear God in heaven, why did I make such a promise? Why don't I have the courage to not let people mess up my life? Why Lord? Why am I such a stupid idiot? What am I going to do now?"

Charlie gets on his bus looking sad and confused. The bus is full. All the kids begin to applaud with great zeal and exultation. Charlie's sad expression disappears and is replaced with a humble, unselfish one. He smiles delightedly. His friends slap him on the back as he walks down the aisle. Dee has a proud and joyous look on her face as he sits down next to her. He looks at her with love and admiration. Everyone begins to sing "For He's a Jolly Good Fellow" as the bus drives off.

His prayers have been answered: he finally gets to share his great deed with the one he loves the most. The moment is bittersweet, though, because he has made a promise that hampers his true wants and desires. As the bus drives down the long highway, all of Charlie's friends say nothing but good things to him. Charlie is very happy. He is finally getting the recognition he has so desperately wanted and needs.

As the school bus begins to let off its passengers, Dee gets a chance to talk to Charlie without being interrupted by anyone. "Charlie, I am so proud of you. I can't even begin to tell you how much. It was worth being suspended three days." She laughs.

Charlie says, "I am glad you're here. It wouldn't have meant a thing if I didn't get to see that happy look on your face."

Dee reaches over and holds Charlie's hand. She looks deep into his eyes. Their eyes reflect love at each other.

She says, her voice like an angel's, "Charlie, do you feel about me the same way I feel about you?"

"Yes, Dee. I feel like you are the most important person in my life."

Dee continues in a gentle, soft voice, "Then why … why don't we just, you know, kinda go steady then?"

Charlie's happy expression turns sour. His voice cracks as he says, "I have been wanting to ask you that question for quite some time now. You see, Dee, I am a real shy guy. I have never asked a girl to go steady in my entire life. It is hard for me to open up and ask such things."

Dee tilts her head sideways, looking confused. "But if you like me so much, why don't you make me your first girlfriend?"

Charlie gives her a disappointed look. "Dee, I have been thinking hard all day long, trying to get the courage up to ask you that. I finally decided that I was going to ask you to be my girlfriend. But then I talked to Melissa Lane."

"Melissa Lane? Who is Melissa Lane?"

"You know, that girl you stuck your tongue out at school a while ago."

"Oh yeah, that floozy that wanted to talk to you in private. Yeah, I remember her. What does she have to do with us, Charlie?"

"You see, Dee, it's like this. I was going to ask you to go steady with me, but somehow that girl made me promise that I wouldn't ask anybody to go steady until I talked to her first."

Dee erupts into a fit. "Do what? You did what?" Dee demands.

"I promised her that I wouldn't ask anybody to go steady."

"I heard what you said! I don't know about you, Charlie. How could you promise someone something like that? How could you promise that?"

"You don't have to keep saying that. I don't know why I promised her that in the first place. I guess I wasn't thinking."

Dee is clearly very mad. Her face is red as fire. "Well, let me tell you something, Charlie Delaney! If you are so stupid to make a promise as crazy as that, then I don't know if I want to go with you! I don't care if you ask me or not. You're not the only guy in the world, you know. I have been asked to go steady with several other guys this year, and let me tell you something else: I'm not going to wait around for you to ask me anymore!" Tears begin to run down Dee's face as she gets up and walks away from Charlie.

Charlie follows her and tries to explain the situation to her.

"Leave me alone!" she snaps.

Charlie reluctantly sits down in the seat across from her. "Please, Dee, don't be angry at me. I didn't know what to say to her. I am sorry."

"Charlie, I told you to just leave me alone."

Charlie watches tears fall from her emerald-green eyes. His heart is heavy with guilt as he gets up and walks away from the sad situation he has created for himself. As the bus continues to make its rounds, Charlie sits back and looks at Dee from a distance. He wants so badly to forget about the promise he made to Melissa and walk over and ask Dee to be his steady. He thinks seriously about it, but with his feelings hurt, he doesn't act on his true feelings. He just sits there quietly as the bus makes its rounds.

When the bus approaches Dee's house, Charlie gets a rush of excitement in his soul. He gets up and walks over to Dee. "Please, will you—"

Dee interrupts, "Will you please get out of my way so I can get off?"

This angry burst discourages Charlie from speaking. He just looks at Dee, hurt, and moves out of her way. Dee's love for Charlie has turned to hate at a time when Charlie's courage was at its highest. Charlie sits down and watches Dee get off the school bus. As she is walking to her front door, she throws all her schoolbooks on the ground, giving a profound message to everyone watching.

One of the other kids who sees Dee throw her books down says, "Hey, Charlie, what did you say to make Dee so angry?"

Charlie says, "I don't think it was anything I said. I think it was something I didn't say."

Some of the kids look around in confusion; others just laugh and joke about it. Charlie simply sits there as if he has lost his best friend. His heart aches with a terrible pain. The happiest day of his life has become the saddest day of his life as well. After he gets off the bus, he goes straight to his room and lies down on his bed. His heart aches as he thinks about how bad he has screwed up his day and possibly his life. His chronic depression sets in and becomes a permanent fixture in his room. He sees a vision of what would have been if he hadn't made that stupid promise. He hates himself for making that promise now. Because he didn't stand up and say no, he now falls into a pit of self-hate. His poor decision making has caused him to feel worthless. He tells himself, "Tomorrow, I am going to tell Melissa that I will ask whoever I want to be my steady." He is mad at her for getting him to make her such a stupid promise. She boosted his ego so much that he didn't realize that she was really manipulating him. Charlie thinks about what took place today and tells himself that he will never let himself fall into such a trap again. He will make the decisions in his life from now on and won't allow anyone to ever make him promise something he isn't sure of.

As Charlie continues to lie there, he thinks about his father. He replays all the good times they had together in his head. Charlie misses his father a great deal now. He feels a void in his life now that his father isn't there. He tries to get control of himself and prepare for tomorrow, when he will set Melissa straight about the promise he made to her. As he thinks about what he is going to say to her, Charlie feels his father's presence in his room, as if his father is trying to help him overcome the problem he has brought on himself. He's learned from this mistake; he will never let anyone talk him into making promises that are not his own.

Charlie passes through another time, another stage of growing up. He is learning from his mistakes and trying to deal with them. He feels the pain of wounds inflicted by his own decisions. Charlie ends this difficult time with a new experience that his actions, and the lack of his actions, can lead him down the path of misery. His shyness and lack of courage will now go through a change. He must learn to be more audacious and find a way to strengthen his character. He must deal with the sorrows caused by those weak traits and make sure he doesn't continue to make them.

Charlie thinks about how to set those self-inflicted wounds right. Charlie is growing up now. As a boy he did things that were wrong and didn't give it much thought, but now he must learn to make an account for his actions, all of them. Strength comes from overcoming adversity. Charlie is becoming a man.

Chapter 5
THE CONFLICTS AND CONSEQUENCES OF LOVE

A s Charlie continues to think, he hears the front door opening, then voices, and then footsteps coming toward his room. As Charlie turns toward the door, Sara and a few other women burst in without any warning. The sudden opening of the door startles him. His room fills with feminine laughter, exuberant excitement, and zeal.

"Charlie! Charlie! Guess what happened today!" Sara says.

Charlie looks at his mother and says, "What?"

"The legislature passed the bill banning the ownership of pit bulls and other vicious animals. Isn't that great?"

Charlie says without much excitement, "Yeah, I know. The principal made an announcement over the loudspeaker today at school."

Sara shakes her head at Charlie. "You're not very excited about the news. Are you feeling all right, dear?" She walks over and puts her hand on his forehead.

Charlie replies, "Oh, Mama, I'm all right. Ever since the news broke, everyone at school has been crazy. It has been one hectic day. I'm just tired. That's all; I'm just tired."

"Oh, all right, Charlie. I'm just surprised that you aren't excited about the fantastic news. I will never understand you men. When something exciting and wonderful happens, you men hold it in like it's something to be contained. You try to hold in all the emotions just so we women won't enjoy ourselves. Well, young man, it isn't going to work this time. I am enjoying the heck out of this news, and there is nothing, not one thing, that's going to stop me from enjoying it! Nothing!"

Charlie just gives his mother a slightly confused look as she introduces the people she has brought with her. "Charlie, I want you to meet a few of my friends, Donna Thatcher, Joyce Marsh, and Cathy Lane. Do you remember Cathy? You met her and her daughter, Melissa, at the swimming pool. Do you remember?"

Charlie looks in fright at Mrs. Lane. She smiles at him. Charlie tries not to let on about the problem her conniving daughter caused for him today and simply smiles back at her.

"Do you remember me, Charlie?" she asks with a slightly seductive gesture.

"Yeah, I remember you."

"Good! I was hoping you would. Have you been seeing Melissa around school?"

He glances at the other women and then over at his mother, who looks happy. He then looks back over to Mrs. Lane and says, "Yes, I have seen her around, along with about three hundred other girls."

All four women laugh wholeheartedly at Charlie's remark.

Sara says, "Dear, why don't you come downstairs and visit with our guests for a little while?"

Charlie hesitates a little bit. "I'm kinda tired right now, Mama. Maybe I will come down later. It has been a long day."

Sara sees that her son is really tired, so she doesn't press him. "If you begin to feel better, dear, come on down for a little while."

"Right. If I feel up to it, I will, but for right now all I want to do is rest."

Mrs. Lane says, "I guess fighting off all those girls will make a fellow worn out."

The ladies laugh a little more as Charlie blushes some and looks on in silence.

"Okay, dear, whatever you want to do is fine with me," Sara says and directs the ladies out of Charlie's room and down the stairs.

Charlie lies back on his bed a little more relaxed now that the ladies have gone. He doesn't want to visit with Mrs. Lane at all. He has developed a dislike for her almost as great as his dislike for her daughter.

He rolls over and thinks about his hectic day once again. He remembers Dee's hurt feelings and expression as she got off the bus. He continues to think until he falls asleep.

He doesn't wake until the next morning. When he realizes that morning has come, he gets up and prepares for school. He takes a shower and puts on his clothes. He then walks downstairs to the kitchen, where he finds his mother reading the morning newspaper at the table.

"Good morning, Mama. What's for breakfast? I'm starved."

Sara doesn't answer his question right off. She turns the page in her newspaper and then looks meanly at Charlie. "You should be ashamed of yourself, Charlie Delaney!"

Charlie looks at his mother with curiosity. "Do What? Huh? What makes you say that, Mama?"

"I had some very close and important friends over yesterday, and you couldn't come down and visit with them, not even for just a little while. I am very disappointed in you, young man."

Charlie shakes his head in amazement. "I told you why. I just didn't feel up to it. Don't be disappointed in me. I was really tired and ..."

"And what?"

"Well, if you must know, I don't care much for one of your important friends."

Sara shakes her head in confusion and anger. "What? You don't care for one of my friends? Who don't you like, Charlie?"

Charlie pauses for a moment. "Well, Mama, it's Mrs. Lane. I just don't care for her too much."

"How come? Tell me what you don't like about Cathy."

"It's a long story, Mama. It's not about Mrs. Lane; it's really about Melissa."

"Did Melissa do something to you at school?"

"Well, kinda. I mean she caused me to have a fight with this other girl who I like a whole lot. I mean, Melissa didn't mean it directly, but she did cause a little friction between this girl I think I am in love with, kinda."

Sara puts her newspaper down and looks at Charlie with great concern. "You mean Melissa is out to get you and this other girl got jealous about it?"

Charlie tilts his head sideways. "Yeah, that's about the size it. How did you know that's what happened?"

Sara laughs. "Charlie, I was a teenage girl at one time."

Charlie smiles back at his mother as she gets up and fixes his breakfast.

As the two eat, Sara says, "Charlie, I don't want to sound like I'm interfering with your love life, but there is something you need to know about us girls. What goes on in the mind of a woman when she has a crush on a guy is something that might be difficult for a young man like you to understand."

Charlie listens to his mother with great attention and wonder.

"You see, Charlie, when a girl really likes a guy, she doesn't want to come out and tell him that she likes him. She wants that fellow to come to her and make it look like he is the one that is creating the relationship. Do you understand what I'm saying?"

"No, not really, but keep going, and maybe I will."

Sara laughs a little as she continues, "A girl will give a fellow she likes some notable signs so that he will get the idea that she likes him. This encouragement is what we girls call priming the pump. Once the pump is primed, she wants the guy to kind of take over things, you know?"

"Keep going, Mama; I think I am catching on."

Sara smiles at her attentive son as she continues, "If the guy doesn't start taking over the situation, she begins to feel as if she is the one conjuring up the relationship. She doesn't want to look like the one responsible for starting the relationship."

"But she is the one responsible!"

"Yes, Son, that is right, but she doesn't want it to look like she is. She doesn't want to look too forward. She wants the guy to think it was his idea all the time. That way she is happy at her ... let's not say *game* but her *quest*. Okay?"

"Okay, I understand a little more now. Melissa is the one who is at fault, and she doesn't want anybody to know about it."

Sara shakes her head sternly and replies, "No, no, no! You are not getting this, son. Let me put it to you another way so you can understand better. No respectable girl wants to look like she is being forward. She wants the guy to be the one that is forward, even if she is the one manufacturing the whole idea. She doesn't want it to look like she is the one who is coming on to the guy. In other words, she doesn't want to look like a fool if the guy doesn't respond. If she comes on too strong and the fellow doesn't follow her lead, she will feel like a fool. No girl ever wants to feel that way. And if she does feel like a fool, she will manufacture a reason to dislike that fellow, even if it is a downright lie. She will find some reason to hate him for not responding to her advances. Does that kind of explain things a little better, Son?"

Charlie smiles. "I think you have enlightened me a great deal."

"Charlie, you understand, though, that I was never like that? Well, I wasn't like that very much."

Charlie smiles at his mother as she gets up from the table. He eats his breakfast thinking about everything his mother said. After he finishes eating, he says, "So if a girl comes on to you and you don't respond to her advances, she will likely manufacture some reason to dislike you, right?"

Sara grins a feminine grin of intrigue. "Well, most of the time. I would say about ninety percent of the time." Sara continues, "Just find a girl you like—not one that just likes you but one that you like. Then make sure she likes you the same way, and then don't let anybody discourage you from what you have decided. Don't let anyone talk you into doing something you don't want to do. If you do that, Son, you will be on top of the game."

Charlie looks at his mother with admiration. "You know something, Mama, I am glad I have you as my mama."

Sara walks over and embraces Charlie in a loving hug. A tear of joy runs down her cheek as she gazes at her son with a loving, affectionate smile.

Charlie walks over to the window and waits impatiently for the school bus. He is eager to make right what he did yesterday. He can't wait to tell Melissa that he has found the girl he wants to go steady with and that girl isn't her. He also plans how he is going to approach Dee. He goes over his plan in his head until finally he sees the bus approach the house. He kisses his mother good-bye and runs out to the bus.

He waits patiently and nervously as the bus makes its appointed rounds. The bus soon arrives at Dee's house. It stops and waits. Charlie worries that Dee isn't going to come out of the door. She finally does, and Charlie feels a bit of relief as she gets on. Dee looks down the aisle to where Charlie is sitting. He waves to her to come to the back, but she just looks at him with an upset look. She sits down in the third row, and Charlie's disappointment comes to the surface.

"Hey, Dee! Come here for a moment," he says. "I want to talk to you."

"I like it up here, Charlie. If you want to talk to me, then you come up here."

Charlie hesitates. He thinks, *Hmmm … If I go up there, everyone will hear me talk to her. I can't ask her to go with me with all those people listening in. Besides, I need to talk to Melissa first. If I ask Dee to be my girlfriend before I talk to Melissa, then I will have to lie. Oh boy, what am I going to do?* As Charlie wonders what to do, time goes by and makes the decision for him. Charlie just sits there alone until too many people get on for him to make his move to sit next to Dee. He feels awful that he didn't act when he had the chance.

When the bus stops at school, Charlie hurries to stop Dee before she gets away. "Hey, Dee. I'm sorry about yesterday. I saw you throw your books on the ground. I feel responsible for making you angry. I just want you to know that I am real sorry for being such a jerk. Will you please forgive me?"

Dee's angry look disappears, and her face lights up with a happy glow. "Yeah, Charlie, I forgive you. I'm sorry too, for acting the way I did. Will you forgive me too?"

Charlie looks at Dee with a happy and loving expression. "You bet! I hope we don't fight ever again. You know, you are the prettiest girl in the whole school. I wish I had come up and sat with you."

"That's all right, Charlie. I don't mean to be trying to get rid of you, but I must go now. I have to get to my locker, and it's on the fourth floor. Then I have to go all the way down to the first floor for my first class."

"I understand. I will see you later, all right?"

"Sure, Charlie, I'll see you later."

Dee and Charlie go their separate ways, except Dee has something else on her mind besides her first class. Dee wants to pay Melissa Lane a little visit. She thinks about where Melissa would be right now. Dee walks around hoping to find her. She looks in the hallways but doesn't find her. She thinks, *I wonder where that snob is. She's in the ninth grade, I think. I'll just go to the office and find out.* Dee goes to the main office, a place she knows all too well.

Dee asks the secretary, "Hello. Could you help me?"

The secretary puts down her pencil and replies, "Sure. What can I do for you?"

"I saw a girl I know drop a five-dollar bill. When I got to the bill, she had already disappeared. I was wondering if you could help me locate her, so I can return it to her."

"Well, that's a nice gesture. I'm sure she will appreciate that. What's her name?"

Dee smiles a devious little grin. "Her name is Melissa Lane. She is in the ninth grade."

The woman gets up and walks over to a computer. She taps a few bits of data into the computer and then says, "Her homeroom is three-three-three. Her teacher is Mrs. McCracken."

"Yeah, I know her."

"If you give her the money, I am sure she will give it to Miss Lane."

Dee smiles with a gleam in her eye. "Oh, that's all right. I want to give it to her personally." Dee snickers softly. "Thank you very much for your help. I will go by there and maybe find her near her locker."

"I am just glad I could be of some service."

"Thanks again! Gotta run now."

Dee leaves the office in a hurry to see if she can find her adversary. She climbs the stairs to the third floor and walks over to Mrs. McCracken's room. Guess who Dee sees standing in front of her locker: Melissa Lane. Dee doesn't waste any time approaching Melissa.

As Melissa is taking a book out of her locker, Dee walks right over and bellows, "Hey, Melissa! Who do you think you are?"

Melissa turns around with a frightened look on her face. She looks confused as she stares at Dee's angry expression. "I beg your pardon?"

"Don't you beg my pardon, you interfering floozy."

"I don't understand. Have I done something to you?"

Dee looks at her with surprise and indignation. "Yeah, you have!

You got Charlie Delaney to make some stupid promise to you so he wouldn't ask me to go with him."

"I don't think that is any of your business."

"Oh, but you are wrong about that, girl! It is my business! Charlie happens to like me a whole lot. You are coming between me and him."

"Are you crazy? You have got a lot of nerve coming here to my locker and talking to me this way."

"That's right. I have the nerve. I want you to stay away from Charlie. Do you understand me?"

Melissa pauses for a moment and then begins to laugh. "Do you think I am going to stay away from Charlie just because you tell me too? Huh! You are crazy!"

Melissa's laughing makes Dee angry. Dee walks closer to Melissa and says, "If I see you making any moves on Charlie, I promise you, I will make sure you get more than you bargain for!"

Melissa begins to laugh uncontrollably at Dee.

Dee erupts with fury. "What are you laughing at!"

Melissa gets control of herself. "Boy, are you silly. You don't scare me one little bit. If you must know, Charlie happens to like me, stupid. That's why he made me such a promise."

Dee just stands there furious as Melissa continues to laugh. Dee begins to attract attention in the hallways.

Melissa says to the bystanders, "Hey, everyone! This girl is making a fool of herself. She thinks Charlie Delaney actually likes her."

Some of the other kids begin to laugh, and more people start to gather around.

Melissa says, "She just can't understand that she is nothing but another bimbo trying to get Charlie Delaney."

Dee can't take the hallway full of kids laughing at her anymore. She clutches her fists into tight balls and then hauls back and strikes Melissa right in the eye with all her might. A loud thud echoes the noise of the punch as Melissa falls to the floor. The blow knocks her out cold.

Soon teachers from nearby classrooms fall on the scene with great interest. They grab Dee and jerk her around and then push her toward the principal's office. The bell for the first class rings.

One teacher stays behind and yells out, "Did anybody see what happened?"

Most of the students scurry away from the scene, but one walks up to the teacher and says, "Man, you should have seen Dee hit that girl! Man, it was a sight to behold. Pow! Right in her eye!"

"Did you see how it happened?"

"Are you crazy? I'm not going to fink on Dee! That girl had it coming to her. She tried to make a fool out of Dee. That's all I got to say."

Other students begin to gather and stare at Melissa still lying on the floor. The teacher tries to revive Melissa. Soon another teacher appears on the scene. The teacher trying to revive Melissa orders the other teachers to call an ambulance.

Before long the ambulance arrives at the school. Right before they put Melissa on the stretcher, she regains consciousness. The EMTs tell her to be still, and they carry her away. She begins to cry. All the teachers are very upset at what they have just witnessed.

When the principal is notified of the incident, he rushes back to his office. The door opens, and Dee looks up. The principal looks down at her sternly while standing still. He shakes his head at her. "So it's you again! I thought I was through with you, but I guess I was wrong."

Dee looks at the angry principal with a frightened look. She starts to cry, and her face gets distorted. Her sad, frightened face is enough to make an angel cry. She looks as innocent as a fawn in the woods.

The principal stares at Dee severely as he walks over to his desk and sits down, not taking his eyes off Dee for one second. "I just can't believe you, young lady! I can't believe what you have just done. I just can't believe it!"

"What have I done?"

The principal looks at Dee with intense anger. He raises his voice in a blaring way. "What have you done? You just about killed a young girl! That is what you have done!"

"Surely not. I didn't mean to hit her. I just couldn't take hearing her run her mouth anymore."

"So that is why you hit her, because of something she said? That sounds very familiar." Dee wipes her eyes as the principal says, "I have told my secretary to call your mother. She should be here soon. I just want you to know, if that girl wants to press charges against you, you might go to jail."

"Jail! You mean I might have to go to jail?"

"You might. It's hard to say for certain. The only thing for certain is that you are going to be suspended from school. I am contemplating just expelling you for good."

Dee's eyes flood her cheeks with tears.

"You should have thought twice about striking that girl, young lady. I told you I don't like people to come in this school looking for violence."

"I wasn't looking for anything. I just wanted to tell her a few things. That's all. I never knew it would develop into a fight. She provoked it. I never would have hit her if she hadn't kept running her mouth. She tried to make a fool out of me in front of everybody, so I hit her."

The principal frowns at Dee as his secretary knocks on the door.

"Come in," the principal calls.

The woman walks in and looks sternly at Dee. She is the one who helped Dee find Melissa this morning. "So that is why you wanted to locate Melissa, so you could beat her up?"

The principal, looking curious, says, "Would you please explain that, Mrs. Elliott?"

"You see, Mr. Golding, Deborah Swanson came by this morning and asked me if I could help her locate Melissa Lane. I got on the computer and located her homeroom. She told me she wanted to return some money she thought Melissa had lost. I see that she just used that as an excuse to find out where Melissa would be, so she could beat her up."

"I didn't want to beat her up! She provoked it. All I wanted to do was have a talk with her. I didn't want a fight with her!"

Mrs. Elliott looks meanly at Dee. "You ought to be ashamed of yourself, young lady!"

Dee's innocent-looking face turns into a mean one. She looks at Mrs. Elliott so fiercely that Mrs. Elliott has to turn away.

Mr. Golding gives Dee a disturbed and acrimonious look and blares, "Is that right, young lady? Did you plot to hurt Melissa this morning?"

"All I wanted to do was find her so I could tell her to stay away from my boyfriend."

"Tell me, young lady, who exactly is your boyfriend?"

"Well, he is Charlie Delaney, kinda."

"What do you mean, 'kinda'?"

Dee wipes her eyes. "I mean if Melissa Lane had not interfered yesterday, he would have asked me to be his girlfriend, so I just wanted to find her and tell her to stay away from him. That's all I wanted to do. She's the one who provoked the fight."

"All the witnesses said that you were the only one to throw a punch. She didn't have time to respond to your violent act. She was knocked out cold. An ambulance had to be called because she wouldn't regain consciousness. She was at her locker, minding her own business, until you came along and beat her up because she was talking to your so-called boyfriend! I just want you to know something: I know Charlie Delaney very well, and I know he wouldn't want a girlfriend that is as mean as you are."

Dee looks on in amazement as the principal continues, "I just can't understand you at all, young lady. You were suspended only a little while ago because you threatened to harm a girl with violence. Now you have made good on your promise of violence to another girl. I just hope the girl's mother doesn't bring any charges against the school."

Dee sits in silence as the principal looks her over real hard.

He says, "I think you need to be punished severely this time. I just can't let you get away with this horrible act! You are suspended for three months, and if you ever harm or threaten another person for any reason whatsoever, I promise you, young lady, your days here at Parker High will be over permanently! Do you understand me, Deborah?"

Dee starts to cry again. She nods.

Dee's mother arrives about an hour later. This time Mrs. O'Brien sits down and has a talk with the principal while Dee is present. She looks at her daughter in confusion. Mrs. O'Brien is angry and very upset at the episode that has taken place. She asks Dee if she is all right.

Dee nods and says softly, "Yes, I'm all right, Mama."

The principal says politely to Mrs. O'Brien, "Please sit down."

"I just want to know what exactly has taken place today! I don't understand," says Mrs. O'Brien.

"What exactly took place is that your daughter beat up one of her fellow students. The girl had to be taken to the hospital."

His stern look angers Dee's mother. "What happened?"

Dee, scared, looks at her mother. "Well, I went over to this girl's locker to tell her to stay away from Charlie Delaney. She then tried to make a fool out of me, so I had to punch her. I only hit her one time, Mama."

"One punch? One punch?" Mr. Golding says. "That one punch knocked her out cold! This behavior problem has developed into something this school will no longer accept or tolerate."

Mrs. O'Brien says, "Oh no! You mean you hit that girl because of this guy, Charlie Delaney?"

"Yeah, I did."

Mrs. O'Brien, looking furiously at Mr. Golding, says, "I think this boy, Charlie Delaney, should be expelled from this school. He is the cause of all my daughter's problems here. I ask you to bring this fellow in this office right now so I can personally give him a piece of my mind!"

"I don't think that will be necessary. He hasn't done anything wrong. He is a hero among his peers. I will not bring him into this appalling situation."

"I demand to see this young man! He has caused me and my daughter a great deal of grief. I demand to see him right now!"

"Let's get something clear, Mrs. O'Brien: you don't make demands in my office! Charlie Delaney had nothing to do with your daughter striking Melissa Lane. I ask you to get control of yourself, right now. We should address the problem without confusing the issue by blaming someone else for your daughter's poor attitude."

Dee's mother gets even angrier. "You let me see this young man, Charlie Delaney, right now! I am going to put a stop to his manipulative ways that are getting my daughter into trouble."

"I will not yield to your demands, Mrs. O'Brien. I will ask you once more to get control of yourself. If we are to have an intelligent conversation, you must first calm down somewhat." Mr. Golding picks up the phone and calls his secretary.

"Now we will get down to the real problem at hand," Mrs. O'Brien says, thinking that Mr. Golding is calling to get Charlie to come to his office.

Mr. Golding says, "Hello, Mrs. Elliott. Have you heard about

Melissa Lane's condition?" Mr. Golding is quiet as he listens to Mrs. Elliott's report on Melissa's condition.

Mrs. O'Brien is getting furious. She feels like a fool now because of the remark she just made. She was trying to impress him with her determination. Now that she is not getting her way, she says, "Hey! I expect you to bring Charlie Delaney to our talk!"

Mr. Golding pays no attention to Mrs. O'Brien's remark. He just continues to listen to his secretary. Soon he says, "Okay, Mrs. Elliott, thank you so much."

Mr. Golding puts down the phone and looks sternly at a very angry Mrs. O'Brien. "I have just gotten word that Melissa Lane has been released from the hospital. Her mother has already picked her up, and she is on her way home. I am just glad she isn't seriously injured."

"Now that your mind is at ease, you can bring Charlie Delaney to our meeting."

Mr. Golding gets very loud. "I thought I told you, Mrs. O'Brien, I am not going to bring Charlie into this. I'm going to focus on the problem at hand."

Mrs. O'Brien then hits the roof. "Mr. Golding, I don't think you heard me! I said I want to talk to Charlie Delaney, right now!"

Mr. Golding stares Mrs. O'Brien in the eyes. "That is it! I will take no more of your anger and immaturity any longer. I want you and your daughter to leave this school at once! As of right now, your daughter is suspended from school for the next three months. If either of you come on campus for any reason, I will personally see to it that your daughter will be expelled from school permanently! Do you understand me, Mrs. O'Brien?"

Mrs. O'Brien cracks into a crying fit. "Why are you doing this to me?" Her tears flow like a child whose candy has been taken away. "Why are you doing this? I work hard to bring up my daughter the best way I can. I have to work hard for a living! I can't stay home and keep an eye on her. I have a job to go to! I will probably get into trouble with my boss because I had to leave work again so abruptly. Please don't suspend my daughter from school."

Mr. Golding shows a little compassion to the crying mother but does not change his mind. "I am doing you a favor by not expelling your daughter right now. I was going to, but I changed my mind after hearing that Melissa Lane is doing fine. The normal procedure when something like this happens is to expel that student immediately. I have taken into account that Melissa Lane did provoke your daughter into the fight. That is why she isn't going to be expelled this time. But you mark my word," Mr. Golding says, directing his next remarks at Dee, "if you ever cause any more trouble with any other students at this high school, I promise you that you will never be allowed back on campus. Do you understand me, young lady?"

Dee with a quiet and sad look says, "Yes. Yes, sir, I understand."

"Please don't suspend my daughter for three months," Mrs. O'Brien says. "Just suspend her for three days like you did the last time. Please?"

"I am sorry, Mrs. O'Brien. Deborah has acted more violently this time. I can't let her get away with only a three-day suspension. I am sorry, but I have a school to run here. I must have discipline for all students. If I only suspend her for three days, I will be giving a message to all the other students to go ahead and act violently because their punishments will be lenient. I just can't give that message to my kids. Sorry."

Mrs. O'Brien erupts into a violent rage again. She grabs an ashtray that is sitting on the desk in front of her and flings it at Mr. Golding. "You are nothing but a stupid man! You don't know how hard it is to raise a daughter by yourself. You men are all the same." The ashtray flies by Mr. Golding's head and hits the wall, knocking down a picture that was hanging there.

Mr. Golding looks afraid as he says, "What is wrong with you? What is your problem? Get out of my office, right now!"

Mrs. O'Brien explodes into an unbelievable, uncontrollable fit. She cusses awful things at Mr. Golding. After about three minutes of this rage, Mrs. Elliott runs into the office. When Mrs. O'Brien sees another woman present, she abruptly stops her outrageous fit. She looks around the room and sees everybody staring at her with confused expressions. The room is filled with complete silence as Mrs. O'Brien gazes over at Mr. Golding.

"Oh my!" she says. "I am really sorry about the manner in which I have acted. I just don't know what came over me. I am real sorry, Mr. Golding."

Mr. Golding looks at Mrs. O'Brien with complete confusion. He doesn't know what to say. He just stands there with a look of fear in his eyes.

Mrs. O'Brien looks over at a bewildered Mrs. Elliott and says calmly, "I am very sorry to you too. I guess I just lost my head. I don't know exactly why I acted that way. I think I had just better go home now."

Mr. Golding and Mrs. Elliott look on in silence with their mouths open as Mrs. O'Brien looks around the room. She says in a soft and delicate tone, "I don't know how much damage I have done to your office, Mr. Golding. I will be glad to pay for any damages. Please just send me a bill, and I will be glad to compensate you for it. Please forgive me for acting like this."

Mr. Golding continues to look on in the same confused state. He still can't find any words to say.

"Mama, I think we should leave now," Dee says.

Mrs. O'Brien looks around a bit more at the disastrous office and then looks over at her daughter. "Yes, Deborah, I believe you are right. I believe we should go now." She looks over at Mr. Golding one last time. "We will be leaving now, Mr. Golding. Please send me a bill, and tell me when Deborah will be permitted to come back to school. I will be waiting for your response."

Mr. Golding, still in a daze, says, "I will do that."

Mrs. O'Brien takes her daughter by the hand, and the two walk out of the office without saying another word.

When they leave, Mr. Golding looks over at Mrs. Elliott and says, "In all the years I have been principal at this school, I have never experienced anything like what I have experienced today. I don't think I am feeling very well. I think I will go home."

"Yes, sir. I don't blame you one bit. I hope you get to feeling better."

Mr. Golding slowly walks out to his car and drives away, not stopping until he reaches his house.

Back at school, the news is spreading like wildfire. Charlie leaves his first class and walks to his homeroom. He is one of the first ones to get there. He sits down and waits for the teacher to take roll.

One of his best friends, Robert Hill, approaches him with a very excited look on his face and says, "Hey, man! Have you heard the news?"

Charlie becomes aroused at Robert's words. "What news?"

"Dee. She got into a knock-out, drag-out fight with some chick this morning!"

Charlie, looking anxious, says, "Do what? She did what?"

"Yeah, man, I was at my locker before the first bell rung and saw the whole thang. Man! She hit the girl so hard it knocked her out cold. They had to call an ambulance to come get her. Man, it was something to see!"

Charlie begins to worry. His worried mind starts asking all kinds of questions. Others in the classroom, hearing the conversation, gather around Charlie to tell him the whole story. The more he hears about it, the more worried he becomes.

After a few minutes go by, Charlie asks the teacher if he can go to the principal's office to see Dee. The teacher hesitates at first but then agrees to his request. Charlie rushes quickly to the office.

He opens the office door and quickly asks, "Miss Elliott, could I see the principal? It is very important!"

"Charlie, you just missed him. He wasn't feeling very well, so he took the rest of the day off."

Charlie looks very depressed. Mrs. Elliott notices his sad state of mind and says, "Cheer up; you can see him tomorrow."

"Oh, it's not really him I wanted to see. It's Dee Swanson. Do you know where she is?"

Mrs. Elliott looks at Charlie with a frown. "I hate to be the one to tell you, but she was suspended for three months because of a fight she got into this morning. She and her mother just left five minutes ago. I hope you aren't too disappointed about this."

Charlie looks back at Mrs. Elliott with a sad, disappointed frown. "I wish I was dead; that's all!"

"Don't be that way, Charlie. Look at it this way: you have got girls fighting over you now. You should feel like a man on top of the world. Don't let her suspension make you feel so bad. You ought to just go out there and find another girl. She isn't the only girl in the world, you know. She isn't exactly of the best quality anyway. You should find a girl who has more ladylike qualities."

Charlie shows a bit of hostility toward Mrs. Elliott with his eyes. She sees the message and says, "I'm sorry, Charlie. I guess that wasn't the proper advice to give. You really like that girl, don't you?"

Charlie's hostile look diminishes. "I sure do. I love her. She is the only girl in the world that I truly care about. Well, except for my mother."

Mrs. Elliott smiles. "I understand now. I hope you aren't angry at me for what I just said."

"No, I'm not mad at you. I'm just disappointed and upset that Dee has been suspended. Do you think if I talk to Mr. Golding he might change his mind?"

Mrs. Elliott pauses for a moment. She gives Charlie a disappointed look. "I don't think he will, but you could try. I will tell him tomorrow morning that you want to speak with him on the matter. Who knows, maybe he will."

Charlie expresses a brief glimmer of hope with a quick smile. He turns to the door and quietly departs the office without saying another word.

After second period is over, word of Dee's suspension has spread around like wildfire. The hallways are filled with conversation about her three-month suspension. Everyone seems to have nothing else to talk about. Anger has erupted at Parker High at a level never seen before. All of Dee's girlfriends are outraged at the principal's decision. Students that were present at the fight have become highly sought-after and valuable commodities for people to hear about what really happened.

As Charlie makes his way to his third class, he looks into the classrooms he passes. He notices a lot of angry students, mostly girls, arguing about something. He keeps on walking and looking, seeing the same thing going on in almost every classroom he looks in.

When Charlie walks into his English class, he finds another fight brewing. Sue Parker and Sheila Boles are standing up and having a few harsh words with each other. The teacher isn't present yet.

Sue bellows out with fury, "Listen here, Sheila! You get away from me."

Sheila is a large, stocky girl with the determination to stand up to anybody, especially when her friends are at stake. She stands right in front of Sue and forcefully says, "It's all your fault. If you hadn't got Dee into trouble the first time, none of this would have happened."

Sheila smacks Sue in the face three times. Slap! Slap! Slap! Sue's face is completely red on the left side now. Sheila then grabs Sue's hair and pulls. Sue grabs Sheila's hair and pulls right back. The two girls are a sight to behold. Their quick motions fascinate everyone in the room. Over half of the class is pulling for Sheila; the other half is just looking on. Charlie looks on in bewilderment. He doesn't know exactly what to do, but since Sue was the cause of Dee's three-day suspension, he just looks on like the others without trying to stop it.

Sheila grabs Sue and throws her to the floor. She gets on top of Sue and begins to slap her silly. Slap! Slap! She just keeps on slapping her. Sue cries out in a state of horror, "Stop! Stop! Somebody stop her! Please, someone stop her!" Her cries are to no avail; no one tries to stop Sheila's vicious blows. Charlie has an expression of enjoyment on his face. He just looks on as the class cheers Sheila on.

"Hey, everybody! Mr. Bishop is coming! Mr. Bishop is coming!" someone calls.

Sheila tries to climb off Sue before Mr. Bishop arrives, but she is still getting up from the floor as he enters the classroom. He looks at the class sternly, and an unhappy and disturbed look comes to his face. He sees Sue Parker lying on the floor crying like a baby. She tries to speak but only gets a jumbled-up, whining noise out.

"What is going on in here? What has happened?" Mr. Bishop asks.

The room is filled with silence as Sue manages to get up from the floor. She points her finger at Sheila. "She beat me up!" She begins to cry uncontrollably.

"That's right, Mr. Bishop; I beat her up!" Sheila says. "She is the one responsible for Dee Swanson's entire ordeal. Sue got away with getting her suspended the first time. Now Dee has been thrown out of school for three months! I take pride in setting the situation right! You can just take me up to the principal's office and have me suspended too. I don't care. Dee Swanson is one of my best friends. I don't think I could have a better friend. If she is going to be suspended from school because of a stupid fight, then let me join her. Frankly I don't give a damn!"

The class applauds Sheila's convictions. Mr. Bishop just stands there with a confused look on his face. After a few seconds he gazes over and sees how bad Sue has been beaten up. He says, "Okay, young lady! Since you don't care, I don't care either. I will not tolerate anyone inflicting harm on anyone in my class. So let's just pay the principal a little visit."

Charlie looks on in silence, knowing that the principal isn't at school. Mr. Bishop leads Sheila down to the office. When they arrive, Mr. Bishop asks to see the principal, and Mrs. Elliott tells him that Mr. Golding isn't there. She contacts the assistant principal, Mr. Matthews, to take care of Sheila. Mr. Bishop briefly tells Mr. Matthews what happened in his classroom. Mr. Matthews listens to the story with intense emotion and concentration. After Mr. Matthews hears the entire story, Mr. Bishop heads back to his class. Mr. Matthews suspends Sheila without listening very long to her story. He doesn't play around at all. He goes strictly by the book. If a student has been in a fight, male or female, that student will be suspended for at least three school days and sometimes even longer. After Mr. Matthews calls Sheila's mother and tells her to come pick up her daughter, Sheila, like Dee, begins to cry. The mental anguish finally sets in. She realizes now that she has made a mistake. She is frightened and worried about how her mother and her father are going to react to her suspension. She cries but tries to hold it in.

By that time third period is over, several more teachers have brought girls up to the office. All have been in fights. The main reasons for the fighting are Dee's suspension and girls taking up for Charlie for what Sue Parker said last week. Talk of the fights spreads throughout the school at a quick rate. After fourth period begins, girls begin to fight for a totally new reason: to win over Charlie. One girl says something about him, and then another one takes up for him. Jealousy begins to deceive intellect. The pride in the hearts of the girls that are fond of Charlie is as fragile as glass. They have fights over the simplest things. They think in their deceived minds that their aggression will win over Charlie's affections. Most girls in the school know by now that Dee won't be around to attract Charlie anymore. They plot their own strategies to win Charlie's affections, even if that means a violent confrontation with a rival female.

By the time fifth period is in process, the hostility has snowballed into another conflict. The girls that have been sent to the office are all being suspended without any compassion at all. Friends begin to turn on each other. Friends fight with their friends who have taken up for those who are being suspended. This sets off a colossal chain reaction. Dozens and dozens of girls who would be sweet and kind on a normal day begin to act vehemently. Some of these girls don't even know Charlie Delaney or Dee Swanson, but they too behave in a hostile manner because they feel the need to take up for their girlfriends who have been kicked out of school.

The assistant principal has his office full of angry girls and upset teachers all day long. He can't understand why all these girls are acting in this violent manner. Just as he finishes with one girl, Mrs. Elliott brings in two more. During fifth period the office is full of angry girls who have been in fights. Mrs. Elliott just shakes her head in disbelief. She can't believe her eyes.

Mrs. Elliott walks into Mr. Matthews's office and says, "What in the world is going on? I don't know what to do!"

Mr. Matthews looks at Mrs. Elliott with a confused look. "How many girls do you have waiting now?"

"How many? There are too many to count! The teachers just keep bringing them in! What do you want me to do?"

"Just stay calm. Don't let them see you upset. I wish Mr. Golding were here. Tell those teachers to stay calm. I will try to handle this ordeal the best way I can. Dear Lord in heaven, help me!"

Mr. Matthews gets on the phone and calls Mr. Golding. The phone rings three times before Mr. Golding answers.

"Hello?" Mr. Golding says.

"Mr. Golding, this is William. The school is turning into a madhouse. It is almost at the riot stage."

"What seems to be the problem?"

"It seems like all the girls have gone crazy! Dozens of fights have broken out all over the school. It really is a madhouse here. What do you want me to do?"

Mr. Golding pauses for a moment. "Just try to keep the school going. Keep the angry girls apart. I don't know what to tell you, but try to stay on top of things. I will be back tomorrow. Just try to keep control of the school until I get back."

"Okay, I'll try."

Mr. Matthews hangs up the phone and goes back to work, doing his best to keep control of the school.

When sixth period begins, the climax of the day arrives. Girls are fighting over everything. Fights are taking place in every classroom, and the fights now have absolutely nothing to do with Charlie or Dee. They have developed into girlfriend taking up for girlfriend. The office is packed full of angry female students and their disoriented teachers. None of the fights have had any boys involved in them. Some of the classes are completely vacant of any girls.

Mr. Matthews manages to keep the school operating. After the bell rings to end the school day, Mr. Matthews tells all the girls that are still waiting to see him to simply go to their buses. He gets them to promise him that they will not fight anymore. When they agree, he lets them leave the office. They leave for their buses with happy sighs of relief.

As Charlie gets on his bus, he is glad the day is over. He is the main topic of conversation on the bus. Everyone seems to have something to ask him. He tries to answer as many questions as he can. He begins to feel a sense of guilt over all that has happened today. He eagerly looks forward to getting home. The bus finally arrives at his house, and he happily gets off. He walks up to his doorstep, glad to finally be home.

As Charlie walks inside to relax peacefully at his home, his peaceable surroundings are interrupted. Dee's mother is sitting on the couch in the living room with his mother sitting across from her in a chair.

Charlie doesn't get a chance to say one word before Mrs. O'Brien says, "So I finally get to see the boy who has made my life a total shambles!" She gives Charlie an angry look.

Sara says, "Come on in, Charlie. We have been waiting for you."

Charlie walks into the living room and timidly sits down on the couch.

"Do you know how much trouble you have caused me, young man?" Mrs. O'Brien asks.

Charlie replies, "What trouble are you talking about?"

"Did you know that my daughter was suspended from school today?"

"Well, kinda."

"She was suspended for three months because of you!"

Sara says, "Hey! I don't think you have to yell at my son like that! He isn't deaf."

"You listen here," Mrs. O'Brien says to Sara. "My daughter has been thrown out of school because your son wouldn't leave her alone. I told him specifically to stay away from Deborah. If he had listened to me, my daughter would still be attending school right now!"

Charlie waits as Mrs. O'Brien gets hold of herself and then stammers, "I haven't done anything to get Deborah suspended. Really! I don't understand why she got suspended."

"She got into a fight with another girl, and they were fighting because of you!" Mrs. O'Brien shakes her finger at Charlie angrily.

She maintains a mean expression as Charlie tries to explain. "You see, Mrs. O'Brien, I like your daughter a whole lot. I wouldn't do anything to get her suspended. After I heard about the fight, I went to the principal's office to see if I could change his mind."

"So you know she was in a fight today?"

"I found out about it during my second class. Some of my friends told me she got into a fight before school started. But I never wanted her to get into any trouble. I think a whole lot of Deborah."

Sara, with a convincing look, gazes over at Mrs. O'Brien and says, "I think your daughter has brought all this on herself, Mrs. O'Brien. I think you are just trying to put the blame on my son so you won't have to admit that your daughter is a troublemaker."

"Troublemaker! I beg your pardon!"

"When you asked to come into my house today to talk to me about Charlie, I had no idea you wanted to falsely accuse him of doing something wrong! My son says he would never do anything to get your daughter into any trouble, so don't blame Charlie for something your daughter has done."

Mrs. O'Brien gets up from the couch and walks over to Sara. "Your son is the one responsible for my daughter's suspension! If it wasn't for his enticing ways, my daughter would never have had a confrontation with that other girl."

"You listen here! You don't run your mouth like that to me! This is my house! I won't stand being talked to like that in my house!" Sara's anger reaches a boiling point.

Mrs. O'Brien viciously turns her head toward Charlie and says, "You stay away from my daughter. Do you understand? Stay away from my daughter or else! The next time you do anything to disrupt her or me, I will have you arrested."

Charlie just sits there with a dumbfounded look. He doesn't know what to say.

"You get away from my son. Matter of fact, you get out of my house! Right now!" Sara yells.

Mrs. O'Brien sees how angry Sara is, so she grabs her handbag and begins to walk toward the door.

Sara says, "Don't let me see you on my property again, or I will call the police and have you arrested. Do you understand me?"

Mrs. O'Brien looks at Sara with a scared and disturbed stare. She doesn't answer back. She just opens the door, storms out, and disappears from the Delaney property without saying another word. Sara walks over to the door to shut it.

Charlie feels bad that his mother had to experience such an awful scene. He looks at her sadly as she comes back into the living room. "I'm sorry, Mama. I hope she didn't upset you too much."

Sara smiles and says, "Upset? Me? Are you kidding? Charlie, I couldn't be happier!"

Charlie looks back at his mother with confusion. "Huh? I thought you would be upset about having to deal with something like that."

"I'm just proud to have a son who has girls fighting over him."

"But you told Mrs. O'Brien that I had nothing to do with Dee getting into that fight."

Sara's eyes sparkle as she replies, "Oh, I just told her that because I was taking up for you. Dee got thrown out of school because she was jealous of another girl and started a fight with her to keep her away from you. I think it is wonderful. I think it is more than wonderful; I think it is marvelous."

Charlie looks dumbfounded at his mother. "Mama, why do you think that? I thought this was a problem, not a victory. You act like it is a celebration that Dee got thrown out of school."

"Oh no, it's not that." She laughs.

"Why do you keep laughing?"

"Everyone is going to have problems in life, but it's better to have some problems than it is to have other problems. I am just proud to have a son who is driving girls to fight over him. I think that is great!"

"But the girl that got thrown out of school is the one I want to be my girlfriend. I think I love her. I mean, I know I love her."

"Charlie, let me give you a little advice: don't let one girl control you to the point where she is the most important thing in your life. You are too young for that. If you let a girl control you, you will be miserable. Play the field, and try not to let one girl dominate your life. At your tender age you're going to meet all types of pretty girls. You may fall in love with one, but you could fall in love with the wrong one. So just take my advice, and play the field like a man of the world. Please, don't let this girl make your life miserable. They will, you know. I made a few guys in my life miserable. Not meaning to, of course."

"Mama! You should be ashamed of yourself."

"I guess I should be, but I kind of enjoyed the attention at that time in my life."

Charlie says, "I don't know if I should tell you, but Dee wasn't the only girl to get into a fight today. The whole school was in an uproar. I heard there were dozens and dozens of fights after the news got out about Dee's suspension. I never saw anything like it before."

Sara looks extremely excited. "Do what? You mean there were other girls fighting over you also?"

Charlie quickly replies, "No, no, no. They weren't fighting over me. They were just fighting. I don't know exactly what the fights were about, but there sure were a lot of them today. Boy, were there a lot of them!"

Sara just falls back on the couch and laughs like a fourteen-year-old schoolgirl. She laughs, then giggles, then laughs, and then giggles. She looks at Charlie with a silly grin and then laughs some more. She laughs until Charlie can't take it anymore.

"You should be ashamed of yourself," he says. "You shouldn't be laughing at them. They all got suspended from school for at least three days. That's not funny."

When Sara hears this, she bursts into another delirious laughing frenzy. She can't get control of herself. She keeps laughing until Charlie begins to laugh too.

"Hey, now! It's not that funny!" he says.

Sara manages to get control of herself just long enough to say, "Then why are you laughing?"

Charlie tries to stop, but his mother is so tickled he can't. They both just sit there and laugh until they get pains in their sides.

The next day at school there is a more relaxed atmosphere. The classrooms are vacant somewhat because of all the suspensions. Everything calms down now that most of the girls are not there. Mr. Golding and Mr. Matthews manage to keep the school in favorable spirits. Since a lot of the girls are not at school, Charlie has time to think about what he is going to do. He still can't seem to get Dee out of his mind. He has been bitten by the lovebug, and the infection has grown into fever status. He decides not to listen to his mother and decides to wait patiently until Dee comes back to school. Many girls play up to him, but he doesn't ask any of them to go steady. He tells himself that Dee is going to be his first girlfriend and that he won't let anything or anybody distract him from this decision. He would feel like a heel if he took on another girl to be his girlfriend now.

As time goes by, Charlie grows fonder of Dee with each passing day. He thinks about her in a more caring way now that she is absent from school. He visualizes her as she was before she had to leave school. His thoughts of her and his admiration for her are powerful. He looks forward to seeing her get back on the school bus. He wants everything to be as it was. He yearns to be with her. The days go by slowly. The weeks seem like months. The three months seems like an eternity. But just like the sun rising in the east and the moon appearing at night, Dee does return to school.

When that all-important day comes, Charlie is full of excitement and anticipation. As he waits on the bus for it to stop at her house, he thinks about all the happy moments he has had with her. The bus stops at her house, and she walks out from her garage and slowly gets on the bus. Charlie is sitting in the front seat today. He looks at Dee with great excitement in his eyes as she sits down beside him.

Dee says to Charlie in a soft, innocent way, "Hello, Charlie. It sure is good to see you again. I have been thinking about you a whole lot. Have you been thinking about me?"

Charlie, still gazing at his lovely damsel, says softly, "I haven't stopped thinking about you, Dee. I have long waited to see you again, with a burden of guilt on my conscience. I have missed you an awful lot. It sure is good to see you again."

Dee smiles at Charlie with a gleam of excitement in her eyes.

"Are you mad at me for all the trouble I have caused you?" Charlie asks.

"No, I haven't been mad at you at all. I'm only mad at myself. I brought everything on myself." Dee shows a look of disappointment as she says, "I know you want me to sit here with you, but I promised my mama that I wouldn't. She is still angry about everything. She told me that she went to your house and had a talk with you and your mother. I hope you don't feel bad anymore about what she said to you."

"That was months ago, Dee. I have forgotten all about that. That is all in the past now."

"Maybe so, but my mama doesn't want me to get into any more trouble. You see, me and my mama are not getting along too good these days. She and I have really had some bad arguments since I've been out of school. It would really set her off if she found out that I was sitting next to you now. I don't want me and my mama to have any more arguments. Do you understand, Charlie?"

"I think I do. I just wish everything had happened a little differently, but after talking to your mother, I understand her feelings."

"I'm glad. I think I will sit somewhere else now. I hope you aren't angry at me for wanting to sit somewhere else. Are you?"

"No, I'm not angry at you. I'm only angry at myself for not doing what I should have done months ago."

Dee gives Charlie a quick peeved look before moving. Charlie is saddened by her look. He is left with another disappointing event in his young life.

As the months go by, Charlie doesn't dare to make any waves between Dee and her mother. He was going to finally ask her to be his steady girlfriend but then decided not to because of her mother. He doesn't want to start any problems between them. Time has a way of working out all problems life deals out, and so it is with Charlie and Dee. Charlie never asks any girl to be his steady, and neither does Dee go with anyone. They remain good friends and talk to one another in class and in the hallways. They don't sit together on the bus anymore but do manage to wave at each other every morning.

Second semester begins, and January sets in, bringing chilly surroundings. Charlie and Dee are sitting across from each other in history class one day. The teacher isn't in the room. Dee is in a playful, frisky mood and begins to joke around. Some of the other kids in the class are also acting a little silly while the teacher is out of the room. Danny Patterson, who is sitting near Charlie and Dee, has his head down on his desk. In her laughable mood, Dee gets an idea.

"Hey, Danny," Dee says, "Charlie says you sleep too much. He says you look like an elephant seal that has washed up on the beach."

A few kids laugh at Dee's remark, and Danny's head pops up. He replies coarsely and sleepily, "I don't care what he said."

Charlie never made the second statement, just the first one. Dee just wants to have a little fun with Danny. Charlie just sits at his desk minding his own business. Danny Patterson puts his head back down on the desk.

Dee thinks a little bit and says playfully, "Hey, Danny, Charlie called you a fag."

Some of the others in the class laugh. Danny raises his head, and with an angry look in his eyes, he jumps up, walks over to where Charlie is sitting, and slaps Charlie across the face. Everyone in the class stops talking and directs their attention to Charlie and Danny. Charlie gets up and slaps Danny back. Danny slaps Charlie again, and Charlie lands another slap on Danny's plump face. His palms makes a loud pop as it strikes Danny's face. Charlie and Danny exchange more slaps. Neither one hits the other with a tight fist, only with slaps. Everyone's attention grows more intense as Charlie and Danny slap it out.

After a few minutes of the slap boxing, Charlie lunges toward Danny and pushes him to the floor. Dee begins to cry. It takes Danny a few seconds to get up. He then picks up a heavy desk and raises it over his head. Charlie, seeing what is about to take place, grabs one of the desk legs. As Danny tries to hurtle the desk toward Charlie, Charlie grabs one of the desk legs firmly and guides the desk to the floor. The desk makes an extremely loud noise when it hits the floor.

Just then, the teacher walks into the room. He looks over the class and notices something is wrong. He then sees the desk on the floor. With a scared look on his face, he nervously asks, "Hey, what's going on in here?"

Someone in the class walks up to him and quietly tells him what has just taken place. The teacher motions for Charlie and Danny to step outside. Dee's tears run like a stream. Her face is full of panic and worry. Charlie and Danny leave the room with the teacher, and the class gathers around to converse about what has just transpired.

"What seems to be the problem?" the teacher asks.

Danny says, "Dee Swanson told me that Charlie called me a fag."

The teacher looks at Charlie and says, "Did you call Danny that name?"

"No, I didn't call him that! I didn't call him anything. I was just sitting there minding my own business."

The teacher sees that Danny and Charlie aren't angry at each other now and says, "You two just stay right where you are."

The teacher sticks his head back into the classroom and motions to a very upset Dee Swanson to step outside. He then asks her, "Did you tell Danny that Charlie called him a name?"

Dee, with tears in her eyes, says, "Yes. I didn't mean to start a fight. I was just joking. I didn't mean any harm." She begins to cry once again.

The teacher sees that Dee is being sincere. He knows about all the trouble she has had this year, so he doesn't make any waves about the incident. He just tells her to go back into the classroom.

"I am sorry, Charlie. I am sorry, Danny. I really am sorry!" she says and walks back into the classroom.

The teacher looks at the boys and says, "Do you fellows think that you can bury the hatchet here and now?"

"Yes," Danny says. "I don't want to get into any trouble over this."

Charlie says, "Me neither."

"Okay, fellows, go on back into the classroom."

Charlie and Danny go back into the classroom with the teacher right behind them. The teacher conducts the class without any further interruptions. After the class is over, Dee, Charlie, and Danny go their separate ways.

At the end of the day, Charlie finds Dee, with red eyes and a worried look, waiting for him in the hallway by his locker. "I am sorry about the trouble I caused you," she says. "Danny won't even talk to me. You don't hate me, do you?"

"Of course not, Dee. I could never hate you. I am a little upset about it, but don't let it bother you."

Dee tries to smile. Her red eyes and distraught expression show that she really is taking this hard. Charlie tries to cheer her up a little as they walk out to the bus. Dee sits with Charlie all the way home. They talk about every little thing. Charlie feels good that Dee is finally sitting next to him. He treasures these times with Dee as the best times of his life. The time goes by fast, and the bus arrives at Dee's house. She gets off in good spirits. Charlie waves good-bye to her, and she does the same. As the bus moves forward, her house disappears from sight.

Charlie feels good about himself now that Dee has shown him more attention. He thinks that he is finally going to ask her to go steady. The bus stops at his house. He can't wait to get back on it tomorrow. He goes inside his house with a new sense of purpose.

The next day arrives before long, though Charlie didn't think it would ever get here. He rushes to get ready for school. He eats his breakfast in a hurry. He sits near the window with his mother with great expectation of seeing the bus come by. He finally sees the long-awaited sight. He kisses his mother good-bye and runs to the bus in a hurry. He plans out his entire strategy to the last detail. He knows exactly what he is going to say. He is going to finally ask her! His long-awaited day has arrived! All Charlie hopes for is that Dee comes back to the back and sits with him. If she doesn't come to him, it will ruin the whole game plan. It's important that she come to the back where nobody will hear Charlie's proposal.

Just before the bus stops at Dee's house, it picks up a seventh-grade student. The boy has taken a special liking to Charlie and has been coming to sit in the back with Charlie for some time now. He is a little pest to Charlie, and Charlie begins to worry about everything when the unwelcome boy walks down the aisle and sits down one seat up from Charlie on the other side.

"Hey, Melvin, why don't you sit up front today?" Charlie says.

"Why?" the little boy asks.

"Because I want you to. I want to talk to someone in private in a little bit, so why don't you just go up front today."

"'Cause I don't want to. I want to sit back here with you, Charlie. I like you, and I like to sit in the back."

"But for today will you please sit up front? I want to talk to someone in private."

Melvin sees that Charlie doesn't want him around, but this doesn't persuade him in the least to go up front. He is more determined to stay in the back now that Charlie wants him to leave.

"Come on, Melvin; go up to the front, just for today."

Melvin shakes his head. "No. Who do you want to talk to?"

"That's not important. Will you just please go up front today?"

Melvin sees the want in Charlie's eyes, and this makes him more determined than ever to stay where he is. Melvin likes the attention he gets from pestering Charlie. So Melvin stays right where he is. Charlie sees there is no use; Melvin isn't going to leave.

The bus arrives at Dee's house, and she gets on. She walks right down the aisle and sits down beside Charlie on the other side. She has a very excited look on her face. She is happy to be sitting next to Charlie again. Her innocent, flirtatious expression gives Charlie an extra burst of confidence.

"I thought I would come back to the old hangout," she says. "I don't care what my mama would say. You doing all right today?"

Charlie notices Melvin taking in every word. "Yeah, I'm doing just fine. I'm glad you finally came back here. It has been a long time, hasn't it?"

"It sure has. It has been a long time."

As Charlie is trying to work up the courage to ask her, Melvin blurts out, "Hey, Charlie, is this the one you said you wanted to talk to in private?"

Charlie's face turns a shade of magenta. "Why don't you go up front and leave us alone!"

Melvin laughs a silly little laugh. "'Cause I don't want to. I want to hear what you want to talk about in private."

Charlie realizes this isn't going to work. He can't ask a girl to go steady with him while a pest like Melvin is present. He remains silent but looks at Melvin as if he wants to kill him.

Dee strikes up a conversation that Charlie gets involved with. They talk about simple things as the bus fills up. Charlie knows for sure now that his plan is ruined. He will have to wait until he finds Dee alone near her locker before he can ask her. He waits helplessly with a strange sense of guilt as the bus continues to make its way to school. The bus stops at the seventh- and eighth-grade school first.

Melvin waves to Charlie. "See you later, alligator." Charlie just gives Melvin a mean look as he walks off the bus.

The bus thins out a great deal as the junior high school kids get off, but there are still too many ears listening in for Charlie to ask that all-important question. He'll have to wait for another time.

When Charlie gets to school, he goes to his locker and then to Dee's locker. He casually walks back and forth by her locker until he realizes that she isn't going to show up. He goes to his first class. When he arrives there, he thinks hard about when he will pop the question to Dee. He decides to ask her that all-important question after chorus class. He will have an opportunity to talk to her after the class is over. So Charlie again plans out his strategy and waits patiently until the time is right.

After Charlie's first class is over, and after he goes to homeroom he proceeds to chorus class. The class goes off without a hitch. Dee, for some reason, doesn't engage in any conversation with him during class. When the bell finally rings to change classes, Charlie waits for Dee so he can talk with her alone. He wants to get what's bother him over with.

"Hey, Dee. How are you doing?" he asks.

"Okay, I guess. How are you?"

Charlie, with perspiration on his brow, has a very serious look on his face. He looks at Dee as if he has something really important to say to her. "Could I talk to you for a moment?"

Dee pauses for a few seconds. She sees the serious look on Charlie's face. "Sure, Charlie, what's up?"

"Dee, you know I have had a crush on you for quite some time now."

Dee listens with complete attention.

"I have been wanting to ask you something for a long time," Charlie says. "You know I am very shy when it comes to talking about serious things. What I am trying to say is I really like you a whole lot, and I know your mother doesn't care for me, but I was just wondering if you would go steady with me? You know, be my girlfriend?"

Dee's smile suddenly evaporates, and she begins to cry. She can't say anything for a few moments, but after a short pause she says, "Charlie, Charlie, I don't know what to say. I have been waiting so long to hear you ask this but …"

Charlie begins to feel a little woozy. "But what?"

"Danny Patterson asked me to be his steady girlfriend right before school started this morning. And you know he was really angry at me yesterday for causing that fight you and him got into. So when he asked me to go steady with him, I told him yes. I am sorry, Charlie. I really am!"

Charlie's heart suddenly disintegrates. He looks at Dee with the saddest look a young man can have. He is devastated. Dee looks at Charlie's sad eyes and begins to cry again. He doesn't know what to say. He just stands there dumbfounded by Dee's words.

Dee tenderly says, "I truly am sorry, Charlie, but he asked me first. I felt obligated to him for causing him all that trouble. I'm sorry."

"I understand. I guess."

"You don't hate me now, do you?"

Charlie doesn't answer Dee. He just can't seem to say anything.

"Please, Charlie, please tell me you don't hate me. Please, Charlie, pretty please, tell me you don't hate me." Tears run down Dee's face.

Seeing her tears, Charlie says, "No, Dee, I don't hate you. I don't. I gotta go now. I will see you later."

"Sure, Charlie. I will see you later."

Charlie walks off with what pieces of his heart he has left. He can't believe what has just taken place. The worst thing that could possibly happen has happened. He is devastated. Poor Charlie Delaney. His mother was right; he should have listened to her. This is Charlie's darkest moment.

The school day seems to take forever. After Charlie puts away his schoolbooks in his locker after his last class, he begins to make that long walk to the bus. As he is walking down the steps, Charlie sees a horrible sight. He sees Dee and Danny kissing each other. What's left of Charlie's heart cracks into tiny pieces that will never be repaired. He turns and walks to the bus with his insides torn, scarred, and broken.

As the school year progresses, Dee continues to go steady with Danny Patterson. They don't break up for any reason. Charlie, on the other hand, doesn't go steady with anyone. He only thinks about Dee and how wonderful it would have been. Dee and Charlie grow farther and farther apart as time goes on. Charlie, disappointed with himself, waits the rest of the year for Dee and Danny to break up. Girls from all over school give Charlie the impression of liking him tremendously, but Charlie doesn't ask any of them to be his first girlfriend. When the last day of school finally arrives, all Charlie gets from Dee is a few nice words in his yearbook. No kiss this year. He remembers the school year as his best one and also his worst one.

After that year, Dee drops out of school because of her grades and family matters. Charlie doesn't get to see any more of the girl with whom he first fell in love. She left Charlie with only a strange feeling of uncertainty and doubt of what was never to be.

Charlie goes to another school the next year and does fine there. He begins to develop into a very responsible young man. He takes on his share of responsibilities and gets a part-time job to help his mother out. Sara is so proud of him for helping out this way. Charlie and his mother become closer and closer as time goes on. She depends on him, and he patterns his lifestyle around her. He doesn't date very much but does manages to take a few girls out once in a while. He doesn't develop any intense relationships with anyone, though. After having his heart broken, he doesn't want to get too close to anyone, except his mother. She becomes the most important person in his life. Besides, he doesn't have much spare time to develop a lasting relationship with a girl anyway. Working part-time after school and studying take up most of his time.

His mother does encourage him to attend church services. He knows the need for church. He believes in God strongly but has never made that commitment to him. Three months before he is to graduate from high school, he starts really thinking those questions all young people ask: What am I on this planet for? What do I want to do with my life? Who am I? What's my purpose? As Charlie prepares for his future, he wants to make that commitment to God, but like everything, Charlie is shy about making such a commitment. He attends church on Sunday several weeks in a row. He begins to ask his mother a lot of questions about how he can become a Christian. His mother helps him out. She became a Christian a long time ago. She was baptized in a creek not far from her childhood home. It was a big thing to be baptized out in the open like that instead of in a pool of water in a church. It gave people who didn't attend church a chance to see the power of faith. It was a real event to see, for sure.

Charlie studies for when he will walk down the aisle and make that commitment in front of the congregation. He has been going to church for a long time and accepted Jesus in his heart a long time ago. But he must come forward in a public place for it to mean anything. He must have the courage to show others his faith. Doing so in a public place will show everyone that his faith is genuine and true. Charlie is just waiting for the right moment to make that commitment.

The following Sunday, Charlie and his mother put on their best clothes and make the drive to church. Charlie feels a special presence of something very powerful as he and his mother sit quietly up in the front of the church. He listens with complete attention to Pastor Riggs.

Pastor Riggs says, "Good morning to one and all. I hope you all had a pleasant week. Something happened this week that has disturbed me somewhat." Everyone is silent and attentive as he continues, "As some of you may know, one of my best friends, Jimmy Fishel, passed away early this week at seventy-two. I want him to be the focus of my sermon today.

"So let me tell you a little bit about Jimmy. Most of his life he was like most people. He went to work and tried to make the best of his life. But early in his life he wasn't actually a very nice man. I don't mean to degrade him any, but there is a reason for me telling you how he was. You see, Jimmy was a very troubled man early in his life. To be honest with you, he was downright mean. He was very violent and spent several years in prison for his violent behavior. But around three years ago Jimmy accepted Jesus as his personal savior. He came forward to me after one of my sermons. He was in tears when he finally came to accept Christ into his life. That was only three years ago—only *three* years ago. And he was seventy-two years old when he died this week."

The church is still and quiet, and Charlie listens with undivided attention.

"It was too bad my good friend Jimmy didn't make that decision earlier in his life. He told me several times that he wished he had accepted Christ as his personal savior sooner. He told me that there was so much he wanted to do for the Lord. He wanted to make up for those wasted years of drinking, swearing, fornicating, and living like a heathen. Those lost years made it hard for him to feel like a fulfilled man. Not long before his death, he told me he only felt like a three-year-old child. He told me that! He really did. And you know something, he was right."

Some members of the congregation look at the pastor with confusion but also with intrigue.

"My good friend Jimmy was three years old when he died." Pastor Riggs walks around the platform and pauses for a moment. "His body may have been seventy-two years old, but his life with Christ was only three. You see, friends, I am really only fifteen years old."

The congregation laughs a little, breaking the silence. They all get quiet again before the pastor continues, "That's right, friends! It may be hard for some of you out there to understand, but I am really only fifteen years old. This body of mine is fifty-five years old, but my age with Christ is only fifteen. You see, I accepted Jesus as my savior when I was forty years old, and then I went to college to become a preacher."

Pastor Riggs pauses for a long time until the church is very quiet and still. He looks deep into his audience and says with a soft tone,

"How old are you?" He takes another long pause so everyone can think about his question.

"You see, forty years of my life was a complete waste. I wish I had met Jesus sooner in my life too. I believe I would have had a much more satisfying life. But I didn't, so now I am trying to make up for all those wasted years, like my good friend Jimmy Fishel. You know, everyone will come to know Jesus sooner or later—in this life or in the next one. It's just a shame that most people in this world will come to know him in the next life. Look at all the people that were born before Jesus walked on this planet. They didn't get a chance to glorify him, but we do!"

Pastor Riggs continues to walk around the stage as he looks out into his congregation. "For the ones who haven't made that commitment to Christ, you need to make that commitment *today*, so you can start living your spiritual life. Jesus once said, 'You must be born again!' That means you must come to realize that only your spiritual life will have any meaning to you. You must be born again so when you get to heaven, your eternal life will be enriched with glory, the glory you will have when you become a part of the body of Christ."

Charlie hardly breathes as he listens. He feels as if Pastor Riggs is talking directly to him.

"You can start living for Christ now! You don't want to be like me or my good friend Jimmy, who have wasted most of our lives. You can start living a life full of purpose and grandeur by glorifying Jesus. Life begins when you become born again."

Pastor Riggs waits for a moment before saying, "How old will you be when you join God? Will you be three years old? Will you be fifteen years old? Or will you be very old? I hope you will all be very old when you join Christ. The older you are, the more years of glory you have waiting for you. It is your decision.

"Christianity isn't like a lot of other religions out there in this world today. Most of the other religions want you to think you are going to go to heaven no matter how you live your life." Pastor Riggs pauses again as he waits for the congregation to absorb his message more thoroughly. "There are going to be a lot of people disappointed when they die. Everyone will one day die; at least, your body will die. But your spiritual life will never die. Some of the religions out there are full of evil and deception! Some of these leaders of these churches, or faiths are misguided. Some preach hate and by doing so give a false image of the truth to their so-called followers. These false misguided religious leaders give the impression that they have the wisdom and the power to get you to heaven. Some of these religious leaders tell their followers to murder, to kidnap, and to do other evil things in the name of God so that one day they will be rewarded in the hereafter. Show me a religion that doesn't have Jesus Christ in it, and I will show you just another religion that can lead you away from the truth. You can make a difference." The pastor points into his congregation with fury showing in his eyes.

After a short pause he continues, "If you know Christ, then you can show the world what he did, what he stood for, what he sacrificed, what he suffered, and, most of all, what he died for! When all the people of this world come to realize that he died for the sins of mankind, then and then only will there be a religion that will stop the powerful forces of the devil's deceiving ways! But as long as there is one religion out there that doesn't understand the need to have sins forgiven, then this world will never have true peace."

The congregation applauds as Pastor Riggs slowly walks back over to the podium. Sweat runs down his forehead as he waits for his church to get still again. After the congregation stops applauding, he looks at them sternly and says, "But let me make it perfectly clear: being saved means more than just being baptized. The baptism is only symbolic of the individual's faith. Jesus baptized people, and Jesus was baptized by John the Baptist, so we as Baptists should practice this ceremony. But it is not the ceremony that will take away your sinful actions but what that ceremony represents when you come to see the glory of what Jesus has done for the world. He sacrificed his life for mankind. He suffered a horrible death so we wouldn't suffer a horrible eternal death. When you are pulled out from that water, you begin to live a new life. You are one day old again. It is up to you to live this new life for Christ. You still make the decisions. You still have to get up every day and go through the same routines. But now your life has a reason. God has a purpose for you. When your face comes out of that water, your sins have all been washed away, and you can begin on that purpose he has laid out for you."

Charlie hardly breathes as he stares at the pastor with complete understanding.

"When you stand in that water, you are standing for Christ. That ceremony shows the world you have accepted Christ. It shows the world your faith. You are deciding, on your own, to participate in such a ceremony. So when you stand before the great white throne, your act of faith will be shown to you."

Sara looks over at Charlie and sees in his eyes something magnificent happening. She looks back over to the pastor and listens to the rest of his sermon.

"We Baptists aren't like other religions in which all you have to do is get baptized and then you are saved. In those baptisms, that kind of religion will then have control over you. As long as you are a member of that type of church, you will be controlled by the leaders of that church. It is easy to get caught up in such a deceiving religion. Jesus once said, 'There will be others who will claim to be me but they will be like wolves in sheep's clothing.' Other religions of the world are like that today! They look right and innocent on the outside, like sheep, but on the inside they are conniving and devious, like wolves, ready to turn unexpectedly and bring evil on unsuspecting believers. When you accept Christ as your personal savior, you will have the power to overcome these deceptions. That's why it is so important to find Christ early in you life."

Pastor Riggs's facial expression becomes more intense as he continues to walk around the stage. "You should ask yourself, where are you going to spend eternity?" He pauses for a moment and says, "Are you ready to meet your maker? Are you? Are you ready to meet your maker, right now? Have you lived this life he gave you the way he wanted you to? Will one of your sins make you rebel from God on that judgment day? There are a lot of people who proclaim to be followers of Christ think they won't have to stand before God on that judgment day. I predict ninety-nine percent of them think they won't have to! But when all is said and done, they too will have to stand before the great white throne. Every sin must be removed from your soul. Not ninety percent of your sons, not ninety-five percent of them, not ninety-nine percent of them, but *all* sins that you have committed must be removed and forgiven. And they can't be forgiven until you first admit they were sins!" Pastor

Riggs raises his hands with strength and determination. "You must acknowledge that you committed them! You must confess that they were wrong! And most of all, you must ask Christ to wash them from your soul! Then, and only then, will you be permitted to enter the paradise we call heaven."

The congregation begins to applaud. Pastor Riggs looks out at them as if there is no applause. His stern expression shows everyone there that he is very serious. "Have your sins really been forgiven? Has Jesus really saved you? Are you really going to heaven when you die? Can you honestly answer these questions? Only you know these answers! You are the ones that must make these decisions. Some of you out there are saying to yourselves, 'Yes! Yes! I am going to go to heaven when I die.' Then let me ask you one more question."

Pastor Riggs pauses for a long time again. "Are you afraid to die right now?" The church becomes very quiet. They all sit very still as Pastor Riggs continues, "Are you afraid of dying? If you know you were going to die right now, would you act crazy? Would you act terrified? Would you be scared to know that your life would soon end? Now, there are a lot of you out there that are thinking, *Of course I would be scared. Of course I would be terrified. Wouldn't everybody feel that way?*"

Pastor Riggs pauses again for a few moments as he walks around and waits for the congregation to think about what he has just asked. "There will be a time when you will die. It is inevitable. You will one day die. There is no use trying to deny this fact. When the Christians of Jesus's time were thrown into the Roman Colosseum, they knew that they were going to die. There were hungry lions, full of fury and rage, that would soon be let loose on them. Those true Christians of that time, those courageous people, weren't afraid to die. You know as well as I know, instead of running around terrified of what was about to happen, they instead began to sing. It is true! Those true Christians sang as those lions were unleashed upon them. They knew that their lives on this earth would soon be over."

The entire church is filled with a deafening quiet. Everyone's attention grows stronger as Pastor Riggs continues, "They were looking forward to eternal life with Christ. They knew, without a shadow of a doubt, that they would soon be with our Lord. They were happy knowing that soon they would be with Jesus. Is your faith as strong as those humble individuals? How many people here would have looked up into the heavens and begun to sing too? Be honest with yourselves. Would you be singing, or would you be crying and pleading to be saved?"

There are a lot of worried faces gazing up at the pastor now, but Charlie's expression is not one of worry but one of strength and admiration.

"I am ready to meet my maker! I look forward to the day when I will stand before Jesus and be with him forever. Your faith in God will be tested before man. God will not put you through anything he knows you can't withstand. That is why he must test us, so he will know what we can handle in life."

Pastor Riggs looks out into his congregation with strength and determination on his face. "I know that there are a lot of you out there who think once you have been saved, you will always remain saved. I have news for you. You are so caught up with going to heaven that you have forgotten about how strong your faith has to be before you can achieve that glorious objective. Friends, I have met many people in my life who at one time were saved by the blood of our Lord. But as time went on, they forgot all about living for Christ. They forgot about having to have their sins forgiven. Matter of fact, they forgot the whole meaning of salvation altogether! They simply thought that once they were saved, nothing could ever undo that decision. I hope and pray none of you folks out there will ever think that way.

"Just as soon as you commit your life to our Lord, your faith will be tested. It is hard being a Christian today. The many temptations of this world are phenomenal. As soon as you become a Christian, the devil will be after you. He will devise a plan to make you one day blame God for all the chaos he has brought forth into your life. So get used to the idea. The devil isn't going to go to all that trouble if he knows you can't be converted. I have known many people who strayed from God. They strayed because of the power of Satan's deceiving persuasions. The devil knows of the great and wonderful plan God has designed for your life, and he will try as hard as he can to prevent you from ever accomplishing this great objective. The devil wants you for his own sinister plan!"

The pastor gets louder as he walks around the stage. "Many have been tricked into joining his wicked army of rebellious demons, even after they have come to know Jesus!" He points his finger at his congregation. "He knows how to tempt you! He knows what things you can't overcome! He chokes the word of the Bible! He gets you caught up in the ways of the world! He lies to you! He turns your friends and family against you! He deceives others to persecute you! His power of deceiving is strong!"

Pastor Riggs's tone gets softer as he walks back to the pulpit. "Will you be able to overcome his compelling plan to get you to rebel against God? Are you going to admit to all your sins before the great white throne? Has Jesus really saved you?"

The pastor is silent for a long time as the congregation thinks over what he has just said. The church grows very quiet and still as the pastor waits. Then he continues, "There are some people in this world who ask for forgiveness but do nothing to rectify their sins. It seems to them all they have to do is say, 'Lord, please forgive me of my sins,' without really meaning it. They want to make it easy and convenient for themselves. They are not very repentant, just saying the words so they can get back to their normal way of life. Then they turn around and repeat the same sins over and over and over again. After they practice these wrongs time after time, they begin to feel comfortable doing them and simply don't care if these things are right or wrong. The only time people fully admit their sins and ask for forgiveness is when they feel the agony of that sin! Then they look up to God and say, 'Lord! Why did you let this terrible thing happen to me?'"

Some of the people of the church acknowledge Pastor Riggs with smiles or grins that indicate they know exactly what he is talking about.

"When you repent of your sins, it is going to be hard to do something about rectifying them. Your self-pride will corrupt you! So be on the alert for deceiving ways. Don't blame God for anything bad that happens in your life. It is not his fault! Most of the problems in our lives are self-inflicted. We bring on ourselves the many problems in our lives. Please don't let your self-pride disillusion your own conscience. It will if you're not careful, so be on the alert! I just want you all not to rebel against God. That is the most important thing in my sermon today: do not rebel from God because of what happens to you on this planet. I want all of you to repeat after me. *I will not rebel against God, ever.*"

The congregation says in unison, "I will not rebel against God, ever."

Pastor Riggs says, "Say it again! I will not rebel against God, ever! I will not rebel against God, ever!"

The whole congregation repeats the words several times before the pastor finally interrupts, "I think you all get the picture. I hope you all remember this sermon when that little voice inside your head tries to get you to blame God for something you have done to yourself. I hope you don't fail God. Remember, God is always right. It is only the deceptions that make you think otherwise. If you will only put Christ first in your life, you will never have to go through that awful period of shame and disgrace when your sins are exposed. You also will never go through the awful period of lying, covering up, and doing anything possible to prevent others from seeing what you have done. Put Jesus first in your life. Then you will have the power to overcome anything that life throws at you."

The whole congregation listens to Pastor Riggs with content expressions on their faces. He waits for the church to become very quiet and still. He looks into the middle of his congregation with a very serious look and says very softly, "Have you really been saved? Have you really accepted Jesus as your personal savior? He wants you to come to him. He will give you a peace that you have never had before. He will give you purpose in life. He will make your life complete. But are you ready to make that commitment? I want to give each and every one of you out there today a chance to come forward right now so you can dedicate your life to him. How old are you right now? This is the first day of the rest of your life. You all were saved two thousand years ago; now is the time to come to realize that. Now ask yourself, 'How old am I, right now?'" Pastor Riggs becomes very silent as the church is filled with a calm, tranquil silence.

He then says, "I want to ask the choir to sing 'Just As I Am' as I give you all an invitation to come forward and ask Jesus to come into your life. The time is now, so please come."

The organist begins to play the hymn. Pastor Riggs walks down to the front of the podium and waits for people to come. Charlie gets up quickly and walks down the aisle. He makes the first move to establish his Christian life.

He walks up to Pastor Riggs and says, "Pastor, I want to accept Jesus as my personal savior. I have thought about this for quite some time now. I want to accept him right now."

Pastor Riggs smiles gladly at Charlie. He tells Charlie to sit down, and someone from the church comes over to gather some information from Charlie. As Charlie tells the man the information, many others begin to come forward also. Seeing Charlie make that first step in turn gives them the encouragement to make that decision for themselves. Ten more people come down, ranging from teenagers all the way up to the elderly. The church service doesn't end for another hour. It is a joyous day! Yes, it is a very joyous day!

Charlie and the ten others are baptized the next Sunday during the evening worship services. Charlie is the first one out of the eleven to be baptized. He is becoming a member of the church. He is the happiest he has ever been in his entire life.

Sara cries when the pastor asks Charlie, while standing in the pool of water, "Do you believe in Jesus as the Son of God and as your personal savior?"

Charlie bellows out, "Yes! I believe!"

The pastor then submerges Charlie in the pool of water. Sara sits there in the front row with tears of joy running down her face. She is happier then than at any other point in her life. She doesn't stop crying until the ten others are baptized as well. The pews of the church are filled to capacity, and there are chairs in the aisle. There are even people standing. They all came to see the great ceremony of faith. It is the most people to be baptized at one time in the little white church. It is something to behold!

After the service is over, all the people in the church shake hands with Charlie and the others who were baptized. A robust energy fills all the people of the church. Pastor Riggs is as happy as he has ever been since he became a pastor. He has fulfilled his ultimate dream: to win over more than ten souls to Christ in one day. All the people leave the church with the spirit of the Holy Spirit. Sara drives Charlie home with a glorious feeling of fulfillment.

One afternoon a month later, Sara is sitting in the living room with an open Bible in her hands. She is waiting patiently for Charlie to drive up the driveway after his hard day of school.

When Charlie comes home, Sara, with a mysterious look on her face, says, "Hello, Son. Did you have a good day at school?"

"Oh, I guess I had a pretty good day."

"You still looking forward to graduating?"

"You better believe it. I can't wait! Me and Wayne have already made our reservations at the beach. Just think, in only one month I will be through with high school for good. Everybody is excited about graduating. We are going to leave for the beach right after graduation. I am so excited! I have never been to Myrtle Beach before. We should have a great time."

Sara sees the exuberant look on Charlie's face. She is happy when she sees Charlie so happy. She gazes at her happy son for a few moments and then says, "Charlie, would you come over here for a moment? There are a few things I want to talk over with you."

He looks at his mother with a little curiosity and sits down beside her.

Sara, with an earnest look, says, "Charlie, there is something I want to talk to you about."

Charlie notices the serious look on his mother's face, a look he hasn't seen in quite some time.

"Charlie, when you joined the church, I got to wondering, has anybody read the Baptist Commandments to you?"

Charlie thinks and says, "I don't think so."

"That's what I thought. I want you to understand what it really means to be a Baptist. Every religion has its own precepts, and the Baptists also have a certain set of rules that you are supposed to follow. I just want you to know what they are." Sara hands Charlie these rules and lets him read them to himself.

After Charlie has finished reading the Baptist Commandments, he looks over at his mother with a shy and somewhat-reluctant look. She sees this look and smiles. "Do you fully understand all of those rules?" she asks.

He hesitates a little bit before saying, "Yes, kinda."

"What do you mean 'kinda'?"

"Well, I mean, I kinda understand them."

Sara stares at Charlie with a serious look and says, "Do you know what fornication is, Charlie?"

Charlie's cheeks turn as red as a stop sign. He stares back at his mother with a startled look. "Yeah, Mama, I know what it means."

"Well then, tell me what it means."

Charlie's face turns a shade of magenta. He looks at his mother nervously. "Mama, I have got to go study right now. Maybe we can talk about this some other time." Charlie rises to leave.

"Charlie! You will do no such thing. We will talk about this matter right now. So you come back over here and sit down!"

Charlie, looking scared, slowly walks back over to the couch like a scolded child. Sara looks at her son with curiosity as he walks back. She waits until Charlie sits down before she says, "Fornication is when two people who aren't married make love or in most cases just have intercourse."

"Mama! I know what it means! I just don't feel comfortable talking about it. That's all."

"Charlie, it is something we must talk about."

"Why?"

"Because when you joined the church you signed a paper, remember?"

"Yeah, I kinda remember signing a paper."

"What you signed was the Baptist Commandments. You agreed to follow those rules by signing your name."

Charlie sits there nervously, and the room becomes silent for a moment. After a few moments, Sara breaks the silence. "I just want to make sure you understand those rules. Do you understand them now?"

"Yeah, Mama, I understand them." He tries to get up and walk away, but Sara grabs him by the seat of his pants and pulls him back on the couch.

"Where do you think you're going? I'm not finished talking with you."

"Mama, I don't feel comfortable talking about this."

Sara gives Charlie a very angry look that scares him.

"Why are you looking at me that way?" he asks.

"Because you need to hear what I have got to say! This is something for your own good! But if you don't want to talk about it, then go ahead and leave. I'm not going to force this down your throat!"

Charlie detects the indignation in her words and expression and is compelled to stay. "I'm sorry, Mama. I will stay if you want me to."

Sara's angry look slowly fades to a more calm and pleasant one. "When you signed those commandments, you promised the church that you would refrain from fornication. Do you understand that, Charlie?"

"Yes, ma'am, I understand."

"So you are telling me that you understand the commandments you signed."

Charlie pauses for a moment and then innocently replies, "Yes, ma'am."

A self-assured look comes to Sara's face. "Charlie, you promised the church you would refrain from fornication; now I want you to promise me that you will refrain from fornication until you marry."

Charlie looks at his mother with scared blue eyes. "I promise you that I will not engage in fornication until I marry."

Sara smiles at her son. "I am glad we had this little talk, Charlie."

Charlie looks at his mother, stunned.

Sara says, "So when you get down there at the beach and begin to see all those pretty girls in skimpy bikinis, you remember what you promised me, young man."

Charlie nods, dumbfounded at what has just taken place.

Sara gets up from the couch and says, "You can run along now, Charlie. I am finished with you for now. Are you all right?"

"Yeah, Mama, I guess I am."

Sara gets up and disappears into another part of the house. Charlie remains on the couch with a stunned and peculiar look on his face.

The next day comes, and Sara once again sits in the living room waiting for Charlie to come home from school. She has the same Bible opened on her lap as Charlie walks into the house.

"Hello, dear. I have been waiting for you," she says. "There is something else I want to talk to you about."

Charlie looks at his mother with a somewhat-scared look.

Sara, with a tranquil glow to her face, says, "Don't look frightened, Charlie. Come on over here and sit beside me."

Charlie, without saying a word, slowly walks over to the couch and sits down next to his mother with a nervous look.

"Did you have a good day at school today?"

Charlie, with a curious look on his face, says softly, "Yes, I had a pretty good day. Did you?"

Sara closes her Bible and says, "Oh, yes, Charlie, I had a very good day. I have been thinking about you somewhat."

Charlie listens even more attentively.

"I was just wondering, what are you going to do after you graduate from high school? You have never said anything to me about your plans."

"Well, I thought I would get a job and make some money."

"But what do you want to do with your life, Charlie? You must want to do something good besides just make money?"

"Well, I would like to go to college but ..."

"But what?"

"It costs a whole lot of money to go to college. It costs a whole lot."

"So you want to go to college?"

"Mama, you know you don't have the money to send me. I know that. That's why I never thought to bring it up. I will just get a job and play it from there."

"You will do no such thing, young man! You don't know how much money I have."

"Mama, I know you don't have enough, so let's not talk about it anymore. Okay?"

"I've done a few things today. One of them is that I liquidated a few assets I have acquired over the years."

"Hey! Where is your diamond ring? No. No! Tell me you didn't sell your ring!"

"Young man, don't you raise your voice to your mother! Do you understand me?" Charlie calms down a little as Sara pauses. She clears her throat and continues, "What is done is done. There is nothing you can do about it, so please just listen. I sold my wedding ring plus several other things today. I raised over three thousand dollars."

Charlie just stares at his mother with a stern look.

"I sold these things so you can have a proper education. So please don't let your pride interfere with what I have done."

Charlie nods and quietly says, "Yes, ma'am."

"I have lived my life. I have lived a good life. The things I sold today have no more use to me. I wanted to turn them into something that will be good for you and your future."

"But, Mama, you didn't have to go and do that."

"Young man, don't interrupt me. These things were mine, and I will do whatever I want with things that are mine, even if that is giving them to you."

Charlie remains silent as Sara continues, "I have opened a checking account for you at the bank. You have three thousand dollars in there. All I want you to promise me is that you will use that money to get a proper education."

Charlie looks lovingly at his mother. "Yes, Mama, I promise I will use it to get a proper education."

Sara smiles at her son with tears of joy in her eyes. "You spend it as you see fit. It is yours now. Just make sure you finish what you start. It would break my heart if you don't graduate. Charlie?"

"Yes, Mama. I promise I will graduate college no matter what happens. I will graduate. I promise!"

"Thank you, Son. I just want to make sure you are ready for this world a little more than I was." Happy tears trickle down Sara's face as she smiles at Charlie. A few find their way on the floor beside the ones from Charlie's eyes.

Sara jumps up from the couch. "Well, that's phase two out of the way." She walks out of the living room and disappears into another part of the house. Charlie is left curiously wondering what she meant by that last remark.

The next day arrives, and Sara once again sits waiting for Charlie to come home from school. She is sitting in the same spot, but this time she has her Bible closed on the end table when Charlie walks into the house. She gazes up and sees Charlie standing in the doorway of the living room.

"Hello, Son. Did your day go well?"

Charlie sees that his mother is in the same mood she has been in the last two days. "Okay, Mama, what do you want to talk about today?"

Sara smiles kindly at Charlie. She pats the seat on the couch and motions for Charlie to come sit beside her again. Charlie walks over and sits down beside his mother as she stares at him with a strange, glassy look.

"I have been waiting for you," she says. "I want to talk to you one more time. This time I want to tell you something that you might think is a little strange."

Charlie looks at her, intrigued. He feels a little strange at the way she is behaving but listens with his complete and undivided attention.

Sara says, "I had a very frightening dream last night. I won't tell you everything about the dream itself, but there is something I do want to share with you because of that dream."

"Yes, Mama. What is it?"

"Now that you have become a Christian, God is going to start to test you. God tests us all so he knows how much we can handle. He will not expect you to do anything you are not capable of doing. When God tests us, it is not going to be very enjoyable. Matter of fact, it will probably be very difficult to bear." Sara reaches over and holds Charlie's hand as she looks at him mysteriously. "You remember Pastor Riggs's sermon the day you accepted Jesus, Charlie?"

"Yes, Mama, I remember?"

"You remember when he said the devil wants you to rebel from God?"

"Yes, Mama."

"When God tests us, it is a test of faith. God wants to see if you will rebel against him. If you rebel against him, you have failed the test. So you must always remember, Charlie: do not ever fail the test. Do you understand?"

"Yes, Mama, I understand."

"Good, Charlie, good. You see, God has a great purpose for you. I just know he does. Call it a mother's intuition. I can't explain it in detail, and I don't know exactly what that purpose is, but I know he has a grand and magnificent plan for you. I want you to promise me that no matter what adversity you go through in your life, you will not blame God. Promise me that you will not rebel against him."

Charlie listens to his mother with great attention. "I promise I won't rebel against God no matter what happens."

"The devil will be after you. He will try to deceive you into thinking that God is responsible for your adversity and hardships. So please, Son, promise me one more time that you will never blame God for anything bad that happens in your life."

Charlie stares at his mother's glassy eyes. He sees something in them he has never seen before. Without having to think much, he says, "Okay, Mama, I promise."

"Wait!" Sara gets up and gets her Bible from the end table. She sits back down and places Charlie's right hand on the book. "Now what were you going to say?"

Charlie marvels at his mother for a few seconds and then stares deep into her eyes and says, "I promise I will not blame God for anything bad that happens to me in my life. I also promise you that no matter what adversity I face in life I will not rebel against God and his commandments. I promise!"

Sara, with a wondrous, glowing smile, kisses her son on the cheek. "Charlie, you have made my life complete today. Ever since you were born, I have waited patiently for you to accept Christ as your savior and to live your life the way God would want you to. I am so proud to have a son like you."

Charlie, still looking a little dumbfounded at the way his mother is behaving, says, "So tell me, Mama, what was your dream about?"

"Oh, it was nothing. Well, it was nothing too much. Let's just say it was a very bad dream."

Charlie gets the idea she doesn't want to talk about it, so he doesn't press her.

Before long, graduation finally arrives. Charlie doesn't have to go to his regular classes anymore. He manages to pass all his classes with no grade lower than a C. He is eager for the evening graduation ceremony. He has to be there at five o'clock. The class of 1979 will begin to march onto the football field at five-thirty. The weather calls for rain.

When Charlie gets up that morning, he walks over to the window and looks outside. It is very cloudy. He begins to have a very negative and strange feeling. He tells himself, "I sure hope the rain doesn't interfere with my graduation."

He walks downstairs and finds his mother sitting down at the kitchen table reading the morning newspaper. He sits down, saying, "Good morning."

"Good morning, high school graduate. Are you looking forward to tonight?"

"Are you kidding? I have been waiting for this day for twelve long years."

Sara laughs. "What would you like for breakfast?"

"What do you mean? Haven't you already got it fixed?"

Sara just smiles at Charlie. "Of course I have got it ready, silly." She takes the cover off the stove and shows Charlie that she has fixed his favorite breakfast, hotcakes and sausage with butter and a full bottle of maple syrup.

"Yum-yum! Oh boy, my favorite breakfast! You had me going. I thought you hadn't even begun to cook anything."

"I just wanted to surprise you. I am so happy that you have finished high school. I am so proud of you!" Her face glows with joy.

Charlie is delighted with her surprise. He wolfs down a couple of stacks of hotcakes, devours a plate of sausage, and drinks down three full glasses of milk.

"Slow down, Charlie; don't eat so fast."

"That's the best part of eating, Mama. You eat fast; then you pour down a full glass of milk in one long guzzle. Yum-yum! You are a good mother. That was the best breakfast I have ever eaten. I hope when I get married, I find a woman who can make hotcakes as good as you."

Sara smiles contentedly as she puts the dishes in the sink.

Charlie asks, "So what time do you want to leave for the graduation ceremony? I have to be there at five."

"Oh, Charlie, you will have to drive yourself. I have to drive over to Aunt Frances's house to pick her up."

"Why can't she drive herself?"

"She hasn't been feeling well lately. I called her last night, and she said she didn't think she'd be able to come." Charlie looks disappointed, and Sara continues, "I told her that you would be very disappointed if she didn't make it, so I volunteered to come by her house and pick her up."

"She lives forty-some miles from the school."

"Yes, I know. I'm going to leave any minute now and stay with her until it's time to go to your graduation. She is the only aunt you have, and I know John would have wanted her to attend, since she is his only sister. If I drive out there so she doesn't have to make that long drive by herself, maybe then she will feel up to going."

Charlie listens with a concerned look on his face. "Okay, Mama, tell her I will be looking for her."

"I'll tell her."

"Is there anything you want me to do before I leave?" Charlie asked.

"No, I don't think there is anything."

"Tonight after graduation a bunch of us are going to a party before we leave for the beach. So I was just wondering if I could borrow a few bucks from you. Please?" Charlie says.

"What about all that money you have in the checking account I opened for you?"

"Oh no, Mama, that money is supposed to be used for an education. I wouldn't dare think about spending that money on anything else."

Sara opens up her purse and shows Charlie a single twenty-dollar bill. "That's all I have, Charlie."

"Oh, that's all right then, Mama. I'll just make do with what I have."

Sara pulls out the bill and hands it to Charlie. "You go ahead and take it. You have fun at the party, all right?"

Charlie feels bad taking his mother's only money but accepts it.

Sara goes into the kitchen and washes the dishes. Charlie goes into the living room and watches TV until his mother walks into the room and announces, "I'm going to leave now. I will see you tonight, dear. Give your mama a kiss."

Charlie just looks at her.

"Aren't you going to give me a kiss, Charlie?"

"If you want a kiss, you'll have to come and get it."

Sara walks over to Charlie, and he kisses her good-bye.

"Drive safely," he says.

"I will. Bye, bye, Charlie. I love you."

"I love you too, Mama."

Sara leaves to go to Frances's house. It begins to rain just as she drives away. It takes Sara a good hour to get to Frances's house. Sara has to knock on the door several times before Frances finally answers it. Frances opens the door and welcomes Sara into the house.

"So how are you feeling today?" Sara asks.

"I feel worse today than I did last night. I don't know what's wrong with me. I guess I am just getting old."

"Don't feel like you are the only one; we all are getting old. Would you like me to fix you some hot tea?"

"That would be nice of you, Sara. I sure am glad you came by today."

Sara and Frances sit and talk about those things women talk about. As the day goes by, the rain pours down.

"My goodness! It sure is coming down now," Sara says. "Just look at that rain come down!"

"It sure is. I don't mind rain so much, but I don't like to see it fall that hard."

In only five minutes, the rain completely stops.

Sara says, "Look, the sun is finally showing its face."

"Yeah, but those clouds up there tell a different story."

In only a brief time it begins to rain once again. This time it rains harder. The sound it makes on the roof is eerie.

Sara says, "Wow! It really is pouring down now. Just hear that awful noise."

Frances, looking worried, says, "Oh my! I wish it would stop. I don't like to hear that noise. Maybe it will stop soon."

After about five minutes of raining cats and dogs, the rain does finally stop. Sara gets up from the kitchen table and looks out the window. "Well, how do you like that? It has completely stopped. Not a drop is falling now."

Frances, looking up at the sky, says, "Yeah, but those clouds still don't look like they are quite through yet."

After five minutes of uninterrupted quiet, the rains begin once more. This time the rain comes down in buckets. It rains like this for another five minutes.

"Oh no!" Frances says. "I think the river is going to flood now! The bridge is just a few miles away, and every time I've seen it rain like this, the river floods the bridge something awful. Maybe you should leave now to go to Charlie's graduation. I'm not trying to run you off; it's just I don't want you to be stranded here."

Sara, showing no look of concern, says calmly, "Nonsense, Frances. Look, it has already stopped again. See, if I leave, I want you to come with me."

Frances replies with a sick expression, "I sure would like to see the boy graduate, but, Sara, I just don't feel right. I don't know what's wrong with me, but I just don't feel like I will be able to make it tonight."

"Charlie will be very disappointed if you don't show up, but if you don't feel well, I guess he will understand."

"I am sure he will understand." Frances gets her pocketbook, pulls out a twenty-dollar bill, and gives it to Sara. "Here, give this to Charlie for his graduation present. I know it's not much, but I want to give him something."

Sara acts surprised. "Not much? He will be tickled to receive this much. Matter of fact, I gave him my last twenty dollars this morning. I will make sure he gets it, Frances. Thank you."

It begins to rain continuously now. It doesn't come down hard, but it does come down fairly steady, and the clouds still look dark. Sara and Frances sit and talk for several more hours.

Frances shows Sara a very troubled and worried look from time to time. Finally she asks, "Sara, what time is it getting to be?"

"It's three o'clock."

"How long will it take you to get to the school from here?"

"Oh, about an hour or so. Why?"

"What time does the graduation begin?"

Sara looks confounded by these questions. "Five-thirty. There is still plenty of time yet."

"If the bridge is out, you will have to backtrack twenty miles. So please listen to an old woman, and leave now. I will feel horrible if you miss your only son's graduation because of me."

Sara gives in to Frances's request and decides to leave a little early. "Okay, Frances, I'll leave now. Is there anything you want me to do for you before I go?"

"No, Sara, I will be fine. I wish I was feeling better so I could go with you."

Sara kisses Frances on the cheek. "I will be seeing you later. I will make sure I give Charlie the twenty dollars. He is going to the beach for the first time, and I know he will be needing it. I thank you for him."

Frances smiles a frail, tender smile. "Think nothing of it, dear. I am glad I gave the boy something. He sure is a fine boy. I will be seeing you later."

"Okay, Frances, you take care of yourself. If you need me, I am only a phone call away. Don't hesitate to call me anytime."

As Sara leaves the house, it finally stops raining. As she drives away, she thinks, *I sure am thirsty. All this rain has made me want a soda. I believe I have enough change to buy me one.* So she stops at a little store. She gets out of her car and heads over to a drink machine outside. Beside the drink machine is a little bench. Oh no, it can't be! But it is—the Old Man! He is sitting on the bench as Sara walks up to the machine.

"Hello, Sara," he says.

Sara is startled when she hears her name. She looks down and sees the man with long, curly blond hair and beady blue eyes. He has a devious grin on his face. He looks at Sara coldly as he sits relaxed on the bench.

"Pardon me, sir, do you know me?"

"Of course I do. You are Frances Delaney's sister-in-law, Sara, aren't you?"

Sara, looking surprised, replies, "Well, that's right. You must know me through her."

The Old Man looks at Sara as if he has something devious on his mind. "Are you going to Charlie's graduation?"

"Why, yes. Funny, you know me pretty well, but I can't seem to place you. What did you say your name was?"

The Old Man stares at Sara with that same devious look. "If you are going to the graduation, I have some bad news for you."

Sara forgets about learning the Old Man's name and asks, "What bad news?"

"It's the bridge, the bridge over Highway 421. It has been flooded."

Sara, looking worried, says, "Oh my dear!" Panic strikes her.

"Frances told me that she was afraid of that. Do you know how I could get to 421 from here? The fastest way?"

The Old Man smiles genially. "All you have to do is go up this road and take the third road on your left. The name of the road is Beguile. You can't miss it. If you take that road, it will lead you straight to 421. That way you won't have to go across the bridge."

Sara, showing a sign of relief, says, "Oh, thank you so much, sir! You are a lifesaver! I will do that."

Before Sara has a chance to ask the Old Man his name again, he says, "You better hurry! Charlie wouldn't want you to be late."

"You are absolutely right! Thank you again."

Sara forgets about her soda and gets into her car and leaves as fast as she can. She goes up the road to the third intersection and sees the sign for Beguile Road. She turns left and proceeds down the road. She thinks, *It is a good thing I stopped at that store. If I had gone the way I was headed, I probably would have had a hard time fighting all that traffic.*

Sara turns on the radio but doesn't hear anything about 421 being blocked off. She says to herself, "That's funny. It seems there should be a news bulletin about 421 being blocked off." The road Sara is driving on begins to go down steeply. *Funny,* she thinks. *I thought this road would be going uphill instead of downhill.*

Sara goes around a turn and sees a bridge at the bottom of the hill. The bridge is flooded. The water is over the top. Sara is still going downhill and is going too fast to stop. A rush of terror runs through her soul. "No! No!" She slams on the brakes and begins to skid. She lets out a terrifying, piercing scream. She screams out, "Charlie! Charlie!" Then the car hits the water. The rushing river flips the car over and carries it off the bridge.

Back at school, Charlie, in dress clothes, arrives for his graduation. As he walks up to the school, he sees someone he knew very well a couple of years ago. She is sitting down on a bench right outside the school: Dee. Charlie stares at his old flame until her eyes meet his. He smiles gladly and walks over. Dee's face lights up with excitement.

"Hello, Dee."

"Hey, Charlie, long time, no see."

Charlie looks down and notices that she is pregnant. Remaining standing, Charlie looks at her glowing face. "I sure have missed you. I see you have been busy."

Dee sees Charlie looking at her belly. "Yes. Me and Danny got married this year."

"Why did you go and do that?"

"Because I love him, Charlie." Dee shows Charlie the ring.

Charlie, nodding, says, "Well, I wish you all the happiness in the world. I really mean that."

Dee smiles.

"Well, I gotta go now," he says. "I'll see you later."

"Sure, Charlie. I'm glad you stopped by and spoke to me. Good luck to you."

Charlie waves good-bye. With a lonely gap in his heart, he walks to his homeroom as he was instructed and puts on his cap and gown.

The class meets in the auditorium at 5:15 p.m. At exactly 5:30 p.m. the class of 1979 begins to march out onto the football field. It takes about twenty minutes for all the students to get to their seats. The graduation ceremony takes place without one drop of rain falling. Charlie receives his diploma. He looks out into the audience to see if he can spot his mother but can't find her. He goes back to his seat like all the other students. He waits excitedly for all the other kids to receive their diplomas.

After everyone has received his or her diploma, the speaker makes a short speech. His voice is mild, and his face is cheerful. "I want to be the first one to congratulate you fine students for your outstanding accomplishment." The students applaud as the speaker gazes out at their happy faces. He waits for complete silence before continuing, "I don't want to make a long, dragged-out speech, but I do want to say something important. When you are ninety years old, I want you to remember what I am about to tell you all. I will sum it up in four words: the quality of life. Now that you young people are fixing to make your own lives, I want you to always remember that the quality of your life is something you make for yourselves."

Charlie listens exceptionally carefully to the speaker's words.

"There was a farmer I knew a long time ago. He was a corn farmer. Every year when his crops came in, he would take his corn to a local mill to be weighed. Well, one year he decided to stand on the scales while his corn was being weighed. He thought he was being slick. His face was full of trickery and pride. The owner of the mill saw what the farmer did. When the farmer went over to be paid for his corn, the owner handed him his check and said, 'I just want you to know that you're not fooling anybody about what you did. Here's your check for your corn and your weight. You just sold your character for twenty-five cents. Don't spend it all in one place.'"

Everyone listens attentively. The speaker waits until there is complete quiet and continues, "You see, graduates, this farmer thought he was going to get more than he should but instead sold his character for a mere twenty-five cents. I hope none of you will sell your character, not even for a million dollars. Because it's not how much money you make in life but how you make it. Just remember: the quality of life. Good night."

All the students jump up and throw their caps into the air. Some also throw the rolled-up pieces of paper representing their diplomas into the air. The atmosphere is exciting and joyous. The students march back to their homerooms to receive their real diplomas.

Charlie wonders why he hasn't spotted his mother yet. He can't wait to show her his diploma. He knows that she knows his homeroom number is 333. He waits for her along with all the other kids waiting for their parents. He can't wait to see her happy expression. The excitement of graduation is one of the most wonderful times in a person's life. The energy that the kids possess is amplified all throughout the school.

But then a big police officer with a giant, shiny badge walks into Charlie's homeroom. He draws everyone's attention when he walks in.

The teacher asks, "Can I help you, Officer?"

"Yes. Could you tell me where I can find a Charlie Delaney?"

Charlie's heart begins to beat fast. "I am he! What do you want?" he sputters.

"Will you please step outside with me for a moment? There is something I need to talk to you about, in private."

Charlie gets a very bad feeling in the pit of his stomach. Charlie, the police officer, and the teacher all walk outside the classroom.

Charlie, looking nervous, asks, "What has happened? What has happened?"

The police officer looks at Charlie with a frown. "There has been an accident. I am sorry to inform you that your mother died just a few hours ago in an automobile accident. I am very sorry."

Charlie becomes hysterical. He screams at the top of his lungs, "No! You're lying! Nooo! It can't be true! No! It can't be true! No! No! No! Dear God in heaven!" He begins to cry, and his screams echo throughout the halls. People begin to gather around him. Charlie falls to the floor and starts to roll around. He cries and screams at the top of his lungs. The police officer tries to get control of him but to no avail. Charlie becomes delirious and makes a scene like no one has ever seen before. The police officer wishes he had taken Charlie outside the building before he broke the news to him, but Charlie had demanded to hear the news immediately. The police officer gets on his portable radio to summon help. Charlie has to be carried off. The other students watch as Charlie becomes hysterical. It is a very bad scene. The upsetting spectacle shocks everyone who sees it. Charlie goes into shock and is put into an ambulance to be taken to the emergency room. The news devastates the entire school. Large groups of people are in tears by the time the ambulance leaves the school.

When Charlie arrives at the hospital, he is given a sedative. He falls asleep until the next morning. He is awakened by his aunt Frances. She is accompanied by a nurse, a doctor, and a police officer. Frances presses on Charlie's shoulder until he finally wakes up from his drugged sleep.

"Charlie. Charlie, this is Aunt Frances. Charlie. Wake up, Charlie."

Charlie is drowsy as he wakes up. He groggily asks, "Aunt Frances, is that you?"

"Yes, dear, it is me. Are you all right?"

"Aunt Frances, what happened to Mama? Tell me what happened."

Frances, looking tired and sickly, says, "Your mother was in a very bad automobile accident yesterday. She is no longer with us, Charlie. But don't you fret none—everything will be all right. You can come live with me until you get better."

The doctor says, "Mrs. Delaney, you go ahead and let Charlie rest some more. He was pretty well sedated last night."

The police officer asks Aunt Frances, "Could you tell me why Sara Delaney was driving down that road?"

Frances, looking confused, says, "I just can't explain it, Officer. She left my house to go to Charlie's graduation around three o'clock. All she had to do was get on Highway 421. I just don't understand why she took the route she did. It just doesn't make any sense."

The police officer, looking distraught, says, "Do you think she might have thought the bridge was out and so taken an alternate route?"

"Maybe so, but what would give her the idea the bridge was out? It never was. This is awful. This is just awful."

"I sure would like to know why she was on that road. I will make sure there is an investigation into this matter."

"Exactly how did she die?" Frances asks uncertainly.

"She had a mild concussion, but the cause of death was drowning."

"Oh my! That's how my brother, Charlie's father, died. He drowned also."

"This is a terrible thing. Tell Mr. Delaney that we at the police department are very sorry about his mother. We will ask a few questions around that area to see if anyone saw Mrs. Delaney drive through there. I don't think we will ever fully understand why she was on that road, but we will do our best."

"Thank you, Officer. This boy sure has gone through a whole lot."

"You say his father also drowned?"

"Yes. It was three years ago when they pulled John out of that lake. It was a terrible tragedy. Now this!"

The doctor says, "I think we should leave Charlie alone for now. He needs to rest some more."

Everyone leaves the room.

Charlie remains in the hospital for three days. The doctors then transfer him to a psychiatric ward. He remains there for three long months. He is given tranquilizers. None of the doctors there ever diagnose Charlie correctly. He isn't diagnosed with depression. They think his only problem is the loss of his mother. All the tranquilizers do is make Charlie sleep. He sleeps most of the three months he is there. The loss of his mother devastates Charlie. The police investigation of Sara's peculiar death doesn't amount to anything. The police question the local residents, but none of them tell the police anything constructive. The police even talk to the owner of the little store Sara stopped at, but no one says anything that would help.

After being released from the psychiatric hospital, Charlie sells the house and moves three hundred miles away. He stays gone for two and one-half years. He goes to a technical institute and receives a two-year degree in business administration, fulfilling one of the promises he made to his mother. After graduating from this institution, he comes back home. He buys a house with what money he has left over from his mother's estate. He gets a full-time job as a business consultant with Steven's Knitting on Broad Street. He lives a secluded life for six years. He doesn't date any women; he remains celibate just as he promised his mother.

But the last promise Charlie made to his mother, the one about not blaming God for the problems and the adversity in his life, is not so easy to keep. He becomes confused about the deaths of his mother and father. He doesn't exactly blame God for his parents' deaths, but he is angered at him for letting it happen. Right after Charlie's twenty-sixth birthday, he begins to come out of his shell again. He has built up a nice savings account at a local bank. He begins to go out and do other things, but the death of his mother prevents him from getting too close to anyone. This deters Charlie from fully enjoying life, but something lives in Charlie's heart. He feels God has a mission for his life, and he feels that mission will soon come to pass. Now he searches his soul to find out what that mission is.

Printed in the United States
By Bookmasters